2022 Best of Utopian Speculative Fiction

Edited by Justine Norton-Kertson

Android Press

Published by Android Press
Eugene, Oregon
www.android-press.com

First Printing, 2023
ISBN: 978-1958121665

Original Publications

"Zen and the Art of Gaia Maintenance" by Jetse de Vries was originally published by *The Mithila Review* in August 2022.

"A Mycologist's Guide to ~~Falling in Love~~ Discovering a New Species" by Shelly Jones was originally published by *Utopia Science Fiction Magazine* in February 2022.

"Space Unicorn and Magic Ovens" by Liam Hogan was originally published by Daily Science Fiction in February 2022.

"Electric Waterfalls" by Ruth Joffre was originally published in *khōréō* in March 2022.

"Worker's Song" by H. Pueyo was originally published in *Mafaverna: Democracy* by Mafagafo Revista, A Taverna & National Democratic Institute (NDI) in October 2022.

"Like Stars Daring to Shine" by Somto Ihezue was originally published by Fireside Magazine in July 2022.

"Icariana" by Wen-yi-Lee was originally published by *Baffling Magazine* in December 2022.

"Taming the Sea and the Wind" by Yasmin Moita was originally published in *Amazofuturo* by Editora Cyberus in January 2022.

"The Moonlit Muse" by Kanishk Tantia was originally published by *Solarpunk Magazine* in November 2022.

"Current Voices in a Convection Oven" by Sarah Ramdawar was originally published by *Augur Magazine* in June 2022.

"The Blink" by Simon Kewin was originally published by *Hyphen Punk* in May 2022.

"She Dreams of Moons and Moons" by Marisca Pichette was originally published by *Strange Horizons* in November 2022.

"Song of the Balsa Wood Bird" by Katherine Quevedo was originally published by *Fireside Magazine* in January 2022.

"Clockwork Dragon" by Toshiya Kamei was originally published by *Wyngraf* in April 2022.

"All The Things You Will Do" by J.D. Harlock was originally published in *The Librarian* by Air and Nothingness Press in December 2022.

"Look to the Sky, My Love" by Renan Bernardo was originally published by *Solarpunk Magazine* in January 2022.

"The Center Cannon Hold" by Holly Schofield was originally published by *Solarpunk Magazine* in August 2022.

"Seven Sisters" by Susan Kaye Quinn was originally published by Grist in *Imagine 2200, Climate Fiction for Future Ancestors* in October 2022.

"The Tides Rolled In" by Christopher R. Muscato was originally published by the XR Wordsmith Solarpunk Storytelling Showcase in March 2022.

"Neyllo" by Naomi Eselojor was originally published by *Omenana Mag-*

azine in July 2022.

"University, Speaking" by Phoebe Wagner was originally published in *Us in Flux* by ASU's Center for Science and Imagination in July 2022.

"If We Can Do This, We Can Stop Asteroids" by Andrew Dana Hudson was originally published in *Our Shared Storm: A Novel of Five Climate Futures* by Fordham University Press in April 2022.

CONTENTS

Introduction: Writing Utopia

Justine Norton-Kertson

In a world where dystopia loom large, where headlines more frequently announce our failings than our feats, stories that cast luminous visions of a hopeful tomorrow are not just desired—they're essential. In the *2022 Best of Utopian Speculative Fiction* anthology, I've curated tales that are the bright stars amidst the inky expanse of speculative literature. These stories dare to dream, challenge the norm, and insist upon the existence of a world where humanity, technology, and nature entwine in harmonious dance.

Every story within these pages shuns the dark, dystopian allure that can so easily dominate speculative fiction and instead embraces a vision of the future rooted in harmony, justice, and equilibrium. Here, hope isn't just an abstract concept, it's a tangible outcome. Whether through innovative solutions to our planet's most pressing challenges or through the portrayal of societies or groups of people who have rebuilt from the ashes and are doing their best with what they have, each tale underscores the belief that a better tomorrow is not just possible, but probable.

You will journey through futures both distant and near, through worlds that might be, could be, and perhaps should be. The authors in this anthology bring forth a unique tapestry of hope, stitched together with threads of creativity, resilience, and courage. While the speculative element remains at the heart of every story, the anthology encourages readers to think, to question, and to dream. If a horror story can cast away its foreboding shadows and step into the light of utopia, then perhaps so can our world. As you dive into these pages, remember that every utopia begins as a dream, and every dreamer has the power to change the world.

As you embark on this voyage through galaxies of optimism, know that with each page you turn, you're not just reading a story—you're part of a movement. A movement that seeks to inspire, challenge, and above all, uplift.

It's my joy and my pleasure to bring you this first annual *Best of Utopian Speculative Fiction anthology*.

Welcome to the future we hope for.

Zen and the Art of Gaia Maintenance

Jetse de Vries

—a quadripartite prelude—

The crisis is big, my children, so big that the distinctions between reality and imagination, impression and expression, even between fantasy and science fiction are dissolving —

The stranger is a presence, an epiphenomenon, an emergent property yet his followers prefer to visualise this ephemeral quadrilaterality as a person, an androgynous icon in zazen, floating in mid-air.

—The four of you must bear witness to the upcoming shift, the change of mental seasons. Short-term blindness, incessant greed, false conservatism and fear are the four hard truths we must face. You must go the East, the West, the North and the South —

Four young adults are listening intently to the Swami of the four new Vedas. Chika Wu from Chengdu, her unruly black hair all but covering her amber face and glasses; João Incanna from Lima, his wiry frame and auburn skin weathered from years of fishing; Grace M'Boku from the Limpopo floodplains, her stature a study in empathy, ebony and elegance; and Saaki Sami from Lapland, his springy red hair complementing his ivory face.

—Sow the seeds of change. Implement the memes of co-operation & entrepreneurship, innovation, long-term thinking & sustainability and hope. Remember the fourfold path — the four new Vedas, if you like — to dharma:

the only constant in the chain of life is change;the protection of the weakest is the new way forward; like biodiversity, multiple strategies need not be mutually exclusive;greatness determines a people's karma, so find a way to improve yours—

Off they go. Wu to the East, Incanna to the West, M'Boku to the South, Sami to the North.

—a quadruple overture: four hard truths—

Chika Wu comes down in Chengdu, Sichuan Province, perched right between the Sichuan Basin and the fertile lands of the Chengdu Plain, a transit area from the Longmen and Qionglai mountains, the Min River convergence area and the extremely crowded cityscapes. The extremely polluted cityscapes.

Like Incanna, M'Boku and Sami, she has to form a team, a team that must focus on one big problem, a hard truth. The hard truth in China's cityscapes is impossible to miss. Pollution, eye-watering pollution everywhere. Breathing masks are as popular as smartphones, and more indispensable.

People are plentiful, perhaps *too* plentiful. Finding the right people might take too long. Yet almost everybody is connected to the internet in one way or another, with profiles, interests and surfing behaviour readily available to those who know how to mine all that data. Wu dives in, searching for the right people, knowing that Chengdu is already a research & development centre for new energies.

—João Incanna remigrates to Lima. In the fishing villages of his youth, an immense hard truth is staring them right in the face. Through a combination of overfishing, pollution and climate change, the Pacific Ocean—the largest body of water on the planet—is slowly dying. Coral reefs are bleaching, fish stock are heavily depleted, huge amounts of plasti —in particular the plastic broken down to small pieces—are disturbing the food chain, biodiversity is suffering and the acidity of the water is rising.

Compared to that, the poverty and lack of job prospects of the Peruvian coastal communities seem like minor problems. Yet Incanna wants to gather a team that aims to solve it all, step by step, little by little.

—Grace M'Boku moves to Gaborone, then to the agricultural communities in the floodplains of the Limpopo River. There are many hard truths in her part of the world, but the hardest are hunger, disease and destitution. Over the last few centuries, her people have been introduced — often forcefully — to new ways. So far, these new ways have mainly helped the already rich and well-to-do, and failed to improve the lives of the most destitute ones, like her community.

Returning to the old ways is not an option. There must be better new ways, ways like the waves of a tide that lifts *all* boats. Even if they have to invent those themselves, even if it means they have to work harder than ever before.

—Saaki Sami shifts down in Luleå. Over there, the winter often covers nasty problems under a blanket of snow. But the winters aren't as long and severe as they used to be, and the blanket of snow is getting thinner by the year.

On top of that, some of the Scandinavians feel guilt about being a part of the problem. Companies like Ericsson and Nokia helped launch the mobile phone revolution, and the billions of discarded phones form garbage patches and landfills the size of small provinces. They helped deplete the Earth of many of its rare metals. It's time to clean up the mess and re-use those precious metals.

—circle the quadrangle—

Chika Wu's team is a weird mix of biochemists whose interests are restless, leaping from topic to topic like magpies chasing anything that glimmers; and physicists whose interests are so singular they almost forget there exists a world outside of it.

Both researchers wish to create their own Shang-tu, while also trying to improve upon already existing products and results. The biochemists wish to develop a thin, organic polymer film that acts like a solar cell. A film that's easy to produce, from materials that are widely available. A film that has a higher efficiency than the current best solar cell technology, and that is as maintenance-free as possible.

The physicists want to develop a room temperature superconductor. Not only that, the material should ideally consist of parts that are readily available. On top of that, a material that can easily be produced as very long strands of wire, to stretch from mountain or countryside (or desert) to city.

As she doesn't want the two teams to be fully isolated, Chika Wu hires a number of interdisciplinary people who shift between the two core teams in an effort to provide both with fresh insights and ideas. The exchange proves so fruitful that a small group splits off from the other two and starts developing a new type of battery with record-breaking levels of power storage density.

—João Incanna has introduced the fishermen of his port to a mixed group of University researchers, start-up entrepreneurs and idealists. While the practicality of the fishermen often clashes with the lofty goals of the idealists, and the can-do spirit of the entrepreneurs often raises doubts with the researchers, a common goal binds them. They wish to clean up and reseed the Pacific Ocean so that its biodiversity can recover — and the starkly depleted fish stock with them — and deliver raw materials to the space-elevator-to-be base floating several hundred kilometres west of the Galapagos Islands.

So they work on a bio-active mega-net. An anti-fishing net of sorts, as it tries to catch the plastic floating around in the Pacific while leaving life — plankton, nekton and fishes — alone. To counter the acidification of the ocean they seed it with novo-plankton, a rich mix of genetically engineered algae, diatoms and protozoans provided with single-celled, alkali-producing algae. The algae will only produce alkali if the seawater's pH rises above seven.

The first prototype of the megabionet has plastic-detecting sensors that err on the side of caution, to be certain no actual living organisms are caught by accident. It lowers their effective catch ratio, but there is so much plastic in the ocean that it's better to launch the first vessels with the original megabionets than waiting and doing nothing. Later generations will be supplied with improved versions.

The first vessels with anti-fishing nets set out on carefully calculated trajectories, from the Peruvian coast to the North and South Pacific Garbage Patches — invisible from space, yet rife with plastic mini-, micro- and nano-particles — and onwards to deliver the captured plastic to the base of the space-elevator-to-be, west of the Galapagos Archipelago.

—Grace M'Boku moves to Gaborone, where she goes after fresh University graduates, innovators young and old and those willing to put in hard labour. In the agricultural communities outside the capital she looks for experienced hands and those well in the know about ages-old cultivation methods.

Her team — her 'agricultural advancers' — a mix of experienced and young people, needs to be wise enough to know what's right, then brave enough to choose it. They dance to the beat of the old world man with the heat of the new world woman. They have to be sharp enough to win the world, and wily enough not to loose it. Above all, as they try to move forward, they need to keep their nature pure.

Grace M'Boku's agricultural advancers must first face five years of hardship. Near the floodplains of the Limpopo River, the land is all but barren, and grand new techniques, together with ceaseless toil, can make it fertile. They must make agrichar and biochar—taking the best from *chitemene*—use new ways of mound cultivation to make the land, square metre by square metre, fertile again.

Not only that. After the land is fertilised, a careful mix of produce must be planted to maintain not only the fecundity, but the re-implemented diversity, as well. Beyond that, they have to make sure that the super-symbiotic neo-agricultures they've developed are also drought-resistant. Otherwise, one single super dry season will undo all their hard work.

She needs initial investments and — like other women, who form ninety percent of all successful applications — gets a microcredit for her project. She fully intents to be among the ninety- five percent who actually pay their loan back. After which she wants to uplift others in her region.

—Saaki Sami gathers people from Finland, Norway, Sweden and Russia—with a few stray Icelanders—to form his research & development team. Reining them in like reindeer, he lures them with the carrot-and-stick approach of old guilt and new challenges.

His team is making something huge that incorporates immensely small parts. Not as big as an iron ore smelter, nor as large as Oulu's paper manufacturing plant, but still very substantial. Small enough to be easily constructed in other places, but large enough to take on big loads.

In their premises overlooking the snow-covered plains of the Scandinavian Arctic Circle, they're developing a high-temperature nano lubricant-cum-dissolver, a grey goo that's extremely resistant to high temperatures, able to penetrate the smallest of chips and circuit boards, with the ability to extract the rare metal needle in the discarded computing equipment haystack. Billions upon billions of computers, smartphones, tablets and other gadgets have been made, used and discarded in quick succession as Moore's Law ran its course. Enormous, polluting landfills where precious metals lay inert as current ores are running out. At some point intricate, intensive recycling will become economically viable. Saaki Sami's team wishes to be ahead of that very curve.

—the eightfold path—

Chika Wu's test project in Chengdu succeeds beyond her team's wildest dreams. Large panels covered with the solar nanofilm cover many square kilometres of the mountain- and countryside near Chengdu, and are interconnected with the cuprate superconducting wires. These same superconducting wires have been laid all the way to Chengdu, supplying the city with over ninety percent of its required energy. A coup emphasising the solar nanofilm's efficiency considering the mostly grey weather of the area.

They also developed a more powerful type of battery. These batteries, implemented both in electric cars and houses have become plentiful enough to store the peak electricity production at day in order to keep supplying everybody with electrical power at night.

The test project is so successful that the Chinese government wants to implement it at a much larger scale in the Gobi Desert, to supply solar power to Beijing, Shanghai and other megacities. Private entrepreneurs are already looking to implement the technology in cities outside China like Tokyo, Seoul, Bangkok and Taipei, among many others.

Five years after the successful test project, the Chengdu Jintang coal power station has been shut down. Chengdu has now the best air quality of any municipality with more than a million people in China, and proudly calls itself the 'green revolution city'.

—After the first five years, João Incanna's fleet is expanding rapidly. Simultaneously, the novoplankton-growing basins of his team are popping up everywhere along the Peruvian coast, even expanding into Chile and Ecuador.

The good they've been doing is surfacing gradually. Fish stocks are, slowly yet inevitably, picking up from their all-time lows. The novoplankton is thriving, both re-invigorating the food chain from the bottom up and countering the acidification of the ocean. Coral bleaching has come to a standstill, and a few coral reefs are steadily recovering. The plastic pollution levels are decreasing, albeit at a rate slower than they wish. His team keeps working hard to improve the efficiency of their megabionets.

The plastic they deliver to the space-elevator-to-be base is fully recycled into graphene and several organic by-products. The graphene is shot into orbit through a double railgun. The first railgun shoots up magnetised ice, most of which (flash-)evaporates in the atmosphere. Right behind it, in the magnetised ice's slipstream, is the real payload that does not burn up in the air. There, in geosynchronous orbit, is where the quadruple-redundant ribbon of the space elevator is produced.

Over time, they gather more plastic than is needed for the manufacture of the space elevator's ribbon, and they deliver the surplus to plastic recycling plants in North and South America. Big oil companies are either slowly dying out, or adapting, modifying their refineries into plastic recycling facilities. Crude oil production dwindles as renewable energy starts providing the majority of the world's energy needs and increasingly intricate recycling methods become competitive alternatives to crude oil's refined products. Slowly, for the first time in two hundred years, CO2-levels in the atmosphere are falling.

—In Botswana, five years of toiling are followed by five years of feeding the people, modifying both their recharring methods and their neo-agricultures to different types of lands and climates. In the original implementation areas — the floodplains of the Limpopo River — hunger became a thing of the past, and people slowly became better off as they were producing more than they could eat, and subsequently found willing markets for their inherently sustainable food.

The hard labour required to set up such a neo-agriculture provides much-needed work. Increasingly, people aren't complaining that they're working so hard, but that they're proud to do such good work for the future of their family, friends, community and — in the long run — for their country and continent.

Their knowledge is made open source, but it doesn't spread as fast as Grace M'Boku and her people like, even as it's made available on every smartphone in Africa. Language remains a huge barrier, and they set up a quick translation app — at first manned by many human translators, more automated as machine learning catches on — that's sponsored by voluntary donations through moola from Mxit and other forms of electronic money. As their livelihoods increase, people are increasingly willing to pay their dues.

As a fortunate by-effect, sub-Saharan Africa starts to develop infrastructures old and new that need less original investments and maintenance such as vacuum Zeppelins for long distance transport, electric quads for short distance transport and Electrified Trees for data signal transport, all increasingly powered by renewable energy. Their economies are growing in a highly sustainable manner.

—After a series of increased fine-tunings, the prototype MaNa—Macro/Nano—Smelter in Luleå achieves recycling efficiencies of over ninety-nine percent, while being energetically self-sustainable and carbon neutral. The refined blueprint, which has been open source from the beginning, remains available to all. Siblings of the Lapland MaNaSmelter are popping up everywhere, worldwide. In a mere five years, the production of the newest device is truly green, sustainable and fair. Fairphone in Amsterdam declare themselves obsolete and start a new project called 'Fairspace'. Landfills are rewilded after their soil has been purified by modified versions of the MaNaSmelters. Most of the mines are closed, their premises re- purified if possible, and rewilded, as well (even if a few are refurbished as *appartements nouveaux*). Eco-diversity is recovering, previously thought extinct species tentatively make a return, and Mercury and other heavy metal accumulation at the top of the food chain are diminishing.

On good days, the MaNaSmelter produces a small surplus of energy. Part of it is fed back into the grid, yet part of it is used for the sauna set up by Saaki Sami's team. After cleaning their minds and refreshing their bodies in the cleansing steam bath, Sami's people roll around in the snow, sky-clad and earth-bound. Is it psychosomatic, or are the winters slowly becoming colder?

—a coda of four kōans—

—If the strength of a chain is determined by its weakest link, how can the chain of life stretch endlessly long? —

—If the survival of the fittest was the grand design behind Darwinian evolution, what's the strategy in the Anthropocene? —

—How is the karma of a people determined? How can you strengthen your own karma? —

—Is it wise to explore another environment while you do not fully understand your own? Is it wise to remain in your own environment forever? —

A Mycologist's Guide to ~~Falling in Love~~ Discovering a New Species

Shelly Jones

Mica had loved Adams before the experiment went wrong. Analyzing the datasets under the plastic dome of the greenhouse, she'd decided it must be love: watching Adams evolve, not understanding how or why, but accepting the outcome nonetheless

"I love you," Mica said one day in the lab, testing the words. The brick-colored moon filled the sky above them as she dripped solvent from a pipette onto the sample cells. For a moment, she thought she hadn't said anything or that her words had been absorbed by the hydronics, nutrients to replace the Earthan soil they would normally thrive in.

"Of course you do," Adams answered, pointing to the fungal ridge growing along the back of his neck. "I'm a *fun guy*." She had shaken her head at his corniness, rolling her eyes and turning away to clean the pipette. But now the words haunted her: had she loved Adams or the fungi that spread along his legs and arms, across his torso to his lower abdomen? How could she be sure which she found more fascinating?

***

At first, Adams' transformation was subtle, a fringe of beige antler mushrooms cresting his temple, a patch of truffle tattooing his arm, black like a bruise.

He had recorded the findings in his daily log but had waited to share them with Mica. Most of the growths could be hidden under his uniform or undetected with the right stance or tilt of the head. Adams hadn't taken the spores seriously in the beginning. "Something else for the memoirs when we get back to Earth," he'd joke.

Mica hadn't heard him. She was studying the tablet in her hand as she compared the data, her brow furrowed. He stared at her.

"Mica, Mica, always so serious." He shook his head disapprovingly, but a grin grew wide across his face, forcing the funnels of fungus around his eyes to dance.

"Why didn't you say something sooner?" Mica asked, still examining the logs carefully, as though trying to understand a language she did not speak. The readings of his vitals and the mineral counts in his blood were all changing, spiking or dipping to unnatural levels. "We should start recording your vitals each hour. I'm going to need to take photos of your body to document the patterns of growth. We can compare them to your pre-spaceflight images on file." She turned to the computer and began a new log.

"Is that really necessary?" Adams asked with a sigh. He stared up at the plastic ceiling of the outpost, ignoring the beeping monitors he was connected to.

"We need to understand how the fungi are spawning in this new environment."

"It's not an environment, Mica. It's my body," Adams said, bristling at her words. But she had already left the greenhouse in search of more supplies.

***

It wasn't until the new phase of the second moon that Adams realized how serious his condition had become. He had slept in, past the alarm, his hand lazily swiping the screen to mute it, before waking again, hours later to

Mica shaking him. His eyes were crusted over with spores, and he rubbed them away.

"Just be still, Adams." Mica was examining him, her hands sweeping over his body for new growths. "We need to get you to the lab."

"Mica, I'm fine. I'm just a little tired." Adams tried to sit up, but his muscles faltered. His stomach twisted and panic surged through him as a cold sweat prickled his arms. "What is happening to me?" But Mica just shook her head.

Later, once he was hooked up to the monitors in the lab, he asked her again.

"They didn't train us for a mycelium mutation," Mica muttered. She tapped her tablet repeatedly and groaned when it didn't respond, spiraling in digital confusion at her many requests.

"Mutation?" He looked at her quizzically, the word heavy on his tongue.

"Adams, look," Mica sighed, turning the screen toward him. "This isn't a bad case of some cosmic athlete's foot. Your DNA is changing."

Mica watched him as he digested the data. Something was growing in the sclera of his eyes. She set the tablet down on the metal tray with a thud.

"How is that even possible?"

"I'm not sure. I don't even know how or when you were exposed to the fungus. I'm the one spending hours in the greenhouse trying to find some species that will grow in these conditions. Shouldn't I be the one with spores growing out of every orifice?" Mica wanted to take back the words as they fell out of her mouth.

Adams lowered his head, his arms folded across his chest. "Are you jealous? Of mold?"

"Adams, I didn't mean that. We'll find a solution. Together." She rubbed his arm lightly, careful not to touch the bracket fungi flourishing on his triceps.

Adams nodded but said nothing.

***

In the waxing of the third moon, Mica entered the greenhouse to discover all of her fungal specimens had aborted. "No, no, no," she cried, rushing to the black synthetic logs where the molds grew. She logged into the database to scan the last biofeedback readings that had been recorded.

"I don't understand," she murmured. "How could this not work?"

She ripped open the plastic that mimicked a dead log, a relic of a bygone era on Earth. She could remember being a child, climbing through the ash, as she tried to map out her neighborhood after the fires: the melted playground, a puddle where the mailbox had been, her bike wheel a twisted grimace. Her parents had warned her not to play in the ash, afraid it could infect her lungs, particulates settling inside her. But Mica had ignored their pleas, exploring the once familiar terrain as if scouting out an unknown territory.

Mica collapsed on the floor of the lab, the spilt soil and wood chips scattered around her. She could not understand what had gone wrong.

"Mica?" Adams called from the doorway. "Are you crying?"

She did not turn around, but remained on the floor, studying the barren samples before her. "The compounds in the soil aren't right. The few spores that grew aborted within a few hours. I don't understand it. They," Mica swallowed her words. She did not want to be the one to tell him what was happening, her words defining him, his mortality.

"What are you saying?" Adams asked, coughing. His voice rasped like dry leaves. Mica imagined his lungs transforming into papery balloons like hornet's nests.

"They found a host in you. In your body. Why?" She turned back and stared at Adams, finials of fungus erupting from his neck and shoulders.

Adams shrugged and walked away.

***

Mica carefully placed the scalpel along Adams' rib and scraped a few samples of the growths onto microscope slides. "Do you smell that?" Mica asked, her nose twitching.

Adams sniffed the air and shook his head. "I don't smell anything."

Mica closed her eyes and inhaled deeply. She could feel the earthy aroma from the smoke snake around her body, embedding itself in her scalp. "Smoke," she said quietly.

Adams looked around the lab for any sign of fire. He tapped at his tablet, monitoring the security status on the outpost. There were no alerts anywhere in the facility. "There's no fire, Mica. Everything is secure."

Mica nodded and resumed taking the skin samples from Adams' leg. With each scrap, she could smell the musty aroma of charred soil. She held her breath as she took the final sample and turned away. "I'll start processing these."

Adams sat back on the gurney and watched the molds knit themselves over the sites where Mica had scraped. For a moment, he felt a comforting warmth he had not experienced since they had arrived at the outpost. He smiled and waited for Mica to return.

***

As a child, after the fires, Mica had wandered into the nearby skeletal woods. There, sprouting from the blackened log, confetti of coral-colored spores dotted the forest floor. She had dug her hands into the ash and pulled up the burnt log. Beneath, a network of mycelium spread out, like fingers outstretched in the dark. Mica had marveled at the vibrant molds thriving in the hidden crevices of the desolated landscape that once was her home. She gingerly touched the mycelium, wishing she could feel the data flowing through her fingertips, signals from one life to another.

***

"Lift your arm," Mica instructed, holding the camera close to him. Adams sighed and did as she asked, lifting his arm to reveal the ghost mushroom unfolding in the cavity of his armpit. Mica snapped a few photos from different angles, reviewed them on the camera and nodded, satisfied. "Now turn onto your stomach."

"Is this really necessary, Mica? Can't you just document what you've seen?"

"I have, but protocol says we need photographic documentation whenever possible." "Well, it isn't *possible* to photograph my naked behind," Adams insisted.

Mica laughed and turned the camera off. "It isn't naked; it's just wearing a new style of clothes. Fungal fashion."

Adams smirked. "This isn't how I thought you'd see me naked for the first time," he said. Taking her hand, he interweaved his fingers with hers, smiling.

Mica blushed, realizing that he was right. She had documented his transformation for weeks, but had not considered his body in that way. She squeezed back, feeling the softness of his flesh like an overripe peach. "Me either," she said after a moment.

Relenting, Adams rolled over on the gurney and let her slip the sheet down to his thighs. He buried his face in the pillow when he heard the mechanical purr of the camera as it flashed into action. Mica pulled the sheet up over him again when it was done.

***

"When did you fall in love with me?" Adams asked on the last night.

Mica hesitated, wondering what she could say. She thought about the cheesy romantic comedies she had watched growing up on earth, mementos from her grandmother. She particularly liked the ones where the dreamy-eyed protagonist's hardest challenge was to tell someone they loved them. Or to realize they were deserving of love. She wondered if there had ever been a romance about a scientist and her experiment that didn't end in tragedy.

"That day in the lab," she replied after a moment.

"Which day?" he pressed. "All we do is spend time in the lab. Before or after the change?"

The monitor beeped urgently, his pulse feeble. His lungs had filled with mold, branching out like a spider web across the last scan.

"The day I touched you," Mica lied, wincing at the incessant blare of the monitor. "You had something in your hair, and I brushed it away."

"I don't remember," Adams managed, his voice raspy.

"You smiled. Grateful," Mica said, envisioning the moment although she had invented it.

He smiled weakly and closed his eyes. *Grateful*, Mica thought again.

The golden moon was waning the night Adams died, the night he transformed, his body overcome by the growth. They had not talked about what Mica would do then. Protocol dictated that his body should be placed in a stasis chamber for his eventual return to Earth. But Adams had not indicated that he wanted his body returned, that there was anything for him to return to. Mica wondered what good it would do, his body abandoned on a planet that would soon be uninhabitable..

Mica wheeled the gurney into the greenhouse. Gingerly, she picked up his body and was surprised at how little he weighed, his flesh spongy in her hands. She placed him next to the plastic logs that she had respawned on a bed of wood chips. She arranged him carefully, a tuft of lion's mane curving upward along his head, his toes honeycombed morels standing at attention.

Mica smiled at him and ran her fingers through her hair, feeling the ridge that had started to develop behind her ear.

It was time, she thought. Downloading the data, she sent an email to the administration: "Adams is dead. Send a new team ready to explore fungal aptitudes in extraplanetary environments. Life can grow here." Her laptop pinged, indicating a successful transmission.

She sat in the silence of the outpost, showered in the golden moonlight, and stared at Adams' body. After a while, she stood up and joined him. Inhaling deeply, she could smell the smoke again and let it fill her, dragging her body down to the floor. She curled herself around him, burrowing into him. She waited for his mycelium to branch and multiply, feeling their way to her, to transmit to the network unfolding between her toes, sprouting from her belly button. Soon they would be tethered together, sharing everything through the mycelium that bound them as one.

Space Unicorn and Magic Ovens

Liam Hogan

I'm sitting with ma as she prepares dinner. It's one of her rules, of which there are more every year. "I don't mind cooking for you, Jem, while you're young," she says. "But I'm not your servant and I'm not working while you watch TV or read comics. So it's either homework, or come keep me company as I prep."

A choice like that is no choice at all, even if it sometimes seems closer to extra lessons than not. She's asking the usual questions about how my day has been and what I learnt at school, which is *so* long ago I can hardly remember, so I tell her what Billy said instead.

Ma lays the knife aside, thoughtful. "Billy, hey?"

I nod. "Right before last class, during break. We'd just had a story-tell about fairies. *Ain't no truth to it,* Billy said. *No truth at all!* Maisie was in *tears.* And... I didn't know what to say to her." I feel heat rising in my cheeks at the memory.

"You could have said Billy's grammar is appalling."

I turn my almost-laugh into a scowl. "So he's right?" I demand. "It is all lies and make-believe? It's just *science*?"

"Didn't your teacher say Billy might be an engineer one day?"

"Yeah." And hasn't *that* gone to his big head?

"Well, Billy is a smart boy." My scowl hardens. "But no imagination. And not a lot of kindness, either."

I don't say anything to that. Imagination and having the wool pulled over the eyes seem to be the same thing. Everyday, whether in class or out, another illusion is burst, another childhood story revealed as fake. And *kindness*? Is that any excuse to deceive?

Ma sighs. She must be able to feel the anger rolling off me. "OK, kiddo. Maybe it's tough to understand, but what if the stories and the science are both right?"

"*Huh?*"

"What happens when I put this dish in the oven?"

Gah. *Science* again. "The microwaves vibrate the water molecules," I repeat without enthusiasm, "and transfer the heat to the rest of the food. That's why--"

She taps my hand away from the sliced veg, where I've been stealing slivers of raw carrot. "So it's not magic, then?"

"Well, *no*."

"Even though it's called a Magic Oven?"

"That's just a *name*."

"Is it? Can you explain how a microwave generator actually works? Why they work so well on water? How the oven stops microwaves leaking out all over the place? Or even why it's got a turntable?"

I frown. It's quickly becoming a very frowny dinner prep, as she places the dish in the oven and sets the timer.

"Do you think Billy could?" she asks.

"Maybe." I shrug, distracted as our meal slowly spins behind the glass door, the smell reminding me how *hungry* I am.

"What about Billy when he was two years younger?"

"*Definitely* no." Ma missed a couple of carrot sticks from the chopping board, and doesn't seem to notice as I pinch them one by one.

"So for Billy-two-years-younger, does a microwave work by science, or by magic?"

I munch the carrot, glad for the excuse to think about my answer. "Science," I decide as I swallow. "But Billy-two-years doesn't *know* that yet."

She smiles and nods. "It's all in the narrative. We tell the stories the listeners will understand. Otherwise, the audience learns nothing."

"It's still not *real*, though," I protest. "Fairies, and... things."

"It's as real as you believe it to be. Or, as real as the storyteller can possibly make it."

"Even if the storyteller knows it's science?"

"*Especially* then. Because the storyteller--me--can't explain to you how a microwave works either. Hardly anyone can. But every single person knows how oven fairies hate metal, right?"

I roll my eyes.

"Which is *important*. Because sparks and fires are very bad in space. That's why, whenever we need a new story--and we always need new stories, it's as much my job creating them as telling them--we work closely with the engineers, with people like Billy's dad, to make sure the story makes as much sense as the science."

I turn to stare out of the porthole, another excuse to think. Somewhere, out there, is the star we left, long before I was born. And somewhere, out there, is the star we'll arrive at, long after I'm gone. I look down and back to the rear of the spaceship and the glittering trail we leave in our wake.

"And unicorns?" I ask, trembling, fearful, ready to have my everything turned upside down yet again.

"Oh, they're real enough." Ma laughs. "And you best hope they never stop pushing. 'Cos ain't *no-one* aboard this spaceship knows how the heck the thing flies.

Electric Waterfalls

Ruth Joffre

A solar panel was malfunctioning in Cluster 4, Quadrant 6 of the Prudhoe Array. Measuring approximately three hundred miles across and hovering one thousand feet above the water, the floating array was co-owned by NOAA, the National Oceanic and Atmospheric Association, and SARC, the Subarctic Regional Corporation, which had bought out the floundering renewables divisions of three oil companies on the North Slope after prospecting was banned in the Arctic and the crude oil market tanked. In news reports, the solar array was always referred to by its government name, but locals always called it Noah's Arc. As in, "Looks like we got another leak on Noah's Arc."

"I got it," Xiomara said, noting that the other part-time technicians had laid out the blanket for a game of snerts and were distracted.

Only Charlene paused to ask, "Are you sure? This looks to me like maybe a two-hour job, plus travel to the Arc, and your shift's almost over."

Xiomara didn't mind. Between panicking about her exams and worrying that her crush, Amka, wouldn't come to her birthday party tomorrow, she couldn't sit still. Better to move, she thought, than to keep reading the same essays on solar engineering over and over without retaining a word. "No worries. I'll take this one. You folks enjoy your game."

Charlene frowned over her glasses. "Do you want any backup?"

"Aww, let her take it, Charlie," another tech said, shuffling the deck. "With her gone, one of us could actually win for a change."

"Have fun," Xiomara said as they kicked off the first rapid-fire round of snerts. With a swipe of the hand, she claimed the ticket in the system and alerted the depot. "I'll need an airmachine."

On the way, she went over her guest list in her head. It was modest, just a collection of family, friends, and colleagues who for one reason or another had never been to the top of the solar array. Amka and her grandparents had recently moved to New Deadhorse from a village in the interior, and Xiomara hoped to impress Amka with her intimate knowledge of the array and its secrets—how if you stood in the center of a cluster, the silvery panels would shimmer like a school of fish; how if you pressed a button at the edge of one cluster you could instruct it to temporarily link up with another, creating a bridge of light across which you could walk for miles in every direction without ever touching the ground.

By the time Xiomara arrived at the depot, her best work friend, Taylor, was languishing on top of the airmachine, their boots kicked up to rest on the handlebars, head flung back over the rear reflector, long blue-streaked hair cascading down the retrofitted snowmachine to dust the floor.

"Showoff." Xiomara smirked, knocking those massive packboots off the handlebars.

With a shrug, Taylor twisted off the machine into a standing position. "Been a slow day."

"Tell me about it. Spent three hours watching anti-reflective coating dry while studying for my A-exams in the shop. Read this article called 'Theoretical Fluctuations in Photovoltaic Efficacy Resulting from Prolonged Exposure to Electromagnetic Instability.'"

"Thrilling. I had yet another wannabe inventor come to me with blueprints for how to make a snowmachine run underwater: propellers, turbines, a big plastic bubble with a periscope on top." Their hands clasped around the handles of an imaginary periscope, spinning it back and forth, until finally they waved a hand in the air. "Had to break it to him that his great idea was basically just a submarine—and a pretty rudimentary one, at that."

"Next thing you know he'll reinvent the bus."

"You laugh, but I wouldn't mind some public transit once they finish the road."

"Public transit to where?" Xiomara points a thumb over her shoulder. "Utqiaġvik is two hundred miles away. Fairbanks is more like five hundred."

"What about a high-speed train to Anchorage? Better than finding a bush pilot."

"I don't think the ground's stable enough. We only got the permafrost back ten years ago."

With a pinch of their mouth, Taylor bobbed their head side to side, then agreed, "You might be right. All I know is I would feel better if I could decide to leave without it taking three days and thousands of dollars to get to the Lower 49." Their packboots dragged across the depot floor to a tool bench, where Taylor picked up various items (wrenches, oil cans, a greasy pair of work gloves), then listlessly set them down again, like abandoned dreams.

For as long as Xiomara could remember, Taylor had been planning to leave New Deadhorse behind. It was a small village on land once overrun by seasonal oil workers and their deprivations. Over the last one hundred and fifty years, SARC had built a new village on top of the reclaimed Prudhoe facilities, and the majority of its residents were Alaska Native engineers and technicians working for the corporation. To both of their knowledge, Taylor was the only trans person in the village. Originally, Taylor had planned to leave for college; then, when their grades tanked in junior year and a basketball scholarship seemed like a distant fantasy, they started dreaming of opening their own shop in Seattle, where their skill as a mechanic could be put to use repairing aircycles and solar-powered RVs instead of airmachines. Each month, Taylor socked away a little money in their GenderFuck-Off Fund.

Their voice dipped low, mumbling through calculations, underlining variables beyond their control while Xiomara gathered the gear she would need on Cluster 4: dimmer goggles, conductive gloves, rubber-soled boots, spare photovoltaic panels roughly the size of her palm, a soldering kit. She stuffed this gear into a storage compartment under the seat of the airmachine, then sat sidesaddle on it, listening. Finally, she said, "I'll come visit you in Seattle once you're set up."

"Yeah?" Taylor twisted around, a big grin on their face. "How will you get there?"

She slapped the saddle. "I bet I could ride this all the way across the Yukon."

They threw their head back with laughter. "Good luck!"

"Thanks. You coming to my party tomorrow?"

"Maybe," Taylor said, without the usual sarcasm. Their elbows settled on the bench, enabling them to lean back and cross their legs at the ankles. "It's kind of a chore getting out there, isn't it?"

"Just rent one of the airmachines. Company's fine with it."

"Are you sure? That doesn't sound like Management."

"One thousand percent; went through official channels and everything. See?" She brought up the approval email on her standard-issue SARC holo-tablet. It sat starred and pinned at the top of her inbox, but the interface had dimmed to minimum brightness to conserve battery, so Taylor had to step forward and squint. "Sorry—I've been meaning to recharge," she said, docking the tablet in one of the airmachine's solar-powered charging stations.

Taylor mimed putting on reading glasses. "Damn. How long is this email?" With a flick of their eyes, they instructed the interface to scroll down through pages and pages of legalese. "If I'm reading this right, this says you're liable for any damages to the solar array and that SARC reserves the right to charge you per diem rates for any outages or repairs on the Arc."

"Yeah, but the lawyer said that's standard and the company would likely choose to exercise its right to waive this requirement," she said, demonstrating with a bored hand gesture.

"And you believed that? Wow, you've fully bought in, haven't you?"

"That's not true." Offended, she dropped her hand to grip the seat. "You know I'm as tired of the legal gymnastics of our government overlords as you are, but I want my party." She raised her eyebrows, as if to say, *I'm not going to apologize for that.*

"You mean you want to seduce Amka with talk of your fancy distance PhD program."

Flushed, Xiomara squeezed her shoulders together with self-conscious delight. "Guilty."

Grinning again, they said, "Okay, I'll come to your party—but only to watch you flirt!"

"Maybe you'll learn something." Her quip was met with a single dry *ha* as Taylor sauntered back to the tool bench, waving farewell over their shoulder. Xiomara donned a safety helmet and many winter layers, then maneuvered the airmachine for takeoff. "See you tomorrow!"

Before she could fly away, Taylor yelled, "Wait!" and then tossed her something.

Xiomara caught the small box, which was plastered with Pride stickers. "What's this?"

Taylor shouted over the sound of the engine, "Early birthday present! Open it up there!"

With that, Xiomara sailed into the Arctic twilight. In November, the daylight narrowed like grains of sand through an hourglass until the North Slope slipped into perpetual darkness, with the bright face of the sun never rising above the horizon again until January. In such long, cold months, the tilt of the Earth's axis threw the Arctic into a state of twilight where you could see rays of light streak across the atmosphere, where you could cast nets across the sky but never catch the sun. During this period, maintenance on the Prudhoe Array was all the more critical because the people of the surrounding villages relied on what little solar power the array pulled down in order to power their smart homes and connect to vital teleservices like immersive 3D classrooms that enabled kids in remote villages scattered across hundreds of square miles to attend regional schools. Five-and-a-half years ago, Xiomara had graduated from the only high school on the North Slope (NSBVRHS), which offered virtual reality vocational classes in advanced circuitry and solar mechanics. She had since enrolled as a doctoral candidate in the University of Michigan's Energy Systems Engineering and Sustainable Systems remote dual-degree program.

On the way to Cluster 4, Quadrant 6, she recited laws of solar mechanics in her head. Upon hitting cruising altitude, she engaged the autopilot and returned to the article she had been reading about the appearance of accelerated degeneration of photovoltaic panels on asynchronous satellites within a specific radius of the Sun. What coating, she wondered, could protect those cells from the endless stream of emanating plasma that was the solar wind? Given modular design, could an array of geosynchronous satellites be installed in orbit over, say, Mars to radically reduce the red planet's surface temperature and thus remake its climate? This was the logic behind the Arctic arrays. Block the sun. Capture the summer light before it can melt the ice that formed over winter and allow the new ice to thicken and fortify itself against future melts. In the twenty-first century, hollow silica microspheres were developed for a similar purpose—to enhance the reflectivity of melting ice caps and buy humanity time. Only after the ice caps had fully melted were the large-scale floating arrays greenlit. One hundred fifty years later, the ice caps have grown back, their

Arctic-blue brims barely visible except through cracks in the international network of arrays.

About half an hour into the flight, Xiomara spotted Noah's Arc floating on the horizon. From up here, the array was like a galaxy viewed on its axis—flat and flashy, most notable for how it manipulated the space around it. Above it, the atmosphere shimmered, primed for an aurora; below, there was only shadow, hundreds of miles of pitch-black ocean getting colder by the minute as frost collected on Xiomara's eyebrows. Sometimes, she longed to slip under the water, to hide in that darkness and see what bioluminescent creatures rumbled to the surface, attracted by the flashing hazards of her airmachine. *What if I just stay here until the party?*, she thought, right before a message arrived from Amka:

Haluu! I'm just coming back from a long fishing trip. Want to hang out?

Oh, fuck, Xiomara thought, *I'm not ready*. She dictated: "I'm actually heading to the array for a job."

Oh, cool! Can I meet you there? Good practice so I don't get lost on the way to the party. [upside-down smiley face]

The emoji charmed Xiomara. *Sure! I'll send you coordinates when I get there.*

Quyanapaq!

You're welcome!

With both hands, Xiomara disengaged the autopilot, resuming control of the airmachine's descent to Cluster 4, Quadrant 6. After landing, she estimated forty-five minutes to an hour before Amka arrived in her powerboat. *Not enough time*, she thought, recalling Charlie's estimate that this could be a two-hour job, but after clipping into the safety vest that anchored her to the airmachine with a rope, she sent the coordinates anyway. Soldering kit in hand, she psyched herself up with a hard shake of her shoulders and a couple rounds of, *You got this. You're amazing at your job. This is great practical experience for your degree.*

Her tablet isolated the malfunction to one panel in Quadrant 6. Upon closer inspection, she identified micro-cracks in the conductive subsurface of the panel beneath the translucent protective shield coating that enabled the panels to bear weight. Without the shield, technicians would not be able to service the array in situ and would instead have to remotely disengage panels, then fly them to the depot to be repaired out of context, without the benefit of instantaneous reboot to know that their repairs worked. Xiomara always carried several spare panels with her in case she noticed any other micro-cracks or malfunctions while on Noah's Arc. She pulled a square panel from the breast pocket of her tool vest, where she had also stored the box from Taylor. Once she peeled back some of the stickers, she realized that it was a cheap cardboard ring box. Inside was a silver-plated thumb ring with a small button and a series of dots on the band that looked like sensors or transmitters. A note with it said: *Press me and say hi!*

She removed one glove to activate the ring. She would not be able to work without the glove for long in this cold. A small red button lit up on the ring when pressed. "Hello? Taylor? You there? It's Xi."

A staticky response trickled through: "Xi? Can you . . . Wait . . . I'll just . . . Maybe . . ."

While her friend tinkered with settings and frequencies, Xiomara laid out her tools in a neat line and began the laborious process of rerouting the quadrant's circuitry in order to safely remove a damaged panel without causing an outage. Periodically, the static would flare up, and she would catch snatches of Taylor's curse-laden attempts to troubleshoot the device. With the white noise, her mind quieted temporarily, and she found herself able to focus on the task at hand for a few minutes without thinking of Amka, only saying "Hello?" and "I'm here" every so often while Taylor worked on their connection.

"Hello. Xi? I think I got it for real this time. Can you hear me?"

"Loud and clear," Xiomara said, getting down on her belly. "What about you?"

"Perfect! I'm sorry about the delay. My transmitter was being fussy so I had to restart."

"No worries. I'm surprised I can hear you way out here."

"Yeah. This bad boy's got a range of a thousand miles." An affectionate thud sounded through the ring as Taylor patted the machine. "If I can figure out how to boost it, we might be able to talk from Seattle."

"That would be so cool. Feels like I'm a superhero talking into some fancy communicator ring."

Taylor started to chuckle, then reconsidered. "Wait, does that make me the sidekick?"

"I think it makes you the inventor with the lab full of gadgets," she said, pulling her dimmer goggles up onto her head so she could better maneuver her slim tools into the shadow gaps between photovoltaic panels. One by one, she disconnected wires, musing, "Well, I suppose we would both be the inventors, actually. A queer and nonbinary scientist tag team."

"We should have a team name. Maybe . . . Xi & T?"

"Like gin and tonic? I love it!"

"When you get back I'll engrave it on the ring."

"About that: I might be a little later than expected. Amka's on her way."

"To the Arc? But the party isn't until tomorrow. Unless I messed up the times?"

"No, she happened to be out fishing and now I'm freaking out. As demonstrated by the fact that I just shocked myself," she said, yanking her hand back and shaking it. Her pinky finger tingled unpleasantly, her hand turning pink from the cold. She blew on it for warmth.

Taylor tried to reassure her. "This is a good thing, right? You get to chat alone, without the pressure of the party."

"Except now it's just us. Alone. With the array storing literal electricity under our feet."

"Wow, okay, you need to relax. I can feel the tension from here and I'm a hundred miles away."

Xiomara groaned and resumed disconnecting the wires. "I'm going to blow it. I know it."

"No, you're not. Just take a deep breath. Finish the repair. And think about what you want."

Nodding, Xiomara counted as she breathed: *in for four, out for eight, one more time, okay.* "What I want to know is whether Amka is comfortable being seen with me in public." On the other end of their connection, Taylor started to reply, then paused to think. Into this gap, Xiomara poured her fluttering anxieties and infatuations, recounting a recent walk on the beach with Amka, how in her awkwardness she began collecting stones in her pocket, not because of their beauty but because without them she would fidget and attempt to hold Amka's hand, and how Amka, seeing her, began dropping pebbles into the same pocket, calling them wishes and, when Xiomara asked, saying that wishes were better secrets and did not need to come true to have meaning. In fact, she remembered, Amka preferred wishes that never came true, because they could be nurtured indefinitely, allowed to flourish and transform in the quiet of obscurity, until they emerged more beautiful and poignant than previously imagined in the course of conversation with a friend. "What if a wish in this context is a crush she never intends to act on? And what if I'm that crush?"

"Okay, I see your point, but . . . have you considered the possibility that she's just flirting?"

It seemed impossible to Xiomara, and yet the thought filled her with sparklers.

"She's not your ex," Taylor continued, bringing her back to reality.

"You're right," Xiomara sighed, thinking of her ex, who had never acknowledged their relationship in public but with whom she remained friendly, understanding the difficulties of being open and free in oft-unforgiving places. A ripple of fear in her chest dissipated, replaced by a tentative glimmer of hope. "Thank you for talking me down."

"Anytime. Sounds like you just needed to work through some things."

"Yes. And now I've got to finish this repair before Amka gets here."

"Okay, I'll let you focus, then. I'll be here if you need to chat."

"Thank you; this is an incredible birthday present," she said, twirling the ring on her thumb, then removing it so the weight of the conductive glove wouldn't accidentally activate it during the repair or her conversation with Amka. In the silence on top of Noah's Arc, she took deep, steadying breaths and then plunged her hands into the hole left by the damaged photovoltaic cell. She worked quickly then, installing the new panel, reconnecting the wires, listening all the while for the rumble of Amka's airboat racing across the Beaufort Sea toward the Arctic Ocean. Only a half dozen wires remained disconnected by the time her tablet dinged with a message from Amka:

Is it safe for me to park my boat up there?

No problem! I always park my airmachine here. Still flat on her belly, she engaged voice command on the tablet so she could respond to future messages without having to pause the repair. A couple minutes later, she heard the turbines on Amka's airboat whirring as it rose overhead, and her shoulder-length hair began whipping wildly around her head like the tails of hungry cats. Windblown and harried, she rose to her knees, trying to comb through the knots with her gloves. "Tablet, engage diagnostics on Cluster 4, Quadrant 6, Panel B-2-1."

Behind her, tentative footsteps grew more confident as Amka approached, her hands tucked into the front pocket of her blackberry-colored atitluq, which was layered over her winter clothes and paired with matching fur mittens. Once within speaking distance, she slipped one hand from the pocket and waved, asking, "Do you need time to finish up?"

"No," Xiomara said, even though the answer was actually *yes*. She jumped up with her tools still in hand and, not knowing what to do with them, stuffed them into the pockets of her down parka. Her shoulders pinched together as she tried to calm her nerves. "You have good timing. I just finished the hard part."

"I'm glad." She squint-smiled at the faint reflection of the panels and the short burst of wind passing between them. For the moment, the weather was on their side.

"Me, too. So happy this worked out," Xiomara said, taking out the spare safety vest for Amka. She thought she would slip it onto Amka's shoulders, but the other woman giggled, and she fumbled through securing the straps before taking a steadying step back. "It's your first time on the Arc, right?"

Amka nodded even as her face began to formulate the question: "The Arc?"

"Oh, that's what the techs here call it: Noah's Arc. Because of the partnership."

"I see," Amka said, with a spark of recognition overtaken by macabre mirth. "It seems grim to nickname it Noah's Arc when the sea levels here have risen so much." Her gaze drifted off to the right, where the icy expanse of the Arctic Ocean was just visible over the lip of the array. "Could you imagine this holding a pair of elephants? Or bowhead whales?" Her mouth pinched as she considered the hundreds of miles of solar panels. "I bet you could fit every bowhead whale on the planet on top of this one array."

"It would crash from the weight first."

"And then the whales would return to the ocean," Amka said, pleased.

Xiomara gave a nervous little shrug. "Noah's Ark didn't carry sea creatures, anyway."

An irreverent giggle bubbled up. "That's true. I always found that rude somehow."

"Same. I've never liked the nickname. I usually call it the Arc. Like an arc of electricity."

"I like that better," Amka said, as she lowered the hood of her atitluq and peered up at the streaks of orange in the twilit sky. Her hand shot up, pointing to what appeared at first to be a flock of birds but revealed itself to be a flight of airmachines most likely headed to one of the nine other arrays jigsawed over the Arctic Circle. All but three of the massive arrays were owned by an Alaska Native Corporation, First Nations tribe, or Russian oligarch; together, they captured approximately 10 percent of Earth's total electricity and 85 percent of its total solar power in summer. Once filled to capacity, arrays docked at former offshore oil rigs long since decommissioned and retrofitted to siphon solar power to massive grids. Offloaded solar power was prioritized to Arctic communities, and SARC's lobbyists had worked on the Alaska delegation to ensure that New Deadhorse and the reclaimed Prudhoe Bay facilities always had utilities available. "It's so nice having guaranteed power. And a pool."

"And a cinema! It's amazing what companies used to do for seasonal workers."

"And what they wouldn't do to save the planet."

"Not to mention the millions they spent popularizing the term 'carbon footprint.'"

Head down, Amka said, "I'm glad they're gone," and poked at the massive array her people co-owned, pressing the toe of her shoe experimentally against the panels, as if testing whether they would hold the weight of their full responsibility. "You know, my father and I debated moving up here for years before we did it. Our ancestors hunted bowheads in these waters centuries before Big Oil arrived on the North Slope. This has always been our land—but it was long put to their purpose. He feared that coming back here, living in their buildings, watching their movies, would perpetuate their memory—their history—instead of ours."

I can understand that. Stories like theirs can be dangerous."

"Stories like theirs are dying. We're indigenizing them, one by one." A smile tugged at the corners of her mouth until she said, "It can be a slow process. But only if you believe in this concept people have come to call 'time.'"

Out of surprise, Xiomara laughed once, musing aloud, "Do I believe in the concept of time? Good question. I guess I believe in how long it takes for a glacier to form. And how quickly it can melt." She gazed down at the ragged patches of young sea ice floating below. "Perhaps time should be measured like that: in events."

"Perhaps." A bright smile lit Amka's face then. "Did I tell you we got an ice cellar?"

"You didn't tell me that. Congratulations! That's a huge step."

Amka giggled, adding, "It has backup solar power."

"Awesome. Have you filled it up yet?"

"The other day. We transferred everything," Amka said, dipping a hand into her atitluq to retrieve a small package wrapped in brown paper. Inside were four strips of maktak, perfectly portioned and color blocked, the pale pink whale blubber meeting the inky black of its skin in a clean line, like elegant patisserie. Her teeth sank into its chewy, boiled skin. Her hunger awakened then, and she endeavored to eat slowly, not wanting to make a fool of herself.

Halfway through their strips, Amka said, "Thank you again for inviting me to your party."

"Of course," Xiomara said, swallowing the resurgent fear that Amka would not come.

"Will there be games and music?" She glanced around, searching for a table and snacks.

"Oh, yeah. We'll have dancing and cake and hologames." In her excitement, she babbled for a while about decorations and arrangements, how she had to account for wind shear and precipitation and the possibility of devices running out of battery if the party ran long, which she hoped it would. She wanted everything to be perfect. She blushed at the nakedness of this desire, then tried to shrug it off and play it cool. "Anyway, there's plenty of time. I'll bring the stuff up tomorrow."

"That's wise. It's supposed to snow tonight," Amka said, her head tilted back to the sky as if to catch the snowflakes before they fell or alighted in her hair. During storms, Xiomara told her, the three-hundred-mile expanse of the Prudhoe Array was disassembled, the clusters disengaging from the totality, then breaking into quadrants, sectors, and finally subdivisions, which all tilted on their mechanical axes until they floated at 45-degree angles in rain and 75-degree angles in snow, so that precipitation would slough off the coated panels, like meltwater off of pointed roofs.

"I bet it looks like a million tiny waterfalls," Amka said, her tone reverent.

"Yes," Xiomara nodded, "but you can only see them when lightning strikes." She lifted her face to the heavens—the streaks of mottled blue and gray coalescing into storm clouds—and as she gazed skyward Amka's right hand slipped out of the atitluq and found her fingers in the cold. Had they ever touched before, skin to skin? Xiomara searched her memories for a graze, a brush, even a soft tap on the shoulder, but found nothing like this. The way their hands fit together as Amka tucked them both into Xiomara's coat pocket and snuggled closer against the cold.

One day, Xiomara hoped, she would show Amka the electric waterfalls. Before the Arctic froze over again, before the air was too cold for thunderstorms, they would rent an airmachine from the depot and fly out to a docking station to watch the lightning bolts arc down from the sky in hundreds. This was not the future her great-great-great-great-great-great-grandparents had pictured when they first moved to New Deadhorse, Alaska, but it was the future she wanted.

Worker's Song

H. Pueyo

Here lies the queen, giant and still, each of her six arms sprawled, open, curved, twitching like she forgot she no longer breathed. Here, in the royal chamber, among us, who only know how to serve, a goddess instead of a woman, a creature so gargantuan that not even dozens of us could move her, she, who covers all, whom we feed since she was born. We, who transformed her into what she is and what she has been, admire her now, not knowing how to continue without her orders telling us what to do and where to go.

Some approach her. The queen's body refuses to rot, frozen in an eternal chrysalis, firm and dry, highlighting what we should have already known: she is grotesque. Lying on comfortable pillows, the queen rests facing the ceiling, her two upper arms extended in martyrdom, her central pair folded unnaturally, her legs prostrated against the walls.

The Great Mother is dead, some of us say—our whispers echoing inside the camber. Others clean her body, wiping the soil and dust off her articulated limbs, polishing the terracotta hue of the royal corpse. The neck ligature of the former ruler has been split, almost entirely amputated, and doubt spreads among us: the stripes of organic tissue look like they have been slashed, a poorly executed decapitation, perhaps. The question remains: what will we do now?

We only hear our own echo for days. Without the duty of work, we aimlessly roam the complex tunnels we have been building for years, and wander the fungal gardens we lovingly cultivated, turned into nothing more than entwined white carcasses. In the nursery, the children toss and turn without the food we used to deliver without fail. The underground booms with the queen's title—the Great Mother—and we cover her chamber with leaves as dead as her.

"There is no reason to leave the body here," says Vinca, walking amid the barren fingers of our monarch. "The royal chamber is far larger than the others. It could house two or three nurseries."

"What is a nursery for, without offspring?" we ask. "Only the queen can give birth to new children."

"An archive, then," says Vinca.

"What is memory without its people?" we answer back. "What are we, without a leader?"

"Or a plantation." Vinca climbs the phalanges of the deceased, walking over the joints of the arm and stopping above the thorax. "It could be greater than any garden. With the humidity and the space we have here..."

"Why cultivate, if we are already dead?"

Vinca gazes down at our mother. The queen lies naked, like she always was on her sumptuous pillows, partially covered by the crimson fabric that spirals from her breast to the middle of her inanimate legs. It makes the body look like the body it should be: beautiful, ample, maternal, immaculate, immense. For a moment, that is how we see her, ephemeral, not the end of our lineage, not an announced calamity, not the imminent destruction of our anthill that now decays without new life.

She is nothing but a body.

The realization is transmitted through our shared network of minds. Our mother is just a body; she is not divine. We keep no secrets from each other—we should keep no secrets—we cannot have them. We are more than individuals, we are the web that ties us, the internal skeleton connecting every dot of this colony, where visions and opinions drip, without explanation, from one sister to the other, streaming from the same infinite source. We have no secrets, but the queen keeps dead, and no one knows who killed her. The grief that controls us is not directed to her, but to ourselves. The desire to live is a thirst; it burns in the throats of our guttural tunnels; it twists the bodies of our children, who cry and plea for attention, activating a mechanism unknown until then: that of the most primal instinct, urging us to survive.

In the nursery, we hear another voice:

"Do we have any princesses? I could swear I saw one or two of them, the other day," says Hosta, huge compared to so many others, but still childlike in front of the queen.

"There is none," we answer. "The queen ate them all."

Hosta's muscular arms are not made for the young, and her mandibles are heavy and inept before the pale newborn. She touches one of the grubs, whose thin translucent pellicle is yet to crystallize in the shape of an adult, and the girl wriggles like she was burned. There are cradles of baked clay scattered across the room, thousands of them, that go from the floor to the ceiling, tiny holes hiding equally tiny creatures.

"Excellent." Hosta leaves the baby aside, and returns to the center of the nursery, where we observe her, as fearful of her harshness as the children are fearful of her size and strength. "If you happen to find one, she must be fed like all the others; she must be raised like all the others, without privilege or special conditions, independently of what she eventually becomes. Do you understand?"

The nursemaids nod.

Those squalid old women surround Hosta, peering at her from the gloom. Something changes within us. In the depths of our home, there are factions that agree with Hosta, while others side with Vinca: why not repurpose the royal chamber? Why should we have another queen? Hosta tears a piece of crimson fabric and ties it to one of her six sinewy arms, and her supporters mimic her, weaving linen and dyeing it with annatto for their own armbands.

Vinca does the same, but instead of tying a red crest around her arm, she covers her narrow shoulders with cloth, an improvised scarlet shawl. Her companions, all of them quick and small-framed workers like herself, paint their exposed thoraxes with the same shade of red ink.

We agree; we disagree; we doubt. We do not know who is wrong or right. We do not even know if Vinca or Hosta have the right to complain or suggest, but their words spread like a forest fire. We, who have dearly revered the queen, now see her vacant and untouched shell and her lengthy symmetrical arms as a threat. We, who braided the waves of her antennae, leave the threads unfurled around the ground, countless brown roots coming out of her regal head.

She, who birthed and governed us, who chose which ones of us were most fitting to serve her, which were too old and should be banished to the nurseries, which were relegated to manual labor, which should dig more and more tunnels that branch into more and more chambers. All from the comfort of her pillows, tall, melancholy and silent, never bothering to even speak. She just lifted a finger, and the order was branded in our head and extended to our comrades: you, strong one, to the squadron. You, architect, mold clay. You, servant, mine.

Our minuscule sisters crawled over her chest, covering one breast with cloth, braiding the antennae that grew longer each year, reaching miles in length. Her three compound eyes, dark and red like the soil of our home, never looked at us, not even once.

Another idea rustles the colony:

"If we want to save the garden, we must bring new apprentices," says Sienna, one of the few elders out of the nurseries. She has a missing leg, but we have carved her a wooden replacement with almost perfect articulations covering the embedded mechanism underneath. The prosthetic limb is pale compared to her rutile complexion, but it allows her to move more freely. "I would like to call some of the squadron girls, since they have so many reserves sitting around."

The gardeners exchange glances.

The ones sucking the fermented wine from sculpted pipes raise confused faces. The ones pruning the longest twigs of the yeast bushes set their tools aside. The ones plucking the delicate bioluminescent mushrooms that light up the underground freeze, their hands rigid around the flat caps or the stems that keep them still.

"The squadron can only do what it was born to do," we say. "They are strong, nothing else."

"They only know what they learned to know," replies Sienna. "They were told they are big and sturdy, so they fight. But they have arms like ours, and they are as capable as us of comprehension, attention and care. We can teach them."

"Not everyone knows how to learn," we insist. "Not everyone wants to."

Sienna walks under the fungal lanterns, bluish sparks shimmering above her head. Her skin is tough and shriveled like leather because of her age, her skilled hands have scarred and fragile fingers. The tools marked her body, excavating grooves like those of a chiseled trunk, and her limbs have burn scars caused by the acid of other women's bites and the toxins of some of the species she farms.

"Everyone *can* learn. Everyone has the right to try."

"The nursemaids are too old to learn. The guards never come down to the chambers, they stay above ground, patrolling, watching a planet that is not ours. The maids were designed to clean waste and serve the queen." The multitude of voices reverberates through the spiraling paths of the anthill. Vinca and Hosta raise their heads, hearing the exchange even far from there. "If we stop being who we are, we are lost. If we change, we die."

"Then we can burn the garden, bury the tunnels and close the entrances," says Sienna. "If we remain as we are, we are already dead."

Change terrifies us. It always did. Fear runs free through our maze, and with it comes the expectation for what is to come. We counted that our mental network of memories and knowledge would be sufficient; that the fabric behind every colony that ever existed before ours, the lineage of queen after queen leading to our dead monarch, would tell us, exactly, the solution to this equation. It does not. Here we are, dizzy, divided between three influences and none. Little by little, we can feel our companions walking away from the mother mind, thinking outside the invisible web that follows us.

Deserters walk down the corridors, painted or dressed, always in red. Royal red is now known as communal red: the color that the workers use to sculpt a new room, the shade that embellishes the stairways that lead to the exit of the anthill, the thread that sews the leaf awnings around the sentinel tower. We cover the children with scarlet bedspreads and label the mushrooms that need to be transferred with annatto.

Without the safe embrace of the superorganism, Vinca feels lost. She never wanted to be a leader. She longed to criticize, yes; she dreaded the Great Mother and the way she sacrificed the workers for the colony. She could not stand to see her surrounded by servants fanning her with leaves, or how the juice from the fruits collected by gatherers dripped from her hypertrophied jaw. She yearned for the day they could all share the perishable goods found on the surface, or the moment they would sleep in spacious and comfortable chambers, like the queen did.

She had no wish to replace her.

Vinca walks out of the shadows of a corridor after hours searching for a moment where she and Hosta could talk alone.

"Despite everything, we agree." Vinca says. "I don't want them to choose another queen. I don't want, in fact, no one to look at us from above."

Hosta stares at her. As a manual worker, small, agile and precise Vinca is almost helpless facing a ranger from the platoon. Her brown antennae are tied with a red stripe of cloth woven to the braid that rests on her shoulder. Her narrow waist disappears under the shawl. Her six limbs square up, alarmed.

"Maybe so," answers Hosta. "What if we do?"

Vinca stares back. Hosta, with her short antennae, her five tiny eyes, her rough and hardened face. Hosta with an old scar cut deep into her forehead, the spoil of a successful battle against invaders. Hosta with red bands around her wrists, red cloth binding her chest. She can attack her, but she will not. She can devour her, but she will not. The superorganism imprinted the good old survival instinct of survival in all of them.

"I also heard that you agree with repurposing the royal chamber," continues Vinca. "Do you have any suggestions on how to deal with the body?"

"If I were to choose, I would chop her in pieces and feed the nursery with the remains." Hosta's voice is fierce, and Vinca tries to pull away when the other woman grasps her by the wrist, twisting one of her articulations, her own arm thin as a twig. "Not everyone seems to agree."

Vinca clicks her jaw, thoughtful.

"The division between us is more worrying than the purpose of the chamber. If we continue like this..."

"If we continue like this, we die," finishes Hosta, releasing her. "Is that so?"

"The others are still prisoners to the affection they felt for the Great Mother. Or, perhaps, the affection they feel for our history..." Vinca forgets their previous animosity, and feels the drastic urge to throw herself in Hosta's arms. She realizes, at last, that she was abandoned by the intricate mental mail that united us. She lacks the solace of our biological connection, the tranquility of exemption. She has to make her own choices and reach her own conclusions. Not even the ancestral traditions woven to our genetic code seem accessible to her, and all she has left is an equal: Hosta. "Maybe that's the problem. The others also matter. We need to hear what they want and, perhaps, concede what needs to be conceded. If the price of no longer having a queen is keeping the memory-body, so be it. We can yield to this small sacrifice."

They exchange looks. Hosta knows she was repelled by the hive consciousness too; and, as hard it is to admit it, she feels the lack of structure inside her thorax. She seizes Vinca's face, touching foreheads and antennae. Equality is comforting. Yes, it is still possible to have what they had before the loss.

"Perhaps, then, it is time to ask," admits Hosta. "But where do we begin?"

We can feel our astray sisters coming back. We hear their steps, ascending the narrow tunnels, crossing hollowed rooms. And, as they walk to the fungal garden to speak to Sienna, we all murmur a distant song, marching toward the royal chamber.

Sienna teaches one of the sentries how to make the yeast rise and turn it into bread, while her aides show a pair of nannies where the bioluminescent mushrooms should be placed.

"We prefer to keep the lights on the nursery floor to keep the children from waking up; in the headquarters, we put them on the ceiling to illuminate the barracks as much as possible."

Hosta and Vinca call the elder in hushed voices, like they knew, instinctively, of our congregation in the middle of the anthill. Maybe they hear the vibration of our steps, or maybe the fragments of collective mentality are saying come back, come back, come back. Our song resounds in the excavated channels, echoing the chorus of thousands of voices like a heart pumping hemolymph.

"Indeed, the best we can do is decide together," agrees Sienna, her two right hands taking Hosta's arm while her two left hands take Vinca's. Age made her warmer than most. "We were all born here, and the ones who have not, were raised here. If the Great Mother has left us any inheritance, maybe it is this place."

United, the three of them go on the same pilgrimage to the royal quarters. They leave the fungal garden, cross the construction rooms, the nursery, the tunnels that serpentine out of the barracks, the stairways that take to the turrets. At last they find us, and we make way for them, our many bodies moving like one.

The queen remains in the same place we left her, but the spasms are gone. Someone arranged her harmonic limbs over the pillows, forever trapped in a deep, peaceful sleep. There are so many of us that we pile over each other, crawling walls, pushing elbow against elbow, sitting on the legs and the torso of this perpetual mother.

The coils of her antennae are adorned with leaves, and her slashed neck is covered by a garland of shimmering mushrooms.

They do not need to call nor beg for our attention. The heavy jaws of the platoons click, clenching teeth, making sound resonate in our cave. The lights flicker. The nursemaids brought the children, the gatherers left a trail of plants and slices of meat on the ground. The workers are stained with soil. Some painted themselves with red dye, others did not. But all of us, even the once expatriated ones, are connecting to the ocher web of our singular mind.

The queen is dead, and we only understand it now.

Without the queen there are no offspring, but some of us remember other lives, where workers managed to replenish the nursery with children. We do not know how, not yet. It is not a problem. Together, we will build patience.

Beyond the realm of possibilities, we have living children. Daughters who wriggle, demanding attention, our little starving mouths. We have sisters who learn, who are more than the limits once imposed on them. The garden spreads through the corridors, invading other chambers, benign. The gatherers know what to bring to enhance it; they even know how to modify the species we already have and include others to the existing crops. The aides want to follow them to the surface. We have never seen it, they say, we say.

Just keep the Great Mother down here, we ask. The empty womb from where we came from. Do not give us a replacement, we require none. We want what we always wanted—what we always have when we are together. Each of the giant arms is a memory we keep. Maybe it is the embodiment of the archive Vinca envisioned. The spiraling antennae reminds us of what we once were. They remind the servants who cleaned, fed and spoiled the queen, and say: never again. They remind the gatherers who sweat and struggle on the surface to bring offerings to the queen: work should not be a sacrifice.

They remind the nursemaids who are banished to constant darkness: aging is not the end of life. They remind the squadrons who invade the colonies of our enemies and defend us from attacks: the time to kill and die is past. They remind the gardeners and the archivists that knowledge must be shared. They remind the workers that they deserve the comfort of the chambers they carved by themselves.

Mandibles are clicking.

The anthill belongs to us, it always did. The anthill belongs to our daughters. It extends across all land that we step on, all clay we mold, all seeds we harvest. It runs through the fructified veins of the garden, it condenses in the marmoreal truffles that feed us. It constitutes our articulated bodies, our intertwined existences. The chorus quiets. The hive reminds us that we are not just a swarm; we are our own organisms. One by one, we look at each other, understanding. Commitment is a laborious burden; never before have we been forced to carry its weight.

Individuality is intolerable, thinking for everyone at all times is restrictive. The queen, reclined on her pillows, remains lifeless. Vinca holds a jug full of honey, once forbidden to all except the royals, and Sienna shares generous portions of sugary nectar in braided leaf bowls. Hosta grabs her own basin and stares at the exhausted face reflected on the viscous amber surface. Her compound eyes, her cropped antennae. When she realizes there is little left for Vinca, she cups her fingers and brings the honey to her companion's mouth.

"We changed," all of us sing, sitting around a circle. There is much to debate, much to learn, much to express. "We changed, we will keep changing, we will always change."

Like Stars Daring to Shine

Somto Ihezue

When the boy opens his housing unit's steel door and the incandescent lights pour into his face, he does not blink away. "Little suns" — this is what everyone calls them. The massive disks hover in the atmosphere, spilling streams of radiant light to the ground. The boy stares into the trees, mere meters from the door, and the forest encaving the unit stares back. A breeze finds him, whistling through the trees and into his dungarees. Threadbare with a Batman logo printed on them, the over-alls belonged to his mother when she was a child.

Peeling his hand off the latch, the boy steals into the bright night. He hurries into the bushes, steering clear of the stone-paved forest pathways, each step sending emerald grasshoppers chirping off the shrubs. In the forest, its canopy a roof of green, darkness collects in patches, but the lights find a way — they always do. Through holes in the dense cover of leaves, they pierce the dark, forming lines of shimmering mist. The trees above crash gently into each other, and the rains that had collected in them fall to the boy's skin in beaded drops. The musk of wet bark, bold and consuming, fills his nostrils as he weaves through the low-hanging palm fronds.

Before the light zones, the world had many green places — rainforests, savannas, mangroves — stretching as far as the eye could see. Not anymore. The Anambra Light Zone, with its damp places and its bird calls, is the only home the boy has ever known. He knows which months the leaves yellow and fall; he knows the poison mushrooms, their caps a vivid toxic scream. He knows the stones that birth the streams; he knows the places the Niger River breaks.

The boy stops when he sees the electric fence of the Multi-Science Research Facility, the words RESTRICTED AREA plastered across it in red. Made up of rows of cuboid structures, the facility stands at the west end of the light zone, with carpets of green algae crawling over it. When they were bored of tree counting, he and the other zone children would sometimes hide in the udala trees and guess at what might have once been the colour of the buildings.

"Vermilion." Kiki, who had a crack zipping across the lens of her glasses, always said the strangest things.

"That's not a colour," some chunky kid laughed.

"Raymond, you thought peanut butter was mashed meat," she replied to the chunky kid without looking over at him. "Maybe sit this one out." She adjusted her glasses, fiddling with the duct tape that was doing a terrible job at holding the hinges in place.

"That was a long time ago!" Raymond looked around to the others, begging to be believed.

"Not long enough, apparently."

Nobody liked going river jumping or antelope watching with Kiki, and this was why. She didn't want them around either, but holed up in the zone together, they were stuck with each other.

***

Thirteen years ago, in the eternal winter of 2125, the boy and Kiki had been born here. They went to the same zonal school, climbed the same trees, and chased the same squirrels.

But Kiki was not one for words, and when she was, the other children ran back to their units in tears. So when she leaned forward in history class and whispered into the boy's ear, "Meet me by the facility, under the udala trees," he thought she'd mistaken him for someone else. But she hadn't. "11 p.m. Don't be late."

"No talking," Mr. Adesua, the geography teacher who also doubled as the history teacher, warned the class, his narrowed eyes jailed behind thick oval spectacles. "Now, where were we?"

He turned to the holographic board. "...Yes, on the 14th of May, 2060, Mount Nyiragongo erupted in the Congo Basin, an eruption that spanned ten months. With increased steaming, rumbling aftershocks, and smoke emissions occurring for the next decade, it was the longest, most intense volcanic disaster after the 1815 eruption of...?"

Mr. Adesua looked around at his students — some doodling on their holo-pads, others fiddling with their glow pens, and only a precious few making an effort to feign attentiveness. "Anyone?"

"The 1815 eruption of Tambora in Indonesia."

"Thank you, Kiki," the teacher sighed, resuming his lecture. "With an endless fount of ash saturating the atmosphere and obscuring the sun, Africa, our continent, truly became The Dark Continent." A trail of dread crept into Mr. Adesua's voice. That same dread found its way onto the faces of his now-attentive students.

"Sulfuric acid aerosols increased the reflection of solar radiation across the globe. Rivers and lakes in Greenland froze over; in Russia, buildings, cities, and millions of people were entombed in ice. And for the first time since the Ice Age, equatorial regions experienced winter...."

The boy's attention drifted as he wondered what Kiki wanted with him. This was the first time she'd said more than a sentence to him. And though he made up his mind not to, he would later find himself hunching by the facility's fence, breaking curfew.

***

Shifting his weight from one foot to the other, arms crossed tightly over his chest, the boy tries to stay hidden. An industrial-grade air filter thrums next to him, sending soft vibrations up his legs. With the incandescent "little suns" blazing bright, it is just a matter of time before the tight security team spots him.

Equipped with a self-regulating heat-yielding capability, the little suns warm frozen landscapes while simultaneously taking over the real sun's photosynthetic role. This made the Anambra Light Zone home to some of the last surviving biological species in Nigeria, as well as the rest of the planet — the reason it's heavily guarded by high-voltage walls against poachers and raiders from outside.

"Boy." The boy looks up to find Kiki hanging from a branch. "You're late." She lets go, and when her feet meet the ground, they do not make a sound.

"This doesn't feel right," the boy says, his breath quickening. "Let's—"

"There's no security on this side. I checked." She takes his hand. "Come."

They slink onto the Facility grounds through a rip in the wired fence and head towards one of its many buildings. At the entrance, Kiki slips out a key card. She slides it across the door-lock, and it buzzes open, revealing an empty hallway.

"My dads work here," she explains, catching the questioning look on the boy's face. "Research biologists."

Half-tiptoeing, half-running, hand in hand, they hurry down the hall. The walls on each side are large glass panes, and behind them are laboratories full of things the boy has seen only in books — microscopes, Petri dishes, titration filters, jars with brownish stuff floating in them — and, in some of the rooms, things not in the boy's books.

Kiki whirls around. "What are you doing?" His hand has slipped from hers.

The boy leaves her to peer through one of the glass panes. "Is that a—?"

"Yes. A prototype. Let's go." She pulls on the strap of his overalls, but he does not budge.

"I want to see it."

"You're seeing it now."

"Up close." He goes to the door, and Kiki knows she's not winning this one.

"I am so going to regret bringing you here." She swipes the key card across the lock. Inside, a little sun fills the room. Far from what the boy imagined, it is not flat but cylindrical, like a bass drum, and insanely massive. And there is nothing ethereal about it. Wires, plugs, and circuits jot out from within it, like twigs on a dying tree. He runs his finger along its dusty metal exterior.

Kiki stiffens where she stands. "We need to go."

With its two surfaces — one plated with blue solar cells, the other made of columns of fluorescent tubes — the little sun is in practice a solar-powered streetlight, only larger and more complex.

"How does it work?"

"I. Don't. Know." Kiki punctuates every word, exasperation working into her voice.

But of course she knows. Unlike the boy, she paid attention in Introductory Tech class. To fight the climate crisis, world governments invented the "little suns." The disks, a hundred times more powerful than the average solar panel, absorb light energy from the sun, converting it to beams too concentrated for the sulfuric aerosols in the atmosphere to reflect. And so, dusk till dawn, the little suns shine, sentries on guard.

"Woah." The boy looks up. A map is etched into the ceiling. "Is that a world map?"

"More like a map of what's left. Come on. Let's go."

"What are those? The red spots?"

"Light zones."

"So few?" He slants his head. "Why couldn't they just shield the whole world?" He gestures to the prototype.

"Do you ever listen in class?"

The boy shrugs.

"With limited time and resources, the advanced multi-purpose billion-dollar design of the technology was not accessible enough to enclose entire countries," Kiki starts like she's reading out of an encyclopedia. The boy blinks at her. "A compromise was reached, and the suns were suspended over arable lands, wildlife reserves, and forests."

"Monaco did it." The boy smirks, crossing his arms. He knows something she doesn't.

"Monaco was a very small, very wealthy nation," Kiki sighs. "They could afford to shield their entire landmass."

The boy looks back up. The area above the US and its five zones is a sheer patch of white. "Mr. Adesua said Canada was a frozen graveyard long before a little sun got mounted."

"The aftermath of the eruption was hardest on polar countries. Most had to migrate their citizens towards the equator, to Kenya, Indonesia, Colombia, and here. Sure, it's cold here, but it's tolerable."

"Do you think the people on the outside are okay?"

"Seeing as they're always trying to get in here, I take it they're not."

"We should just let them in."

"We— We can't."

"Why?"

"There's barely enough room and resources as it is. We can't risk an overpopulation crisis. Our parents are only here because the work they do is important, nothing more."

"My mum doesn't work here in the facility like your parents. She's down in agriculture."

"And without her, we'd all starve, including those on the outside relying on us for monthly supplies." Kiki takes his hand again. "I want to show you something."

***

They head to the end of the hall and down a spiraling metal staircase. The stairs empty into a mass of interlocking pipes and dripping tanks that comprise the central grid of the drainage system. A chemical stench hangs in the air.

Kiki lifts a sewage lid like she's done it a hundred times before, and the lights spill past her, into the dark below. "Get in."

"No." The boy backs away. "I'm not jumping into some random sewer." His astonishment at seeing the prototype is long gone at this point. "I knew I should never have come."

"So why did you?"

"I don't know. I thought maybe you— I don't know." He coughs once, scratching the side of his neck.

"Oh god, you thought I wanted to kiss you?" Kiki's expression cannot decide between disgust and shock.

"Ye— No— That's not what I meant."

"Just get in."

Too embarrassed to protest further, the boy climbs down the greasy wet ladder. Following him, Kiki closes the lid, and the sewer goes pitch black. In the forest, under the cover of the canopy, the boy has experienced shades of darkness, but nothing like this. This is encompassing, ripping him of his sense of space, of being. He cannot tell where his body ends and where the darkness begins.

"Kiki, where are you?!"

"Relax, I'm right here." She shines a headlamp in his face.

"I want to go back."

"Not yet." Handing him a lamp from the row of others hanging on the sewer wall, she trudges ahead, dispatching puddles of water with every step. The boy follows. Walking with a knowing sway, Kiki does not pause when the tunnel splits in three, and — unlike the boy — does not shriek when a rat scurries over her toes.

"How many times have you been down here?"

"Hm," Kiki mutters, and nothing else.

The air starts to smell of river rocks as the pipes, mucky water, and defined walls give way to a larger, rough, cave-like exterior. Kiki stops.

The boy bumps into her. "Are we there?"

"Turn it off," she says, switching her lamp off. "They don't like the light."

"Who?" The boy hesitantly does as she says. "Who doesn't like the—" Then he sees it: a speck of light afloat in the dark. Another follows, twirling and glinting, up and up. A third comes, then a fourth, then a thousand.

"Fire— Fireflies." The word leaves his lips as a whisper, his breath catching in his throat.

"Have you ever seen anything like it?" The swirling lights glint off the lenses of Kiki's glasses, casting her entire face in a scintillating glow.

In the cave's immensity, swelling with the euphonic hum of lacy wings, swarms of fireflies dance, a rain of stars. No, the boy has seen nothing like it.

"But..." He finds his voice. "My mum said... She said they all disappeared when she was little. She said the lights blinded them. She said—"

"I know, I know. The lights made their mating glow invisible and, unable to evade predators or reproduce, they went extinct. I know." Kiki lets her impatience show. "But look, they're right here!"

"How did you find them?"

"I didn't. My dads have been coming down here for months, studying them, how they've survived this long."

"I guess the warmth from the little suns helped." The boy inhales the fresh warm air.

"About that..."

"What?"

"Don't freak out, but we're not in the zone anymore."

"Where— Where are we?"

"Where do you think?" Kiki scoffs.

It takes a minute, but it comes to the boy. His eyes widening, he spins around, frantic.

"No, no, this is a good thing." She reaches for his shoulders. "We're outside the zone, but it's not freezing down here. Don't you see what that means?"

"We can't— We can't possibly be that far away?"

"We've been walking for hours." She beeps her timepiece in his face. "It's 6 a.m." The boy gasps. "I'm usually faster on my own, but thanks to your side quests, we are definitely getting caught. Point is, the earth is healing," Kiki says, her voice charged with something the boy cannot describe. "My dads say soon we might not need the little suns anymore."

"Really? How soon?"

"They're not sure." She pauses for a minute. "But can you imagine? Seeing the oceans, a sunset, the moon!" Her hands tighten around his shoulders, and she shakes him. "Boy!"

"Zaram."

Kiki raises a brow.

"My name is Zaram." The boy stares down at his fingers.

"And all this while I thought it was 'Boy.'" She lets out a mocking chuckle. "I know."

Zaram looks up at the fireflies. "Kiki, why— Why did you pick me?"

She does not look at him, but not in the same way that she doesn't look at the other zone children, like Raymond. "Well, out of everyone here... I hate you the least." A shy humming silence builds in the space between them. "What would you like to see, Zaram, when the earth is normal again?"

"I— I—" He has never thought about it. This — the light zone, the little suns — is his normal.

"It's alright," Kiki smiles. "You don't have to think about it now."

Zaram smiles back. And they stay, watching all the little things daring to shine.

ICARIANA

Wen-yi Lee

I find her by the riverbed after the end of the world, wings tucked under her grubby ribs. Some new kind of being, or else some rich maniac's attempt to engineer homo deux before it all went down. Or went up. Tides, lava, nukes, spaceships. Those last ones, especially, aren't ever coming back down.

I've come across my fair share of bodies, but none of them alive, and none of them winged. She blinks groggily as I carry her out of the scorching sun. Home is a cave dressed up like one. I lay her down on the mattress—she weighs less than the portable generator—and fetch a cup of water.

She sips with puckered lips. She's hollowed out—hungry, exhausted, dehydrated if the fourth cup is anything to go by—but she doesn't look much older than me under all of it. Slim brown eyes and shorn dark hair, roundish face, and of course the wings, spilling from the slits in her dress. They're like grimy clouds across my bed.

"What's your name?"

I don't know if she can speak; her motor control seems fine but—

"Seraphine," she says.

All right, that's a little on the nose, but I'll take it. Seraphine's voice is surprisingly smooth, low and clear like a warning bell. Everybody else—the few there are left—rasps like they swallowed the generation ships' dust clouds. "I'm Kya," I reply. "Let me get you something to eat."

***

Seraphine doesn't remember much, but she says she remembers flying. She tries some experimental lifts, but her body crumples before she can get a foot off the ground. Her wings shed feathers that fall mutely as I catch her. "You need to get your strength back."

"Flying," she murmurs desperately into my chest, half-conscious, less a behaviour than an instinct, some immutable part of her she needs to exert over and over again.

"Strength," I reply.

Strength is food. I can scrounge up a decent amount. There's not a lot of variety, but I'm not picky. My goat Mantle does the heavy lifting: cheese, milk, everything silky and creamy. I know where to find cactus and nuts and dates if the season is right. There are dwindling bags of beans and tough grains from the last time I stumbled on a caravan. Water is precious. After her first day, we drink in small measures. These are the blightlands. The sun came too close, and we do our best not to shrivel.

I get used to cooking for two, and to sitting opposite someone while I eat. Seraphine eats like a bird of prey: sharp, tearing bites. Fortunately, she's not picky either. She likes the cheese. I start making more of it.

I show her how to cut open saguaros and scoop out their insides. She's deft with her fingers. I demonstrate how to make nut paste and milk curds. Once she asks, "Is there anything you miss eating?"

Anything with flour. Beef. Carrots. Rice, unthinkable in this dryness. *Chocolate.* But instead I find myself saying, "Strawberries." Luxurious, sweet things. I had them once as a kid when trade was on its last legs and the growers hadn't yet been packed off past the atmosphere.

"A fruit?"

I wonder again where she's from, what hole she was locked up in. So many things seem new to her. Not the abandoned planet, though; that she never asks about.

"Yeah, fruit." I describe it, and think of Mom. "Maybe they have it way up north still, but it wouldn't grow here."

Seraphine gets stronger every day. I start thinking about going upstream. There's rumors it's less scorched there. That things actually grow. I haven't wanted to before, because I've built too much safety here to abandon for maybes. But now that Seraphine's practically healthy, my encampment seems less safe than stale compared to the way she moves through it. Like my world is too small to fit her. In my quiet moments, I look at her and think we could risk the maybes.

Then one day she says, "I want to fly again."

"Oh," I say.

Somehow I'd forgotten.

***

We stand on the cliff above the caves. There's a decent northeasterly wind, a little cloud cover. Seraphine's tried some jumps and experimental flexes, but this is showtime.

I realise I'm terrified, but before I can speak—I don't even know what I want to say—Seraphine steps off the edge.

The world tumbles, and then her wings snap out and my breath swallows itself. *Whoosh* and a twist and a laugh and a burst of white feathers arcs past me. Seraphine slices through the air. Her wings burn with the reflected light of the sun, the glow almost harsh.

She circles before darting skyward again. Suddenly she's tiny. Then she's diving again, wingspan eclipsing the sun. But while I'm staring at her, she's staring at the horizon. "I need to fly out further," she shouts.

My euphoria crashes. "How far?"

She shakes her head, half a shrug, face obscured by feathers and motion. "As far as I can go!"

It's a lack of a question that hurts the most.

I want to grab her legs, hold on, never let go. Even if it sends us both plummeting into the scorched earth.

But I don't. I make a gesture that I think means *okay*. I smile. I let her fly.

Slowly, she vanishes from sight.

Girls with wings were made to soar. Girls with nothing get left behind. That's the way the world works, even after it ends. I make my way back down the cliff. I have so much space, and too much cheese.

*****

Seven nights later, there's a thud outside. I freeze, slowing on the butane crank. There isn't another sound, but I know better than to trust silence. I grab my prod and climb up to the cave entrance just as a shadow descends.

Even when Mantle bleats happily, I can't bring myself to believe it. But Seraphine is there tucking her wings in as I gape. She smiles like my head isn't spinning to pieces, and lifts her cupped hands. "It took longer to find than I thought."

Strawberries, fat, red, still dewy.

"Where?" my mouth asks, even though I know.

"North," she says. "Just like you said. There's people up there, Kya."

In this moment, I don't tell her about all the times when she was gone that I started thinking about jerky and portable rations. Things I'd have to leave and things I could bring along to go after her, to go anywhere that wasn't still and scorched. Right now, I just show her how to pluck the leaves off the fruit.

There's only six. Three each. Every burst of juice makes the lump in my throat grow. They taste like somewhere I've forgotten. Somewhere I could know again. When the berries are gone and my hands are sticky, I ask her to tell me all about it.

She begins, "Far up the river, there is a field…"

Taming the Sea and the Wind

Yasmin Moita

The *Maçariquinho*, a nacre-colored fishing submarine with its name painted red, moved like a *tralhoto* fish under the Atlantic waters. Inside the underwater machinery, a sixteen-year-old in a deep blue full-body uniform cheerfully navigated as she had been lucky enough to find a shoal up for grabs around the canal.

She rose to the surface, looking at the swamp, then to the city of *Salinópolis*, and then back to the bottom full of muddy seawater that simmered with life.

The day was June 16, 2247. At seven in the morning, Yara listened to and sang an old song called *Carimbó Modernista* as she finished her work for the day and decided to roam around the sea afterward.

Today was a decisive day! At nine, they would decide on the main singer for Cassava Day! She wanted to be the ONE!

This holiday was a massive festivity on the eve of Saint John's Day. There would be banquets, music, dancing, boat racing, fried fish, *beiju*, *tapiocas*, sweet cassava cake, fried sweet cassava, *tacacá*, *maniçoba*, cassava flour and *açaí*.

However, the holiday history was not so full of food and fun since it started before the *Pluripolar* Age, when the exploitation of the *Imperial* Age recked the Amazon, causing climate change, deforestation, and pollution. Similar to other parts of the *Global South* at the time.

The *Imperial* Age is the historical period between 1492 a.C. and the end of the 4th World War in 2157. The war began with the *Catalaxia* Vírus; a biological weapon used simultaneously in 10 countries. But it did not take long to uncover a very curious fact: while people died in the *North*, the people from the *Global South* who ate organic foods from their regions did not get sick. And, (of course!) when people found out, the 4th World War changed its pathways, becoming an endeavor to conquer the *South*.

Still, the battle was short-lived, and the *South* soon rose to power. *Southern* countries managed to get war compensations and technological exchange, which led to the signing of the Lagos Treaty in 2157 when humanity entered a new phase: the *Pluripolar* Age.

Cassava, among other foods, was considered a savior of humanity. It made the *Amazonic Republic* rich and outside the modes placed by the Imperial Age; since it was the base of the survivors' diet. So, to honor nature for saving a good portion of the old *Global South* countries, people created Cassava Day.

Moreover, for many Amazonians, that miracle was the unexpected fulfillment of the *Ybymarã-e'yma* Legend, the Land of no Evil. And now, the Lagos Treaty completed its 90th anniversary.

The submarine boat was back on shore. The vessel's A.I., nicknamed NAIÁ, assisted with maneuvering and unloading the fish in an autonomous car on standby. Yara oversaw the process with attentive eyes. Soon, the vehicles would send the fish to the houses that needed them, as pre-established in the automatically handled collective distribution of resources.

Since she met her fishing quota, Yara went to the vessel's bathroom and changed her beautiful and helpful uniform to a combination of shorts and a blouse. It was a 4-hour job. She only fished when the city needed food.

A brown face with dark curly hair looked at her in the mirror, bags under its eyes. She put lip gloss on the thick lips to make them reddish, put on her iron bracelet on top of the satin ribbons, and feather earrings to complete the look.

Now, she just needed the guitar to rehearse with the band after the test, so she looked for it in the trunk. *Aaah, I forgot it at home!* She kicked herself while getting out of the submarine boat as she was leaving the port in a hurry. The Grand Port had been renovated and was three times the size of the older one. Small vessels, amphibious vehicles, other submarine boats, and bigger ships docked there.

The girl went fast down a street flooded by palm trees and other such plants from the Atlantic Rainforest, which would drift to Amazonian plants if one cared to enter deeper into the Continent. Then, she saw an empty microbus with no driver and signaled it to stop; afterward, she pinpointed her house's location.

***

As soon as she reached the ninth floor of her building and opened the door, the dog *Caramelo* showed up. He gave her his usual warm reception, full of scratches and tiny kisses. Behind the dog, the highly annoying figure of a white child with straight black hair and slant eyes presented itself.

It was Caíque, Yara's brother.

"Stop stalling and eat!" shouted Luciana, Yara's mother. She was also white with slant eyes, but her straight hair was brown instead of black.

"I'm not hungry, mommy!" shouted the boy back.

Luciana stood up and pulled the boy by his arm until he was seated at the table with his plate of *crepioca*.

"No wasting food, not happening. You have no idea how lucky you are! Do you know how many children are starving in the North right now?"

Yara smartly evaded the scene going straight to the bedroom and taking advantage of the fact that she was at home to put her uniform and tools out of her bag. Then, she proceeded to pick up her guitar in her bedroom. Soon, she ran outside while her mother shoved the *crepioca* inside her brother's mouth.

***

At school, it was finally time for the test.

"Yara Pereira Tupinambá!" announced the speaker. The girl went on stage, confident. She sang one of the five lyrics allowed, the '*Esse Rio é Minha Rua*.' The competition was decided by five judges — who raised their eyebrows when Yara sang — and by the public, whose ratings also counted for the final score. Marlucia Ticuna, the Amazonian ambassador, was among the judges. She was Yara's idol.

Marlucia was a famous singer when she was a teen. And, not so long ago, she had been the Cacique.

Yara, sadly, received few applauses by the end of her performance. She would get the score only after the last candidate presented, and the line behind her was still great.

"Keila, how was I?" asked Yara to her friend when she came back to the audience's space.

"I-I think you need to train a little bit more... It must have been the nerves," answered Keila.

Suddenly, a young man left backstage. Actually, it seemed like somebody almost pushed him out of there. He started stammering a song in *nheengatu*, the other official Amazonian language, and a celestial voice filled the hall.

The audience's reaction was quick: many shouts of encouragement all at once, leading the voice to improve confidently. Yara burned with rage as the boy received a standing ovation; seeing that even the judges seemed impressed, the girl felt tears coming down her face.

Yara said goodbye to her friend briskly and gave up on the rehearsal. She ran towards the school's entrance and continued on foot until the *Caranã* Park. Some people asked if she needed help, but she just ignored them.

In *Caranã* Park, she sat on a stone bench between dense trees and flowers, close to the lake built by the fountain. Feeling distraught, she stared at the trees dancing with the wind.

Suddenly, she observed a remote hibiscus start to move strangely. The next thing she knew, standing precariously on the branches, an older black woman fell to the floor with no strength. Seeing this, Yara ran towards the old lady at light speed.

The woman was dirty with blood all over her dress, whose origin seemed to be from a deep wound in her stomach. Yara started to call 911 immediately, with her hands trembling as she pressed the buttons.

"What happened? Can you tell me what happened?" she tried to pry when she felt a sudden pull from below.

The old lady grabbed her bag and pulled it with full force toward herself, almost making Yara fall face-first on the floor beside her. Now that was a strong woman.

"Listen to me." gasped out the woman in a low voice. "Cassava Day! The Clown is setting a trap to kill all our current authorities and Fiji's as well... they will attack civilians too... He is with the Oranges... There are outsiders involved... They want to... restore the Empire,... make war and enslave us. Here, this will help you." gasped the lady again.

The irony was not lost on Yara as she accepted what seemed to be a tiny pocket mirror from the old lady's hand; the lady was the one who looked like she needed help, not the other way around. However, as Yara's hand brushed against the lady's, she felt the touch of astonishingly soft and young skin which did not match the older adult she saw in front of her. The woman was wearing a disguise!

While Yara was still processing the shock of this sudden realization and the sight of blood, the lady lost consciousness. A few minutes later, the ambulance arrived, and the rescuers ran to help. As they left for the hospital, Yara sat down and hid the little mirror in her bag.

It was then that she saw a middle-aged brown man approach. Well dressed and with curly dark hair combed to perfection, contrasting with a huge burn mark on his round nose and mouth. Similar to a clown...

The girl gulped when she realized the person approaching her was no other than Belém's lead representative in the General Board of Leaders, accompanied closely by his bodyguard. He stood up in front of her and introduced himself as Álvaro Silva.

Following his introduction with "Have you seen anything unusual young lady?"

"No" said Yara swiftly.

"I see... you are right, you know?... Certain things should never be spoken out loud... to anyone."

The politician's bodyguard was about to reach for something in his pocket... but stopped immediately after a group of children and their teacher started to take pictures. Yara saw an opportunity and swiftly said her goodbyes to the Clown, as the public nicknamed him, and ran.

***

At the same time, a plane from the State-owned company *Vanua* Airlines, which was transporting a Fijian delegation, arrived at the Salinópolis airport—giving the city a lot to talk about. The delegation would be doing a presentation at *Caranã* Park that evening, and the hotel they were staying at was right beside Yara's home.

Yara was left in front of her house by the bus when she saw a group of five boys and three girls pass by. They were coming from the hotel. The tallest and darkest approached her as she was about to enter her building.

"Excuse me" he said in English.

"Do you know where the Corvina beach is?" his pronunciation was a little off but easily understandable.

Yara turned around and checked the boys out, paying closer attention to the one who approached her. She was about to give them the address, but after seeing that friendly face with lovely curly hair (and bod), she stopped in her tracks and said:

"I can take you there if you want..."

"It would be very kind of you." praised the white boy beside the first one.

The Amazonian smiled while pressing her cell phone three times to call for the bus.

***

On their short trip to the beach, she found out that the small group was actually from Fiji and that most would go to the *Caranã* later at night. Yara heard each of their names, but only Tomasi Waqa and Lavenia Waqa stayed in her mind, as they were the names of the boy who first approached her and his older sister. His sister was an engineer in the incredible *Tokavoki*, a machine that generated eolic energy through strong winds. It was as if they were really taming and stocking up on wind!

The Fijians shared that they would stay in Salinópolis for ten whole days, and Yara was having a great time, a break from the last moments that now seemed unreal. But, unfortunately, she had to go back home to prepare lunch. So, when they finally arrived at *Corvina* beach, she said goodbye to the Fijians and called for another bus.

***

Yara just started dressing up for the *luau*. After lunch and a bath, she began to style her hair. And as she was doing so, she remembered what had happened that morning. She picked up the tiny mirror inside her bag and stared at it, reflecting on what she should do. Tell or don't tell?

She took a deep breath and decided it was better to tell. But, as she was about to open the tiny mirror to see inside, Yara was surprised by Lavenia, who showed up in the window dressed in a 4th World War combat suit. The Fijian girl aimed her pistol at Yara.

"Drop it, or I'll kill you." threatened the girl.

Yara shook nervously but did as commanded.

"I know what you know." she continued. "And you will keep your mouth shut."

"But... with your plan, we will die anyway," said Yara as she took her distance and stood against the bathroom mirror.

In the blink of an eye, Lavenia was millimeters away from Yara. Then, a sudden sharp pain shot through Yara's body, radiating from her pulse to the entire body like a fire. She tried to scream, but Lavenia shut her mouth with a rag. Yara struggled, but Lavenia was much stronger.

The agony seemed to last an eternity until the doorbell rang. Lavenia let Yara go, and the girl screamed as the Fijian stole the tiny mirror and ran through the window. Juçara, Yara's other mother, and her uncle Peri came running to help.

Yara was in shock when they came in. Not much time passed when she started to tell them everything at once, in a single long trembling narrative—ranging from the future attack to Lavenia's intrusion in the bathroom. Uncle Peri, who worked at the Cacique's office, soon contacted his network and returned to work to investigate and possibly prevent the plans shared by Yara.

Meanwhile, Juçara decided that Caíque would no longer go out by himself and asked for leave from her job in the afternoon with the excuse of personal problems. Moreover, even though she was petrified, Yara thought to herself that now she could go to the *luau* almost at ease. She dressed with all the care in the world, thinking she would have a great time and forget everything tonight, and that's what she told her mothers when they questioned going to the *luau* altogether.

Her picks were a chintz electronic skirt with prints that changed randomly and a top to match, leaving her belly button on display. A sandal and a plastic flower completed the look.

Since Yara took a long time to get ready, the whole family arrived late at the park when the Fijian prime minister Amaya Singh was finalizing her speech. Soon after, part of the group Yara had met earlier started to present themselves on stage dancing *meke*, a traditional *iTaukei* dance. As they were about to end the performance, Yara enthusiastically hurried toward the dressing room.

But before taking another step forward, she was grabbed by her mother, Luciana.

"It's a pity you like boys. But since you do, be careful: Men are not trustworthy."

"Mom, I know him" said Yara.

"Even so, take care" was Juçara's advice for her child.

"Ok, mommies. I will take good care of myself" said a grumpy Yara as she went away.

Tomasi and the other dancers descended from the stage, still in tribal clothing. Yara's heart skipped a beat when she saw him shirtless. Fishing time had begun!

She waved to call Tomasi's attention. And that was a Big fish!

"*Bula*!" he shouted.

Yara's eyebrows went up. What a weird thing to say... Why was he shouting about medicine leaflets in Portuguese?

"Hi!" she exclaimed, ignoring the strangeness of his greeting. "Is everything ok with you?"

Now apparently was his turn to make a confused expression, as if Yara's question had been something weird to ask.

"I'm in great health" he answered in Portuguese.

Everyone in the park heard a guitar playing an old popular song, 'Sinhá Pureza.'

"Do you want to learn *Carimbó*?" asked Yara, smiling and changing the subject.

"Yes, of course!"

She spent a wonderful time teaching him *Carimbó* and *Brega* while having a friendly chat. Then, the music changed to *TecnoBrega*, then, *Lambada*. Yara moved her hips close to his and felt his hands on her waist. She was feeling like a magnet, magnetism dripping from her pores.

Yara looked him in the face, illuminated by the beam of white light from the big red lighthouse in her field of vision. He touched her back and pulled her closer. Now their faces were almost touching. Satisfied with his response, she stole a kiss from his lips, a sweet passionate kiss. And he stole another right back, with intensity. Seeing that she had caught the big fish, she held her arms around him tightly. She hoped for a very long and fun make-out session. It was going to be amazing...

"YARA!" screamed Juçara, almost bawling and being consoled by Luciana. "Did you see Caíque?"

Yara begrudgingly stepped back from Tomasi.

"No"

"We can't find him!"

Yara gulped hard. She hastily said goodbye to Tomasi and joined her mamas in the search for her baby brother.

***

The neighbors united in search of Caíque the next day without results. Mothers and daughter came home late, and when they did arrive, their phones vibrated simultaneously. A Great Kiskadee signal! It was a whistle that imitated the bird's singing, giving the GPS location of the person using it.

But the location was vague...

***

Yara walked with her spirits low to school the following day, feeling like a failure. She noticed her own shadow walking beside her, and that shadow slowly became two shadows. She screamed when she realized it. Her ears buzzed with the sound of the projectile that passed dangerously close to her head, and she felt pain resonating inside her ears while she ran.

Looking back for a second, Yara saw a man in a suit similar to Lavenia's, and he was now falling on the floor. His implants seemed to be going haywire. She kept running until another person in a combat suit appeared in front of her, under a chestnut tree's safe shadow—a woman with a rifle.

"Calm down" the woman said, "and come closer."

Yara obeyed hesitantly.

The woman relaxed her posture against the tree while looking at Yara. She identified herself as part of the Baquara Agency, a secret intelligence service of the Amazonian Republic, and asked Yara if she was ok.

After that moment of sensibility, the woman put a suitcase in Yara's hands.

Inside the suitcase, Yara found the suit she usually used for work alongside a note stating that the uniform dated back from wartime and was more than what it seemed.

"Now, wear it after school, ok? Go home, and preferably, don't go out anymore. Got it?" The woman was stern in her speech; she was not someone to be taken lightly.

The agent escorted Yara, and the girl arrived safely at her school. During recess, she chatted with several classmates, asking if they had heard any Great Kiskadee the day before. Keila, who lived in *Destacado*, said she heard it, but it was too distant. The signal seemed to come from the grand terrain of the abandoned mansion; people believed it was a haunted house.

And, right then and there, a tough choice presented itself: Go home and have the chance to die in anonymity or go to the scary mansion accepting the risk of making a colossal mistake and dying famous?

By the end of the recess between classes, Yara went to the bathroom to change clothes. While getting changed, she wondered how nice it would be to turn invisible at that moment, and her arm disappeared as soon as she thought that. She almost fell butt first when she realized what had just happened. What a suit!

Then, she sneaked out of school and saw Tomasin on the street.

As soon as she saw him, her heart skipped a beat again, and she turned visible. Not only that, her suit lighted up in a deep blue color. Tomasi was startled to see her show up out of nowhere and asked what was going on. She answered, saying that she was still looking for her brother.

"Oh, I'm the same. I'm looking for Lavenia. She is missing too." he said.

"No Tomasin, she is not. I'm sorry that you get to hear this from me, but... Your sister is a mercenary. She is helping the people who kidnapped my baby brother! She's probably at the same place he is right now!"

"No... That's impossible... Lavenia is not like that..."

"Tomasin... you're being fooled, but if you want to see for yourself, you can follow me."

He accepted the proposal without a second thought, his eyes determined.

Maybe he was working for the Oranges this whole time? She carefully looked at him.

He was being sincere.

The blue light of Yara's suit went out, and they went to the abandoned mansion together.

***

As they got closer to the place, walking by the swamp, they heard gunshots from the mansion's backdoor and drones flying toward the residence.

They advanced carefully while a conflict ensued at the main gate. A strange Great Kiskadee was activated, and Yara pulled Tomasi towards the entrance with brute force. There were no guards.

And so they entered through the unlocked door. The room inside was empty, except for two dead men.

Nothing could prepare Yara for the painful blow she received when Lavenia flew in her direction and threw her against the window, breaking the glass in the process. Yara was down with glass shards all around her, and when she looked up, she saw a glimpse of Caíque running down the stairs on the other side of the room.

Tomasi put himself between his sister and Yara.

"Stop this now!"

"I need to do this, Tomasi! The Pluripolar Age is throwing away our potential. We are going backwards!"

"Lavenia, if we go back to being an Empire, there won't be a loser and a winner. Everyone will lose!"

"You're worthless!" his sister shouted while taking hold of his wrist.

Tomasi fell on the floor, feeling excruciating waves of pain all over his body.

Seeing Tomasi suffer, Yara stood up.

Lavenia was ready to fight the Amazonian, leading with her fists and giving massive punches to the girl's face. Yara was terrified and desperately tried to defend herself from every blow. But the blade inserted in Lavenia's arm ended up piercing her thigh, making her fall again and shriek on the floor like a wounded animal.

At that exact moment, however, Caíque had managed to get his hands on the whistle that had fallen on the ground and used it with all the strength inside his tiny lungs. Yara didn't think much as she hastily put her hands around Lavenia's neck, squeezing with all her might. Then, Yara's suit began to glow in a scary gleaming purple tone. A high-voltage electrical current ran through the uniform. Lavenia convulsed painfully while going haywire and burning. The engineer's implants started to let out a cloud of black smoke, like the ones from the Imperial Age.

The painful waves Tomasi felt disappeared.

And when Yara saw her opponent's motionless burned body on the floor. Something inside her broke.

She started to sob while Tomasi covered his mouth with his hands. Caíque got closer, hesitant.

"I'm sorry." she gasped.

"It was you or her. It's ok." Tomasi almost whispered to himself.

Yara felt out-of-balance and weak. Her vision slowly got darker until there was nothing left to see.

***

Yara woke up slowly.

She saw her mothers' by her side. A significant part of her family, neighbors, Tomasi, and even people she didn't know were waiting for her to wake up. Emotional and relieved, she did something she would never have done before: she hugged her mamas in public without fear of looking like a child.

She had a quick recovery because of the current advances in Medicine.

Now was Saint John's Day, six days after the fight. Cassava Day went on without a hitch. And her doctor shooed the busybodies, telling Yara that she would be in observation for a while but that she showed every indication of a full recovery.

***

Later, Yara had the chance to talk with Marlucia personally, who thanked her for her service.

Amaya Singh awarded her all the honors and said she was more than welcome in Fiji.

Tomasi would go home on the 26th, so he stayed with Yara the last two days before the trip, oscillating between pain and joy when he was with her. They had long conversations about trivial things, finding unexpected things in common between their languages and cultures.

On the tenth day of the Fijians' stay, they made one last presentation on the sidewalk in front of the *Maçarico* beach. After the performance, musicians played a farewell song: '*Isa Lei.*' Yara saw everything with tears in her eyes, as she felt deeply for Tomasi, who had to leave without his sister by his side.

"I love you" she said when it was time to say goodbye.

"I love you too, very much, Yara."

They kissed under the sunset, a long and steady kiss that Yara wished would never end.

***

Then he left, and Yara called her mothers for a vital talk. They sat on a bench close to a coconut tree that swayed with the wind.

"I don't know what to do. I thought I had a path and now I feel lost."

"I think I know what it is," said Luciana. "You always want to control every aspect of your life, lovey. Have you never thought that there is no right path in life?"

"What do you mean?"

"Simple," answered Juçara. "Tell me something, sweetie. Is there anyone who can stop the rain? Or hold the sea in place? We invented automatic containment barriers to protect ourselves. But they still need to adjust to the flow of the waves to be in harmony with it. In Fiji, they even managed to take advantage of cyclones to generate energy, but they can't control them. They can only avoid damage. Life is like nature. We must maintain harmony with what comes our way, adapting as best as we can. If we try to control everything, we won't be able to enjoy the ride."

"You're still too young and full of potential. I'm sorry if I ever pressured you. I should have listened to Ju," said Luciana. "And I understand why you want to keep your distance. I'm too controlling... I know. But on the bright side, it's never too late to change your ways. Can we do that together?"

Yara was in tears again.

"I just know that I love you guys," she said as she hugged them. "And thanks to you two, I feel free and ready to live through anything that comes my way." She took a minute. She remembered the Cassava Day contest, which was so very important before and so futile now... So she decided to add one last thing: "Maybe not everything. But whatever happens, I will find my way."

The Moonlit Muse

The dust swamp roiled before Nahar, silver powder swirling with lifelike intensity. She prepared herself, chose her paints, touched the canvas with her brush, and then stopped. How could she portray such raw power?

Movement at the far edge of the swamp, visible even through layers of thick plexiglass—a glimmering blue iguana chasing its prey. Bioluminescent tentacles thrashed as it darted under the warning signs ringing the sunken swamp. Nahar couldn't see the prey but guessed it was one of the silvery hares native to Epsilon's rocky terrain. The iguana, however, had invaded the moon settlement. A few dozen accidentally stowed away on a cargo ship from Epsilon's twin moon, Zeta, a decade ago. As the only carnivores on Epsilon, their population had exploded, and the local herbivores had only recently learned this new species was an existential threat.

The glowing sapphire speck dashed for the center of the swamp. As the iguana gained ground, the silver dust shifted violently, enveloping it. The iguana's anguished cry shattered the silence, and the speck winked out.

Nahar frowned. Attempting to capture the dueling savagery and elegance of the swamp was an exercise in futility. Hours spent powdering mushrooms to make her paints, painstakingly threading and restoring the bristles of her paintbrush, and camping out on her little artist's stool, alone, watching the swamp, to end with nothing but malformed blotches on canvasses destined to compost in the dirt.

Her colors felt dull. Her brush felt meek. And whenever she moved towards her easel, the frigid fingers of indecision gripped her, freezing her in place.

"Damn this." She grumbled as she rose, dusting off her patchwork smock. She packed the brushes into a handwoven waist-pack and snuck the canvas under her arm. The problem was, the Dust Swamp was over *there*, and she was over *here*, perched on a stool behind sixteen layers of reinforced plexiglass and a dozen signs that cautioned against moving closer. Nobody knew why the swamp attacked, but everyone knew it could swallow a person whole. The viewing dome would keep her safe.

And safety would suffocate her.

How could she paint the Dust Swamp when she couldn't even see it? Any marks she made on her canvas were lies, pretty lies daubed in purples and blues, but still lies. An approximation of an approximation.

Safety be damned. She needed to get closer. She needed to be inside the swamp, to feel the brunt of its wildness instead of cowering in fear.

Day and night meant little when Epsilon's twin hung eternally against a backdrop of pure darkness, but it was late enough that Nahar was alone in the observation station. Not that anybody would have stopped her anyway: Freedom of movement was a founding tenet of Epsilon, an inviolable right. The signs didn't even prohibit her from entering the swamp, they just strongly suggested that she shouldn't.

Ten minutes and a dozen digital waivers later, Nahar exited the observation deck and breathed the chilly night air. The scent of the swamp pervaded Epsilon, but it was strongest here, right at the edge. The air carried a tendril of damp sand, not overpowering but insistent. Breathing in some more, Nahar could pick out an undercurrent of fungal growth, the strong herbal smell of toadstools and moss. Back home in the central settlement, spices and perfumes masked the earthy spray. But the central settlement was hours away. Here the swamp reigned supreme, brashly announcing its presence.

Outside the observation deck, the swamp looked like it was drinking in the moonlight, bending and refracting it as the specks of shining dust floated on the air. Under the obsidian cloak of the night sky, the swamp was awash with the silver light of Zeta as the pale disc watched over its twin. The dunes of the swamp melted and reformed, like candle wax reshaping. The air shimmered and glistened, and Nahar clutched her canvas a little tighter.

Goddess, she hoped she had enough silver paint.

She edged closer, and closer, until the particles of swamp dust danced just a few feet away from her. A final wooden sign urged caution, but the effort was half-hearted, printed in faded letters used to being ignored. Anyone who made it this far had already proved that mere words wouldn't impede them.

The ground changed underfoot. The crackling of dry grass softened into the rustle of fine dust. Nahar's fibrous boots nearly sank into the swamp before she found purchase. She was bigger than an iguana, so maybe the swamp would leave her alone. Gingerly, one step in front of the other, she proceeded towards the center. So far, so good.

The observation center turned the swamp into a subject, a scientific curiosity best looked at from a distance. Here, standing on a mound of fine, gray dust, Nahar could see that the swamp was alive. A mild breeze made particles dance in the glimmering light, millions of motes that fluttered to a melody only they could hear. Her footsteps sank stark against the smooth, untarnished surface, accompanied only by the jagged claw prints of the iguanas and the padded paw prints of hares. Here and there she saw white bones and scraps of blue scales.

Power thrummed under her feet. Nahar's tentative steps turned bolder as she moved with greater surety. The dust conformed to her movements, practically leading her. She didn't know where she was going, but she trusted the gentle pull and push of the swamp, feeling intoxicated by its natural magnetism.

White trees dotted the nearby landscape, birds flitting in and out of their branches. The chilly air swirled around her, dust obscuring her view of the distance. Not that seeing where she was going was imperative. Nahar had no illusions of control. As the swamp guided her, the shimmering in the distance grew closer. At first, she'd thought it was an illusion, or a result of the oddly refracting lunar light, but no. Each step brought her closer, until she stood one pace away. The swamp paused its push and pull, leaving the last step for her.

A curtain of shimmering light, like a veil over the very fabric of reality, lay before her. What lay beyond? She didn't *have* to know. She could simply leave the mystery alone. Certainly, she had accomplished the motives of her art, hadn't she? She'd seen enough of the swamp now, enough to capture something close to its true nature.

Close, but not close enough. If she left now, she left with a lie and a question that would prick her at every waking moment until she returned.

"Geronimo, I guess." Nahar steadied her breathing, one hand on the canvas and the other on her pack, and stepped forward.

"Oh good, I thought you'd never get here!" The woman was tall, dressed in a black bodysuit and silver *dupatta* that looked striking against her brown skin. Thin white lines decorated her face in an intricate pattern of spidery lines and dots. She looked directly at Nahar, but not in surprise. Her expression indicated that she'd just been waiting.

The woman projected an aura so uniquely powerful that, for a second, Nahar forgot the mechanics of speech.

"The name is Sabine, dear." The lady, Sabine, waved a hand in front of Nahar's face. "Pupil dilation is normal; eye movement is excellent. You feeling okay?"

"How are you here?" Nahar asked. Not the most eloquent question, but her personality was still rebooting.

"I walked."

"Me too." Not a brilliant response, but Nahar had suddenly become aware that the woman's eyes were piercing into her and couldn't think of anything else. "Walking is good."

Sabine laughed then, a piercing, echoing peal that washed over Nahar like water. Nahar looked at Sabine, and then at her canvas.

Goddess, she hoped she had enough silver paint.

***

"About seven years ago. I just felt...exhausted. So tired, all the time." Sabine nursed a small clay cup of tea, inhaling the rising steam. She had invited Nahar to her home, a small hut within the shimmer. Nahar, no longer able to tell up from down, had accepted. "I left. I thought the swamp would swallow me. I wanted it to."

Nahar sipped from her own cup, feeling the warm, subtle sweetness of mushrooms and chamomile play on her tongue. "Instead, you found a hut and a farm and settled in?"

"Something like that." Sabine smiled, the white lines on her face crinkling. "Insane, huh?"

"Not even a little." Nahar stretched her legs out, feeling the coolness of the spongy floor on her skin. Goosebumps formed on the exposed flesh, and a shiver ran through her spine. "Do you ever get back to central? For market days or festivals?"

"Sometimes. I enjoy looking at the shops." Sabine got to her feet and gently stroked the glowing fungal walls of her house until the temperature rose. "*Boletus caliditas*," she explained. "It heats up if you touch it."

"Wait...aren't they normally tiny?" Nahar rummaged in her pack and took out a portable handwarmer: a small plastic bag filled with *Boletus Caliditas* spores. "This tiny, to be exact?"

"If you harvest them, sure." Sabine sat back down, a little closer this time. "But this one must have been growing for decades, hidden under the shimmer."

They luxuriated in the silence and the heat for a while. The inside of the mushroom hut smelled faintly musty, comfortable, like an old library, or the smell of home after a long trip.

"Sabine?"

"Mhmm?"

"Why didn't the swamp swallow you?"

Sabine looked at Nahar. Her eyes were pools of black, and Nahar could see her face reflected in them.

"I don't know. Why didn't it swallow you?" Sabine shrugged. "It's picky. Eats a lot of iguanas and no hares. Eats some people, not others. It didn't eat me, and, thankfully, it didn't eat you." Sabine tilted her head. "Now, tell me, what led you into the swamp?"

They spoke into the small hours of the morning, words ebbing and flowing without the need for conscious effort. The spongy floor was soft and imparted a delicate coolness to Nahar's skin. Soon, without even knowing it, her eyes closed, and she slept, bathed in the moonlight.

***

Nahar prepared herself. Slow breaths, washing away the indecision that had become a familiar, if unwelcome, companion. Sabine had helped her make fresh supplies, laying the bounty of the swamp at Nahar's disposal. They had powdered toadstool shavings by moonlight to make pigments. They had scavenged and sharpened iguana spines to make palette knives Together, they had brushed dozens of hares, gathering loose strands of fur to make Nahar's brushes. The canvas still lay untouched, but this time, Nahar knew the blankness to be temporary.

Sabine sat on an overgrown toadstool in her garden, its midnight blue cap streaked with bioluminescent purple that glowed at frequent intervals. "Which way should I turn? Left? Right?"

"Left, please. A little more." Nahar propped her canvas and judged the scene.

The sky was a dark violet. A haze of pure, white light descended from Zeta, setting the world before Nahar ablaze. The swamp, drenched in shining moonlight, stretched out behind her, the wind rising and falling, sapphire specks appearing and disappearing between the elegant, slender white tree trunks. Every so often a hare, fur streaked with patches of glittering obsidian and solid white, zipped past, spraying the dust into the air, making the moonbeams dance. The trees bent and waved in the breeze, their creaking echoing through the silence. Specks of glowing dust settled into her paints, imbuing the colors with the unyielding life of the swamp.

Carefully, Nahar chose her paints.

Sabine's dark hair billowed out behind her, strings of luminescent grey seaweed woven into the fine strands. Dust speckled her shining black boots, giving them an ethereal glow. She wore a *sari* of gossamer silk and turquoise lace, nearly translucent under the benevolent watch of the twin moon. The thin lines of white paint on her face and shoulders stood in stark contrast to her brown, lunar-kissed skin and infinitely dark eyes.

Nahar's muse waited.

Nahar touched the canvas with her brush, and this time, she didn't stop.

Currant Voices in a Convection Oven

Sarah Ramdawar

Elbow deep in sticky overwatered dough, Molly scraped the pastry mixture off her lithe arms and flicked it back into the mixing bowl. The girl's bones carry more mass than you'd think. The fine mesh net on her head barely contained her curly hair—her frosted tips poked out from behind her ears and crown, wet flour spackled across the bridge of her nose and cheeks, creating a new layer of freckles—it was impossible to keep the human parts out of the food parts. Who would mind if a few arm and head fuzzies got worked in with the cold butter; how else would the judges know the sweet confection was from her, from her toil and time and love?

Hands are the secret ingredient to anything scrumptious, my dear. We've been perfecting and iterating deliciousness as long as anyone's been doing anything else. Mix and mash and turn the pot around and inside out; then something different, deckled, and delicious comes out, perfectly imperfect, like you.

Now this particular currant roll recipe was Molly's mother's from a half-remembered Trinidad and Tobago—the people surviving while the island masses themselves were long since swallowed up by the water. The child—no, young woman now—hoped to make her mother's memory proud. She was nervous having reached the final round of the bicentennial edition of the Sweet Memories: World Bake Competition. She started strong and won full points with a callaloo served with roti. The sound of greens, smooth coconut, and sea crab with the slight grittiness of sand were bright and cheerful. They talked of days at the beach, back when they were cherished for their horizons rather than their encroaching prisons.

Molly faltered in the second round making bake and saltfish. The fry of her bake was too oily and drowned out the booming clear voice of the dry hot sun on a clear sky; the saltfish too salty for cooling sweat running down a forehead. Even so, she made it to the final four—the dessert round.

On the bench to her left, a croquembouche was being hurriedly assembled by a man whose square hard face clashed with his airy choux. One puff at a time sighed as he pinched and placed them each with his thumb and forefinger. The bench to her right was lost in a pink-purple iridescent haze, clouds of evaporating liquid nitrogen and powdered sugar obscured where their groans were coming from. The person dancing at the bench in front of her swirled and twirled ribbons of bright orange jalebi, their sweet singsong serenade engulfing the entire space.

Molly, determined, rolled up her loose linen sleeves to her shoulder, dusting board flour on her clavicle in the process. She sifted more flour into the dough through finer and finer sieves. As she did, she heard the multitude of tiny particulate voices, fighting to pass through, not to be considered too lumpy or clumpy to be discarded and forgotten.

She would be food too, one day—this is what the currants collected in her bowl said. Hundreds of round, monotone, tart voices dusted in cinnamon and brown sugar, love reminding her at this stage in the recipe,

□"Like us," said one currant

□□"you too," said another

□□□"will be"

□"folded,"

□□"and rolled"

□"away,"

"inside something else,"

□"for someone else."

Molly kissed her teeth at the dried up fruit and got on with it. She took some yeast—oh, this dalliance is not part of her mother's recipe—feeling that the dough needed something more to lift up these mouthy currants. She thought the billions of yeasts—new and ancient at the same time, all eager to eat, chatter, and degas—might enliven the whole thing. She bloomed the yeast and worked it into the dough, kneading and folding and pleating itself into its self over and over. Then she rolled it out into a rectangle and spread the currants in an even layer on top. With stalwart hands, she raked her fingers through the cinnamon sugar and currant filling sitting on the dough surface and rolled the rectangle into a taut spiral, muffling the despondent noise. After proofing the log, Molly set the convection oven to preheat, hot air blowing, preparing to lick itself around her creation.

When the temperature was set and the time was right, Molly placed her currants roll alone in the centre of the oven. In the silence she knelt in front of her oven waiting for whatever the final judgment would be, knowing she made it her own way.

Savouring the remaining sweet cinnamon from her thumb, her tongue curled and stuck to the roof of her mouth. And as her eyes closed, tasting the sugar melting in her, she heard voices. Not the currants, and not a memory, but from inside herself—present today, present from the past. From the microscopic mitochondria that dwell within her, us engines that turn sugar to energy to life, she hears us say, she hears her grandmother say, she hears all the greats and all of us who hid and folded ourselves away say,

"Rise."

THE BLINK

Simon Kewin

The light of the seventeen suns washed the sides of the purple mountains as Efemi, breathing heavily, calf muscles burning from the climb, slumped to the flat, rocky surface of the peak.

Seventeen suns: the single, larger disc of the true sun, setting now, flattened and orange as if dropped onto the horizon, and then the sixteen smaller red stars of the Halo, arcing overhead. He climbed the pre-dawn hills every year to see it. The Blink. The moment the artificial stars flashed off and on in sequence, a celestial lightshow to match anything the natural world offered, up there with solar eclipses or aurorae. Every year, at the moment of the summer solstice in the southern hemisphere, midwinter in the northern, they flashed once in a complete circuit. You could never see it all from the surface, of course; you'd have to be in space for that, positioned above the poles on some satellite. But you could take in eight on a clear day, especially when you were high up and near the equator. As he was now.

"So, ready for the divine display?"

Oni arrived to slump beside him. She was also panting from the long climb, but less than he was. The setting sun made the yellow fabric of her tunic glow. His father had brought him up here to see the Blink when he was ten, but since then he'd made the journey alone. Until today. Today, he and Oni had come together. He'd wanted her to see it from this place.

Efemi breathed in the cool mountain air. Distantly – tiny, tiny sounds – he could hear the drums being beaten for the festival as the moment approached. Down in the valley, verdant from the irrigation system's network of underground pipes, his people were gathering – as they would be the world over, in field and street and square. He held out his hand and she took it, lacing her fingers through his. She was teasing him with her question. She planned to go to University in Lagos in a year; her head was full of engineering technicalities and the explanations offered by physics and mathematics. He, on the other hand, was the one who saw the world through the lenses of metaphors and the transcendent. He was the one who wanted to write and sing. He was the one who had time for the divine.

He played along, amused at her words. "God blinks to let us know he's still up there. I am ready to witness that."

She smiled, nestled her head against him. He was intrigued to know what she thought, what explanation for the phenomenon she saw. She was clever, so very clever. They'd grown up together, and he'd lost track of how many times their teachers had sighed and, stopping their teaching, said, *Oni, I'm sorry, there is nothing more I can give you to learn*. She was driven, too. Maybe that was the real difference about her. Most people, himself included, graced a life of minimal effort, drifted along. She, though, strove constantly to *understand*. It was as if she felt some urgent need to prepare for imminent danger, some calamity just around the corner. It was a wonder she was with him. He sometimes thought he was no more than another puzzle she was attempting to unravel.

She shrugged. "You really want to hear mundane technical reasons?"

"If they're coming from you, yes."

She sat up to look at him, directly into his eyes. She stroked the side of his face. "The stars in the Halo, you do know they're fusion reactors in geosynchronous orbit, yes? They're not eyes or fires or angels; they were built to supply us with all the energy we need. The desalinators, the decarb plants, the lights, the irrigation pumps, everything."

"Oh, sure. That's what they say."

"But they're just machines," she continued, ignoring him, "and machines need to be tested from time to time. This is a power cycle. The reactors go offline for a second and diagnostic routines kick in. Maybe software updates get applied, relays tested. That's all we're seeing. It's perfectly logical."

"There's no poetry in your soul," he said. "Billions of humans the world over stop and gaze in awe at a power cycle?"

"Just because you know what's going on doesn't make it any less breath taking. More, if you ask me. *We* did this. People like you and me. Well, like me, anyway. We built the Halo and we saved the Earth. Without the secondary suns up there, beaming down all that energy, what would we be? I'll tell you. We'd be clinging to existence, starving and frozen, a few million people at the most, a few thousand, killing each other for resources. More likely, we'd be dust, all dust. The Halo builders saved us."

"Only after they nearly killed us all."

This was one of her favourite subjects. "*They*? Who are *they*? Corporate greed and a system geared towards overconsumption nearly destroyed us. Countries slaughtering each other over scraps of land. It was the collective effort of thinkers and campaigners and builders that saved us. Scientists, yes. The simple cooperation of people across the world."

He loved to hear her talk. A light came into her eyes when she explained the achievement of the Halo. She was *fearless*. Of course, he knew the truth of it. They all grew up being taught about the old tech and power corps holding the world to ransom. He liked to hear her describe what had been achieved. He envied her the depth of her understanding, in truth. But, among the many things the builders had given them fifty years ago had been the freedom to pursue other paths in life. Five decades previously, humans had been concerned only with survival. Dwindling food supplies; the floods and droughts of environmental destruction; mass population migrations; pandemics sweeping the globe: all had taken their toll, and humanity's long story had nearly petered out. Limitless free energy had solved many problems. Now they were thriving, comfortable, at peace, and one such as he could waste away his days writing words rather than fighting for food or trying to save the world.

"Ten seconds," he said. "Whatever the Blink is, we don't want to miss it."

She nodded, her head back on his shoulder. He hoped they could always come up here, an annual pilgrimage. Perhaps, in time, if the world unfolded as he hoped it would, they could bring their children to see.

He hadn't mentioned this to her yet. He had no idea if her plans were in any way similar.

The true sun was an orange glow in the western sky, now. In the valley below, pyres were flaring as the festivities continued. Even on a planet made viable by technology, people liked to gather around fires and sing and talk and stare into the flames. This was what they were.

She gripped his hand tight as the first star, low on the eastern horizon, blinked out, followed by the next, and the next. Overhead at the zenith, then down the western sky. For a moment, the stars came out, a speckle and scatter of the hard white lights that were normally lost in the glow of the Halo. There were so many of them, their patterns familiar and strange. He'd witnessed the sight every year of his life, but still it was unexpected, alarming, beautiful beyond his power with words.

Efemi held his breath, as he always did, for the moment, the brief moment, when all the artificial stars went dark. The pause. The Blink. He turned his gaze back to the east, waiting for the first to blaze back into life.

He waited. And waited.

And waited.

It was Oni, finally, who moved. Afterwards, he often thought he might have stayed there forever, frozen, holding his breath. Reacting, saying anything, was to acknowledge the truth.

Instead, Oni – pragmatic, sensible Oni – was the one to speak. "They're not coming back on."

"They will," he said. "They must. They always do."

"No," she said. "It's too long. Something has happened."

"What could have happened?"

He couldn't see her features, but he could hear the alarm in her voice. "I don't know. Something. Something bad."

***

She hid in the shadows of the doorway while the mob raged past, shouting their chants. The smoke from their torches smelled of petrol, an acrid tang catching in the back of her throat. She knew what would happen if they saw her. People the world over were banding together, fragmenting into *us* and *them*, forming their gangs and their nations to fight against other gangs and nations. The world was unravelling to what it had once been.

Heavy, thick rain fell, splatting into the mud of the Lagos street. That would help, keep some of the crazies off the streets while she searched.

"Oni! Where are you? We need to go now!" Dr Wu's voice sounded in Oni's inner ear, relayed to her cochleas via her neural implants. Comms networks were failing the world over, but the local Lagos loop was running. For now. The voice of her supervisor was clear to Oni, but the mob wouldn't hear. She didn't respond, stayed back in the shadows.

A scrawny cat wound itself around her feet, begging for food. She had no food to give it. No one had enough these days, not since the suns went out. She thought about Efemi, that day nearly three years previously they'd climbed the hills to see the Blink. She often let her mind drift to those precious moments. How happy she'd been to have beautiful, witty Efemi to herself. Efemi who was always happy for her to be herself, who would do anything for her. Three years? It seemed more like thirty. Three long years. They hadn't seen it, but their contented lives had been built on straw. How quickly everything had fallen apart.

Some said it was divine retribution – the sort of nonsense Efemi might have talked about – but she knew there had to be a real reason. That was why she was cowering in the shadows of this backstreet when she was supposed to be suited up for the launch of their cobbled-together, desperate mission. The builders would not have done this to them. How could they?

"Oni!" Dr Wu sounded angry now. As she might: she and the others would be at the launchpad, the lift-off threatened by endless technical headaches and the anger of marauding gangs. If they didn't leave now, there was every chance they never would. It still seemed mad that she, Oni, was even a part of the mission; she hadn't learned enough in her time at the university to justify her slot. There were experts and specialists better suited to the work, but they were mostly frail relics from the old days, the construction of the Halo. It was up to people like her, now.

At least the mob had moved out of earshot so she could speak. "I'm here, Dr Wu. I'll be with you in an hour."

"We need you here. There is no time for your nonsense; we're running final preps."

"There are answers here, answers we need."

She could hear the exasperation in her supervisor's voice. "And I told you, you're chasing phantoms with your nonsense. The answers are up there, on the Halo. That's where we need you. This is an engineering problem, nothing more."

"I'll be with you. I promise."

"Our blast-off window is confirmed for 22:00. We're leaving with or without you – her supervisor's voice softened – but... I'd prefer it if you came. Please come, Oni. No one can program a fusion array controller like you."

"McTavish can. Seng understands the physics better than anyone."

"None of them has your breadth of understanding, and you know it. You see patterns in the numbers no one else does. Not McTavish, not Seng, not me."

"I'll be there."

"Be sure you are. Please."

Dr Wu closed the connection. Time to move. Oni pushed off from the wall, hurried down backstreets, around blind corners, across muddy urban streams strewn with empty food cartons and the occasional carcass of a dead dog. The map in her head showed her the way.

Ten minutes later, she found it. The house must have been grand, once: the stone-built villa where Professor Amuna had lived, raising his family while working on the focused beam propagators that had supplied the planet with energy. Now the building was a ruin, half-collapsed, burnt out. She'd been delighted to learn that one of the revered builders of the Halo had lived in Lagos, had worked at the very university she'd come to. Of course, he'd disappeared early in the effort. People said he'd succumbed to the mental health problems that had plagued him all his life, and his contributions had been largely forgotten. But Oni, delving into the designs and early calculations, the core routines, had seen the dazzling genius of his work. She felt like she knew him, catching glimpses of him in the elegance of his code. A quiet, self-effacing man who'd calmly gone about the work of saving the world.

Shattered glass crunched underfoot as she walked up the path to the dark house. She pushed through the sagging wooden door. She'd brought a torch, because they were all used to the darkness, now. The interior was a shattered ruin, everything destroyed. She crept into a hallway, a sitting room, shutters still hanging over the windows.

She didn't notice the concealed switch she triggered by stepping on it. Didn't detect the radio signal it sent out.

Instead, as she passed from room to room, she saw that Dr Wu had been right. There could be nothing here, no answers. She'd been so sure. Because Professor Amuna had been the perfectionist, had written beautiful multithreaded code that *couldn't* have malfunctioned. And then he'd left his flaw in the core routines. The fundamental weakness. It was subtle, a timing bug, easily missed, but once you saw it, it was obvious. It *couldn't* be a mistake, because Professor Amuna didn't make mistakes.

To Oni's eye, it looked deliberate. It also looked very, very carefully concealed. And the effects had been catastrophic. This was the weakness that had been exploited, she was sure of it. This was how someone had hacked the Halo, uploaded their own routines during the brief outage of the Blink – and broken the world.

Her light picked out a picture frame on the floor. Picking it up, careful of the cracked glass, she saw Professor Amuna and his family as they'd been: happy, smiling, posing in the sun. The man himself tall, a shock of hair about his head as if his brain was fizzing with electricity. They stood in front of the house, this house. It was huge; much more than she'd thought had been destroyed. The sight confused her, even as the warmth of the smiles delighted her. His parents, she knew, had been tailors, a skilled-enough trade, but certainly not one to make you rich. University professors did not make a fortune, either.

"How did you afford all this?" Oni said out loud. Professor Amuna, in the picture, refused to reply, simply smiling back enigmatically.

She was about to return the picture to its resting place when her fingertip felt something underneath. A metal object, taped to the back of the picture. She removed it to study. She knew what it was: a key. Before the Halo lit up the world, in the bad old days, people had used them often, locking away everything that was theirs, keeping others out, hoarding. Another artefact of a world where energy resources were limited. She held the key up to the light. The question was, where was the lock?

Ten minutes later, she found it: a cavity in the stone floor with a little hinged metal door. It had been covered by a moth-eaten, faded rug, worn by the damp so that the outlines of the stone flags were visible through it. The flags and the perfect square of the safe.

The key slid easily into the keyhole and turned, but there was also a combination. The lock wanted her to enter twelve digits. She had to leave, had only minutes, and knew well it was futile to try combinations at random. Even if she could enter a different number once a second, it would still take her – her brain ran through the maths without being asked – getting on for 32,000 years.

Then it occurred to her what the numbers had to be. She'd spent long enough immersed in his algorithms to know what number he'd pick. The golden ratio. Surprising how often it had shown up in his work. It was irrational, never-ending, but she knew the first twelve digits of it (and more besides) without having to think. The little dials were stiff with rust, but she got them all to turn eventually.

There was the softest click, and the safe door opened to her pull. Inside was a crystalline data fleck, the sort they'd used on the Halo to store code and data. She had several with her, those she was carrying to work on, one or two she wore as jewellery simply because they were beautiful. They were a non-degrading storage mechanism, and the Halo's systems depended on them, but why was one here, locked away? The live systems were obviously fully backed-up; there could be no need to keep this copy offline.

She held the little sliver of glass up by its edges, as if she could read the data it held by her flashlight.

The crystal glowed red as the aiming lights of three guns picked it out. The voice from the darkness was metallic, amplified.

"Hand the fleck over."

Damn. Damn, damn, damn. She slipped the object into her closed hand, used her other to shade her eyes to try and see into the gloom. Her heart pounded as she spoke, but she tried to sound calm.

"Who are you and why do you want it?"

"Hand it over and no one needs to die here. In fact, scratch that, we'll just shoot. No one is going to come looking for you. No one is going to care."

She persisted. She had to keep them talking. If they talked, they weren't shooting. "Why is this fleck so precious to you?"

"Precious?" There was a fuzzy, guttural sound that it took her a moment to identify as laughter. The shooters who'd come looking for her, the soldiers, appeared to be enjoying their moment of triumph, their power over her. "No, no. It's not precious, not at all. In fact, we're going to destroy it. There was always the chance he'd left other copies lying around; he resisted us to the end. And you: we should thank you for finding it."

"It wasn't that difficult to track down. How hard did you look?"

"Bait too well-concealed doesn't attract the vermin it's intended to destroy."

"This is his original code, isn't it?" she said, taking a guess. "The version without the flaw, the loophole. He couldn't bear the thought of destroying all copies of his work, could he?"

"It doesn't matter; we're going to destroy it now."

"Why?"

"Isn't it obvious? So the Halo stays dark. So the world remains lost in these new Dark Ages."

"Why would you want that?"

The laughter came again. "Limitless free energy. Do you have any idea how troublesome that is to the power and energy corporations?"

"There are no power and energy corporations."

"They've been… quiet, it's true. These fifty years: they've given humanity a glimpse of paradise, and now it's been taken away again. Do you have any idea how much people will pay for reliable electricity these days?"

"This is all about money."

"What else is there?"

"You can't hope to produce even a fraction of the power the Halo gave us."

"No. True. But scarcity is good, drives up the prices. Once the mothballed fission reactors are running, people will pay any price for what we have to offer, now that they've glimpsed the possibilities."

"So, why haven't you killed me?"

There was, she thought, a pause. A brief pause. Maybe they were conversing among themselves, these three high-tech soldiers in the darkness. Maybe they were receiving orders from someone far away.

"We know who you are, Oni Yahaya."

"Am I supposed to be impressed by that?"

"You're like him, like Professor Amuna. He was ferociously intelligent, too. He proved useful. Our hope is that you do too. He took our money, lived a life of comfort and luxury. You can as well. Is that so bad? Someone like you will always be useful in our new world. Your life can be filled with delight."

"He died young, far too young. Was that you?"

"If he'd stayed true to us, he'd have been allowed to live out his life. Consider that to be a lesson."

Oni forced herself to laugh. "Well, you're too late. I've copied the fleck already. Uploaded it while you were babbling on."

She showed him two crystals to prove her point: the two she'd slipped from her bracelet with her hand by her side. Perhaps not many people in the world habitually carried a fleck-reader around with them, but she did: a fact that they might well believe if they knew anything about her. She just had to hope they didn't know comms were currently down, the damned Lagos loop offline.

"Ah, that's disappointing," said the disembodied voice. "Well, no matter. If you aren't with us, you're against us. Now it's time for you to die. One more sad death among so many. I told you: no one will know. No one will care."

Oni opened her mouth to shout as the shots splintered the flecks she held into shards before – the bullets' velocity barely reduced – thudding into the soft flesh of her body. The pain of it was incredible. She was thrown backwards, thumping to the ground by the momentum of the rounds.

She lay gasping for breath while the three soldiers stood over her, their boots filling her world.

"Dr Wu." She spoke inside her head with the last of her strength. The conversation ran quickly, at the speed of thought. Finally, gloriously, comms came back online.

"Oni. Where are you?"

"I'm not going to make the launch after all. I'm sorry."

"Where are you? Are you near?"

"Stop talking. I'm uploading a fleck image to you. Take it with you. You have to take it with you."

"What fleck?"

"Take it with you, you'll need it, I'm sure of it."

"Oni..."

Then the universe faded, and Oni talked no more.

Efemi sat on the top of the hill. He still liked to keep up his routine, his ceremony, even though it had been three years since the suns of the Halo had blazed. Three terrible years. At least he was fitter now, the climb nothing to his muscles. Three years of labouring in the fields, pumping water, fighting off marauders, had made him strong. He'd barely written a word, and the loss of that part of him burned, the frustration of it, but survival came first.

He thought about Oni. So much for his naïve dreams. She'd left soon after the Blink – the *Long Blink* as they'd called it at the time, in their desperate optimism – had begun, determined to help with the effort of restarting the Halo. They'd never made the pilgrimage together again.

But then, everything had broken that day, and his small sadness barely mattered. People had lost too much. God hadn't blinked; he'd closed his eyes permanently, turned his gaze away.

He heard steps behind him. Instinctively he reached for the iron bar he carried with him at all times for defence. If he had to fight, he'd fight.

"You won't need that, idiot."

He stood frozen, unable to understand. Oni stepped into the light of his little fire, the one he lit every year because it felt like the right thing to do.

"What are you doing here?" he managed. "I thought you were... gone."

"Been busy. But that's over, now."

"I don't understand. Last time you got through, you said you were going on the Halo mission."

"That didn't work out."

She sat on the ground. He saw the wince of pain on her features as she talked.

"You're hurt."

"It's fine, don't stress. I... got shot."

"What?"

"Three bullets, but none hit anything vital. I'll survive."

"What happened? Where was this?"

"They bribed him, you see, threatened him, too. That was why he did it. One way or another, it killed him in the end, but not before he left a little counter-exploit of his own. An unflawed copy of his code to replace the compromised algorithm. He couldn't bring himself to turn away from his ideals completely. And, now they've shown their hand, stepped back into the light, people aren't going to let them get away with it, are they?"

"Who are *they*? What are you even talking about?"

"We stopped being afraid of them, you see, reduced them to clichéd villains in our stories of the bad old days. But they were still there, waiting in the shadows."

"Who?" His thoughts were still reeling, trying to catch up.

"Hush, now. Stop talking. Come sit beside me to watch."

"Watch what?"

"Hush."

They sat in silence, her head resting on his shoulder as it had three years previously. Fires burned in the valley, but they were no longer for celebration. Fires burned constantly now.

After a moment, she spoke again. "One day, we should bring the children up to see."

"The... children?"

"I've given it a lot of thought. It's time for fresh beginnings, the return of life."

"But I don't..."

"Quiet, now. Watch. Put what you see into words, the beautiful words you have in your head. Capture the moment to preserve it for ever. I've done what I could, now it's your turn."

Overhead, above the eastern horizon, a single light flickered, then flared red into fulgent life.

A moment later, the next artificial sun in the Halo lit up. Then the next, and the next.

She Dreams of Moons and Moons

Marisca Pichette

Oma said ours was the only house on the firefrost. She had carved it from the husk of a durian, so the spines would keep the bats away.

Despite her warnings, I climbed onto the roof at night to gaze at the moon. The firefrost sparkled around me, crystalline fields stretching all the way to the violets in the north, and the cliffs to the south. I loved the view from the roof under the moon, everything turned luminous green, the dull buzz of the frost flies reminding me that we were not alone.

As far back as I could remember, Oma warned me about the bats. She said they would eat me if they found me exposed at night. But I knew the green light of the moon would protect me, even when I was still smaller than Oma.

The moon has always protected me.

During the day Oma took me out across the firefrost, to the violets. I held the basket while she plucked grubs and mushrooms from the soil. The violets towered over us, their sprawling petals bathing the forest in purple shade. They were the largest growing things I'd seen, though Oma said there were many forests across the world, of many different plants. I sat at the base of one of them, staring up at its huge green leaves and the distant purple bloom. When Oma pointed out lichen on its stem, I scraped it off into the basket. It was almost as bright as the firefrost.

The lichen was poisonous. It helped keep the bats away.

I wanted to explore the violet forest, but Oma never brought us in further than the edge.

"Civets will be hunting," she said. Sometimes I saw things moving deep in the violets, even larger than the bats. Their eyes were flat and blue.

"What do they hunt?" I asked, when I was almost as tall as Oma's stooped shoulder. She laid three long roots in the basket I held.

"At night, they hunt bats. During the day they hunt people."

"Are there people in the violets?"

"No, but there are some on the other side of the forest. It's not as safe there as it is for us, in the firefrost."

Before I could ask more questions, she brought us back out into the orange gaze of the weak sun, and we walked home.

Oma told me she came right after the sun was raised. We were the first people to settle the world—Oma with her notebooks, and then me. She said the moon and I are about the same age.

"There was a beautiful valley," Oma said after we got home, emptying the basket onto the table. She sorted mushrooms from lichen, took a knife and began peeling the roots into strips. "Many people went there, but they weren't alone. The valley was filled with beetles as large as this house.

"There were also tall mountains, which of course the beetles couldn't reach. Some people settled there, but when night came, so did the bats.

"That's why the firefrost is the best place. The beetles don't cross the violets because of the civets, so they can't reach us. And the bats dislike the light of the firefrost."

"Why didn't anyone else come here?" I asked.

Oma wrung oil from a root into a bowl. "Many people love the valley so much that they will fight the beetles every day. Others like the mountains enough to risk the bats every night. There are other places to go, and lots of people went far, far away from here. But everywhere, there is danger."

"Why did they make the world dangerous?" I asked. "Why couldn't it be safe for everyone?"

Oma set the root aside and took my chin in her hand. "People need danger. Otherwise, they forget to be clever." Her thumb left a smear of oil on my skin. It smelled of dirt and violets.

"Some people did try to come to the firefrost after us, but they didn't know how to please the frost flies." She took the oil to the counter, where jars were lined up and waiting. "Did you put out the bowls?" she asked as she poured the fresh oil into the jars.

I nodded. Every night I filled three bowls with violet sap Oma and I collected from the forest during the day. Before it got dark enough for the firefrost to light, I put the bowls outside around the house. At night, the frost flies came to drink the sap. They didn't bother us, so long as there were bowls to drink from.

Oma never told me what they drank if there wasn't sap.

Oma finished filling the jars with oil and wiped her hands on her apron, smiling at me. "Good boy. Now, to bed. I feel the sun going down. Soon enough, the moon will rise."

***

I waited until it grew dark in the living room. When Oma went to bed, I snuck out through the front door, into the green night. The first thing I was aware of was the murmur of the frost flies.

They were roughly the size of Oma, and just as hunched. In the never-dark, they clustered around the bowls I'd put out, drinking violet sap. Their wings were iridescent green, reflecting the moonlight and the glow of the firefrost that surrounded our house.

They didn't look up from their meal as I climbed the rough side of the durian Oma had made into a home. I settled at the apex, snugged between two spines.

The moon was waiting for me. It hung in the sky, shining almost as bright as the sun. Green reflected off distant clouds and set the firefrost alight. Crystals shimmered all around the house, their sparkling only interrupted by the coming and going of frost flies, drinking their fill from the bowls I had put out. They flew to the places where Oma and I had walked, our feet crushing the delicate facets of the firefrost. Under the moon, the frost flies repaired the damage.

Each night, it grew brighter.

Oma told me that the moon would soon be as brilliant as the sun, and then more. She said this was planned, that the moon would take over when the sun ran out of energy. I saw it happening—every day dimmer than the one before. Oma worried the bats would start coming out before the sun had a chance to set, and it would no longer be safe to make the journey to collect sap to appease the frost flies. We had to travel slowly, her body stuffed with aches, her eyesight worsening so she increasingly relied on me to select the correct ingredients to put in the basket.

Sitting on the roof, I thought the moon was already bright enough. I hadn't seen any bats for several nights. I wondered if they'd flown away to the mountains, to hunt the people who hid in the caves and didn't have the moon and the frost flies to protect them.

Distant booming echoed across the firefrost, momentarily disrupting the steady humming of the frost flies. Nervous, I slid down between the roof spines and went inside.

When I asked Oma about the noise the next morning, she said the mountain people had figured out how to make explosions, and used them against the bats. I watched as she wrote it down in her notebook.

***

While we were collecting in the forest, I heard new sounds coming from deep within the violets. Sharp cracks and a screeching that set the hairs on the back of my neck rising. Oma paused in her work, brushing soil from her wrinkled fingers.

"The valley people have developed long-range weapons," she said thoughtfully. "Hand me my notebook."

I fished it from the basket, along with her pen. Oma leaned against a violet stem, writing. "Hear the screams? Those are the beetles. The bullets are powerful enough to break their shells."

I nodded, picturing it, though I had never been beyond the forest. I didn't ask how Oma knew what was happening on the other side of the violets and the hunting civets with their blue eyes. After her writing was finished, she drew a sketch of the weapons we were hearing, next to a beetle with broken skin.

She had never visited the valley, not in all my life. She was always here, with me.

The sounds grew quieter, and Oma handed the notebook back to me. I put it into the basket with the jars and roots, and Oma leaned on my elbow as we walked back across the firefrost. The sun hung pale in the sky, its orange light faded to beige. Shadows stretched in front of our feet, sliding into the spaces between crystals.

We had to stop many times for Oma to rest. When we did, it was as if the sun stopped with us, hovering in the sky until we moved on, and it sank, exhausted, to the horizon.

***

That night the frost flies glittered with near-blinding brilliance, the moon a green beacon in the sky. I sat staring across the firefrost, realizing I could see further than I could during the day. The moon had finally surpassed the power of the sun.

No bats came. When the frost flies finished the sap, I climbed down to the door and went inside.

Oma was waiting, notebooks stacked on her lap.

"Oma," I said, surprised and ashamed. She had told me many times never to go out in the dark.

Though now it was brighter at night than during the day. My skin prickled with the memory of the moon's green heat.

"Sit down," she said, nodding to the chair beside her. I walked over and sat. I was now much taller than her, strong and healthy, while she shrank every day, her eyes veiled with age.

"I'm sorry, Oma. I know you warned me never to go out at night—"

"Night is now day," she interrupted. She slid one trembling thumb into the notebook at the top of the pile, flipping it open and pressing her palm to the pages. The notebook was filled with her cramped handwriting and sketches of the world.

"When the frost flies were designed, they were made to be perfectly suited to the firefrost. They are the only species that will never go extinct, no matter what the settlers invent to change the world."

She turned the notebook pages. I recognized images of the valley and the mountains, the violets and their lichens. "It is right to befriend what will never go away. That way, you'll not be lonely."

I looked at her, confused. She closed the notebook and handed it to me.

I turned the pages while she opened the next in the stack, older and neater than the one I held. "Does anyone else know to gift them violet sap?" I asked.

Oma smiled, wrinkles doubling. "If the settlers thought to befriend the creatures on this world, we wouldn't hear explosions and screams."

"Someone should tell them!" I fumbled through Oma's notebook, passing her notes on caring for the violets so they would always give sap, on changing where we crossed the firefrost so as not to crush too much underfoot. "There must be something that would charm the beetles, or the civets. Don't you know?"

"I know," Oma said. She looked at me. "And so will you. But we can't interfere. We can only keep ourselves safe."

"They're killing each other!"

"One day, they may figure out how to stop. If not, things will end in another way. We can't tell them what to do. If we tried, they wouldn't listen. And the sun is running down. Things will change."

I stared at Oma, then at her notebooks. I turned to the back of the current one, my own handwriting following Oma's scribbles as she dictated her observations, her fingers too cramped to hold the pen anymore. There were a few blank pages left, but not many.

"We made this world to change," she said, her voice strained. "I've been taking notes since its birth, since before the settlers came. Everything changes. Everything grows old."

"Even the sun," I said, taking the notebooks from her. She smiled, moonlight carving lines of shadow across her face.

"Even the sun."

I helped her to bed, leaving the notebooks stacked on the table.

The next day, the sun barely crested the horizon. Oma was too weak to rise.

"Take the basket and make the journey to the violets yourself," she said, holding my hand. "You know what to do to stay safe."

I crossed the firefrost alone for the first time, crystals crunching under my feet. The frost flies would fix them when the moon rose, excreting the sap we fed them and shaping new crystals from shattered dust.

Under the violets, I collected everything Oma used to gather. I filled the basket and wrote down what I heard in the notebook. The sun set before I had finished, the moon lighting my way back.

When I returned home, the basket heavy with ingredients, Oma pinched my chin between her fingers. "You're strong. You'll shine for a long time."

***

The moon blazed across the firefrost. It never set but hovered against the horizon, nearly blotting the sun from the sky. The morning was green.

Oma stayed in bed. I visited her before trekking across the firefrost. "It is bright enough now," she whispered, cupping my cheek in her hand. "Don't go into the forest, even now. The moon can't protect you from the civets, or guns."

"I'll stay safe," I told her.

The sun set before I left, and the moon guided me to the violets, green light warming my back.

Gunfire and movement in the forest drove me back early. When I got home, Oma was asleep.

***

She sleeps still.

I follow her directions. Each morning as the moon rises I rise, taking the basket and my notebook and crossing the firefrost to the violets. I collect sap and listen. With every sound, I take notes. I return home and prepare bowls for the frost flies and pack lichen into the soil around the house to keep the bats away.

After a year of silence from the mountains, I stop collecting lichen. I record the extinction of the bats in a notebook I sewed from violet leaves.

In the evenings, while the moon blazes through the windows, I read Oma's notebooks. I start with the most recent, and work my way back through time. Half of her notebooks include me; the other half were written before the moon was born.

In three years, I reach her earliest notebook. Its spine is cracked with age, the pages brittle. I paint them with oil as I read, preserving them for the gaze that will follow mine.

It is in this notebook that I find the recipe for the moon.

Sitting in green light, I copy it out onto a new page. Oma sleeps upstairs. The sun has faded to nothing, but the moon now shines bright. It shows no signs of failing, but everything changes. Everything grows old.

***

The next day I venture into the violets and collect everything I will need to make a moon. Lichen, sap, roots, and petals. Beetle shells and civet teeth. I am afraid, but I read in Oma's notebooks how to charm the beetles and the civets. They donate their dead.

Back home, I wait for night. The final ingredient I need is a frost fly wing, glittering with green light.

For this I trade a jar of sap, fastened around the frost fly's neck with yellow ribbon. It crawls away into the firefrost with its payment, to await the regrowth of the delicate wing I now hold.

Oma sleeps.

I take a large bowl from the kitchen and crush the ingredients together. Using a broken crystal, I mix them into a paste that is almost clay. It sticks to my hands as I mold it—teasing out arms, craters, skin, light.

Oma sleeps.

I lay my creation on the windowsill to dry in the green gaze of morning. I leave with my basket and notebook, collecting what I need to survive in the world Oma made.

When I return, she still sleeps. The moon still shines. But everything changes, and everything grows old.

On the windowsill, a new light is being born.

SONG OF THE BALSA WOOD BIRD

Katherine Quevedo

I followed my mother through the open-air market, weaving between stalls of wallets, pan-flutes, and knitted ponchos in crayon-garish colors. Tourists' sunblock and perfume overpowered the stink of fresh leather from the stalls. I inhaled those foreign scents, let their promises of escape permeate my lungs and quicken my heart. They conjured distant cities, those aromas, with more skyscrapers than colonial façades. A million different futures for my teenage self. But for now, my mother and I sought gifts for my cousins abroad, trinkets for their college dorms. Llamas were all the rage over there, they claimed, but they wanted *authentic* ones.

A table of animal figurines caught my eye. The seller, a tiny woman with two long braids, leapt from her stool and greeted me with the customary, "A la orden." At your service. Wrinkles gathered upon her face like tree rings.

I gave her a quick smile, then examined her merchandise. In one row stood animals made of stone and in another, of tagua nut. Behind those rested bright creatures of painted balsa wood, light as corks, nice and inexpensive to ship. I didn't notice any llamas, but I spotted a curious birdlike creature carved with the plumage of macaws, the great, scaly feet of an iguana, the long neck and beady eyes of a tortoise. But its beak, oh, its beak! Majestic curvature to rival that of a toucan, in flame-orange—I'd never seen such vivid, shimmering paint.

When my mother looped back to find me studying it, she clucked her tongue. "Alondra, that's not what your cousins want."

They always got what they wanted.

She turned to leave. When I didn't follow, she paused. "Looks like you've found a knick knack for your own dormitory, and only five years early."

I blushed. My mother attempted to barter the woman's price down, as expected for us natives. But the seller scowled, and somehow those wrinkles deepened. No haggling for this little bird. She'd charge us a foreigner's price, which only made me covet the sculpture more. I clutched my mother's arm, begging her with my eyes not to insult this woman.

My mother sighed and opened her purse.

***

I'd guessed the carving was a Quetzalcoatl from the Aztecs or Maya or some other culture way up north, but back at the house, my abuelo took it in his leathered hands and, upon examination, declared it none other than Etsa, ruler of all birds. The name seemed familiar, probably from an old school lesson, but my recollection ended there.

"Ruler of birds?" I asked.

Abuelo shot my mother a disappointed look. "Have we grown so far from the jungle that we can't bring a bit of it with us?"

She pretended not to hear him and went out back to tend the avocado tree.

He continued, "According to legend, a demon named Iwia terrorized the rainforest. He orphaned an infant named Etsa, deceived the young boy, and raised him as his own. Poor Etsa had to go hunt birds each day to bring for Iwia's dessert."

"Ew." I squirmed.

He stifled a grin. "The rainforest grew quieter, less colorful without the birds. Then one day, Etsa befriended a dove who told him the truth about Iwia being a demon and having killed his parents. Etsa also learned he could bring the birds back if he blew their feathers through his blowgun." Abuelo perched the wooden figurine in his palm, fingers open and non-threatening as if he held a live creature. "The part of the legend you don't often hear is that when Etsa freed the birds from the demon, the boy was transformed into this shape as a reward, to escape the sadness of his past. They gave him this magnificent beak to signify the tube he'd used to save them. They say it produces the most superlative birdsong of all, because it carries the gratitude of every bird species of that jungle."

My pulse rushed at the thought. I desired nothing more than to hear it, that song of escape, of freedom.

***

That night, I placed the figurine next to my pillow and stared at it in the humid, sweaty dark.

"Please, Etsa," I whispered, "let me hear your song."

The beak gleamed back at me, as still and silent as the rainforest must've become while Iwia consumed all those birds. My heart sank. I knew too well that feeling of a place being devoid of something. Whenever the topic of my future came up, I could see the resignation my mother tried to hide from her eyes even as she talked about college. As if the demon Iwia had gobbled not just the birds from the jungle but also the wealth and opportunity from around us. I didn't want that resignation to creep into me. What would it take to restore greatness, to make real change?

"Only once," I pleaded.

The carving moved. I bolted upright, gripping the bedsheet. I fumbled for the light switch, my eyes never leaving the figurine. As light flooded the room, Etsa stretched his wings and neck. They rippled with iridescence. He blinked at me with eyes as dark and precious as black coral. Finally, he opened his beak.

The birdsong trilled against my eardrums, channeling his memories straight into my mind. I saw the human Etsa surrounded by trees, so many branches waiting to be perches again. I watched him lift his blowgun to his lips to make it more instrument than weapon. And out from the wooden tube streamed thousands of birds—over a hundred types of humming-birds alone, plus macaws, toucans, motmots, tanagers, and curassows. They warbled and trumpeted and chirped. The foliage trembled with their song. They fluttered and soared and dashed to freedom, sparkling like gemstones spilling across the green fabric of the rainforest.

My eyes blurred with tears from the beauty, from the emotions – Etsa's and the birds' – that their song carried. Notes of gratitude, as Abuelo had promised, but also of sadness and of regret that things had reached this point.

When the song ended, I found myself weeping into my bed sheet, my hair plastered to my forehead and neck. The figurine had become motionless balsa wood once again. The best kind of wood for Etsa. Weightless like a bird's bones, taking up space with the type of presence reserved only for taking flight.

I took that figurine with me when I followed in my cousins' footsteps to college abroad, as my mother had predicted. I took it with me afterward, too, through my studies and travels, in my backpack for every hike, on my desk where I work now designing green infrastructure. Always keeping a bit of the jungle with me. True to my word, I never asked Etsa to sing again. When you hear something that powerful, and listen with an open heart, you never have to. You've already been transformed.

Clockwork Dragon

Toshiya Kamei

The miniature dragon let out a mechanical groan, and its beady eyes glowed amber. As the dragon thrashed its pointy tail on the tatami floor, Hijiri looked at Yumehiko and smiled. He placed his hand on her shoulder and smiled back. On a low, wooden table, the flame of a lantern flickered, and their enlarged, conjoined shadows fluttered on the white wall.

They hardly exchanged a word. Orphaned at an early age, Hijiri was a bit of a loner. It didn't help that Yumehiko was a laconic man. Even so, after several weeks working together, she was almost certain that their hearts grew closer.

"It's very clever," Hijiri exclaimed with delight. She glanced at Yumehiko again, clapped her hands once, and held them together under her chin. "Do you have to wind it?"

"Yes. But mind you, it's not a toy," Yumehiko said, sounding a bit offended.

"It's not?" She took her notebook from inside her kimono and jotted down a few things. Licking the tip of her pencil, she considered what else to write.

"No. Far from it. Wait till you see a life-sized dragon." Yumehiko glanced toward the wooden sliding doors. Beyond them there was a shed that served as his workshop where he spent most of his waking hours. "Let me show you the blueprint." He spread a piece of paper on the low table.

"I can hardly make head or tail of it. But it's an airship, isn't it?"

"Correct." He pushed out his chest, proud. "It's steam-driven."

When she was little, Hijiri had ached to escape her dreary life in the orphanage. She'd wished she could fly away.

"When will it be ready?"

"Soon. Of course, as my official biographer, you'll be the first to know. Don't you feel privileged?" Yumehiko half-joked, looking up into her face. "Say, how's the book coming along?"

"Quite well. I'm adding final touches now."

"What are your plans after this?"

"I don't know yet, but something will come up." She smiled faintly, expecting him to make overtures.

"It's been nice having you around. I'll miss you," Yumehiko said. His gaze lingered on her longer than usual. She blushed and looked away. It was the first time he'd said something resembling *I love you.*

"Me too." Hijiri cleared her throat with a cough and managed to keep her tears at bay.

The following morning, Yumehiko led Hijiri to his backyard. He pulled off the cloth draped over a large object and revealed a dragon-shaped airship. The early morning sunlight shimmered off its metallic surface.

"Let's give it a test flight," he said and put on an aviator cap. He handed her a pair of goggles, a map, and a compass.

"Where are we going?" Hijiri asked.

"Wherever the winds take us," he answered. "Cancel all your plans. I'll show you the world." He opened the gondola door and invited her in.

"Wonderful," Hijiri said.

As the airship floated into the bright azure sky, her heart soared with hope and excitement.

All The Things You Will Do

J.D. Harlock

Whenever Dr. Kassar found herself restless on one of those long nights that left her cold and empty, she would traipse the cobbled roads that lead to the Hayyan Alchemical Library. On her way, she would make sure to pick up an ibrik of chai peppered with cinnamon and lemon from the student cafe and then hurry along lest it grow cold and stale for its notoriously punctilious recipient. There, as sure as the dawn would rise one day on these lands, she was certain to find Akila Saloum with her nose in some ancient tome or another that never failed to impress with its obscurity, and of course, its page count.

On this particular sleepless night, eager to see her pupil after a breakthrough that the Department of Applied Alchemy had shamelessly made light of, Dr. Kassar rushed by the new librarian who noticed and said nothing, only smiling to himself as if amused. Dr. Kassar promptly backtracked with a tinge of shame, returning to the reception desk, where she gently placed the ibrik on the counter.

"Goodnight." Dr. Kassar nodded respectfully. "Or should I say good morning, a'mo."

"A goodnight and a good morning to you, habibti."

The librarian smiled under his bushy mustache and Dr. Kassar smiled back with warm ease, as if the old man had worked here for ages and knew every single attendee by name. Something about him was strange, but it was the kind of strange that was most welcome at the Lebanese University of Arts, Sciences & Magicks, home to the brilliant but not prim and proper enough for the Modern Magicks University of Beirut.

"Is she in?" Dr. Kassar nodded in the direction of the alumni work-benches. Then she grinned. "I hope you don't mind the ibrik."

"Of course, she is." The old man winked, then put down his book and adjusted his spectacles, "And you're more than welcome, as long as you pour us a cup."

"A'mo, you don't even have to ask!"

"Thank you, habibti."

The librarian pulled out two flower-adorned porcelain cups from a leather satchel on the table before pausing and pulling out a third. "Will you be joining us tonight?"

"Oh, I'm afraid not." Dr. Kassar shook her head. "I have a lecture early in the morning, and the wife worries if I'm gone too long."

"That won't do." The old man shook his head, sending his parchment-white beard fluttering. "You will join us for one cup."

Dr. Kassar, by now familiar enough with the resolve of Lebanese hospitality, knew better than to argue with it, and bowed her head in assent.

"Shall we," she said, then picked up the ibrik off the reception desk, and led the way to the alumni workbenches.

⁕⁕⁕

Even though she could easily lose herself in her work for hours on end without rest, Akila, out of respect, made sure to stop anything she was doing whenever Dr. Kassar paid a visit. As soon as she heard her voice coming down the stairs, Akila put the ampoule down on the bench and eagerly awaited her arrival.

"I don't think I've seen you outside of the library in ages."

Dr. Kassar remarked as she carefully placed the ibrik on the table by the workbench, making sure not to disturb the chaotic order of the books, beakers, and test tubes.

"All the better!" The librarian exclaimed, his laughter echoing through the hall as he carefully made his way down the creaky staircase. "This is where she belongs."

"Thank you for checking up on me, Dr." Akila responded out of habit, then paused and realized that the following words were long overdue: "I appreciate it—more than I could ever and have ever expressed."

"No need, habibti." Dr. Kassar tried to say before Akila promptly hugged her.

Though the rest of the faculty was more than aware of what had befallen their star pupil, they had turned their backs on her once she had forfeited the generous studentship they never failed to remind her of. Dr. Kassar alone offered her unwavering support for a student who, up until then, had failed to make much of an impression on her outside of an academic context.

"Thank you."

"Ahm...." The librarian cleared his throat as courteously as he could. "We've brought over some chai. Just the way you like it."

"You shouldn't have." Akila rubbed her eyes in disbelief. "Really...."

Dr. Kassar clasped her hands enthusiastically.

"Now, now, we must celebrate."

"What?" Akila seemed more flustered than surprised.

"Don't be so harsh on yourself, habibti," the librarian remarked as he poured chai for the three of them. "We must celebrate, and we all know why."

"I read your latest publication in the *Journal for Alchemical Remedies*." Dr. Kassar picked the cup off the table and breathed deeply of its wonderful aroma. "I must say I'm impressed and—if I may allow myself the honor—more than a tad a proud of you...."

"The department isn't." Akila tried to sound bitter, but her tenor betrayed her hurt. "Maybe, they're right...."

Oh, forget them." Dr. Kassar swiped at the air in frustration. "In time, they'll come to their senses."

In saying this, she had hoped to rouse Akila, but Akila just sighed, and the look in her eyes tore Dr. Kassar up inside. Silently, the librarian walked over to the workbench, set aside the ampoule, then placed the cup in its place.

"Though I believe the sun would sooner rise in the west and set in the east, allow me to propose the following toast."

The librarian cleared his throat. "Let us drink to the department someday coming to their senses."

Akila raised her cup with a brave smile. Her guests followed suit. The new librarian always found the right words, and when he did, she always realized how desperately she needed them.

"What's that you've got there?" The librarian leafed through the tome Akila had recently discarded in frustration. "Seems promising...."

"Oh, not at all. If anything..." Akila turned to the tome and sighed. "It's more of a dead-end..."

"Still, a marvelous read." With great care, the librarian silently estimated how much of the book she had left to read. Then he looked up at Akila. "I'd highly recommend you finish it. Or get to the thirty-second chapter. At the very least..."

"Have you read it..." Akila tried to address the librarian by name only to realize that she did not know it.

"Oh yes." The librarian fluttered his fingers.

"I wouldn't call this light reading."

"I've dabbled in the alchemical arts. You could say I, too, was once a scholar."

Akila's eyes widened. "Did you specialize in Eastern or Western Alchemy?"

"Western, of course." The old man pulled proudly on his suspenders. "Hence, my employment as the lowly librarian here."

"Oh, that's sure to please young Akila," Dr. Kassar exclaimed, surely as delighted as her former pupil. "She's one of few western-concentrated alchemists active in the region—myself included, of course."

"Of course." The librarian nodded. "I'm familiar with your work. Both of yours, actually."

Lighting up, Akila gestured to the ibrik. "There's enough in here for three! Will you join me — both of you?"

"No, I'm afraid not." Dr. Kassar yawned. "I just came down to see how your research was coming along."

"I wish I had results to report more often." Akila nodded toward the book and then back to her teacher. "I wish I had something to report tonight at all."

"Don't make light of your discoveries, no matter how minor you find them." Dr. Kassar put her hand on Akila's shoulder. "You know the state of our field! Do you think anyone in the department—or anywhere else—is making as much headway as you?"

"But—"

"Breakthroughs take time. We both know that." Dr. Kassar brought her forehead to Akila's and smiled. "Don't doubt yourself. There are those who have great faith in you and what you may someday accomplish."

Hearing this, Akila tried to smile back, only for her to tear up instead.

"I'm not even close," was all she could say.

"Akila, it took immense courage and conviction to have stood before the scholarship council and explained to us why you were forfeiting one of the most generous and coveted studentships the university has ever offered. Few would have dared to stand before their elders at so young an age, all to pursue what they knew was their path. I will always remember that as the day I watched, with my own eyes, one woman enter into the annals of history."

"I'm not after fame."

"No great alchemist is."

"If only I could have him back...." Akila broke down. "If only I could have started sooner, worked faster, harder, my brother would still be...."

"Akila." Dr. Kassar bent down on one knee and stared into her student's eyes with a sympathy Akila had never known from her before. "That's in the past. All we can control is our future."

"Some future..."

Dr. Kassar smiled. "You know, not everyone can work all night, every night for years without giving up."

"Well, I'm about to."

Dr. Kassar caressed Akila's cheek, as she would have her own child's. "Maybe if you believe in yourself, as much I do in you."

Akila, reining in her tears, tried her best to smile.

Dr. Kassar slowly rose and walked over to the staircase before turning back one last time: "Just imagine it. Imagine all the things you will do...." She then knocked on the handrail three times for good luck and was soon out of sight. "Goodnight, Akila."

"Goodnight, Dr. Kassar."

The librarian watched Dr. Kassar depart. Once she was out of sight, he pulled out one of the chairs and took a seat, leaning into it quite comfortably for a man of his girth. After taking a deep, long breath that had his mustache fluttering, he picked up the ibrik and poured himself another cup, drank it slowly, then poured another and sat back.

"Are you alright, habibti?" he said.

"I guess so." Akila wiped the tears from her eyes. "I'm sorry for the—"

But before she could say it, the librarian raised his palm and waved the entire thing away. He would hear nothing more of it, and Akila was comforted by that.

"You have a lot on your shoulders. More than you know."

"Thank you." Akila took a deep breath. "I'm sorry, but I've failed to remember your name."

"That is because I have failed to share it. But do not worry.

It is of no importance." The librarian blew the steam off his cup. "Yours on the other hand...."

"Oh, don't listen to Dr. Kassar." Akila frustratedly reached for the ampoule, hoping to toss it into the pedal bin, only to realize she'd forgotten where she'd placed it. "I haven't published much, this latest 'breakthrough' means absolutely nothing, and my name is of no importance either."

"Maybe not now, but...." The librarian winked as he sipped from the cup, "I would hold my breath."

Akila grimaced. "You think so? From those papers?"

"Not just from those papers..."

"You mean all these nights I've wasted here have given you a reason to believe in me too."

"You sound as if you don't believe in yourself."

Akila shrugged. Then she stood up and dusted herself off. "It's time for me to move back home and find something else to waste my time on."

Tilting his head forward, the librarian, frowned. "That would be a mistake."

"You really think so?" Akila's voice was pleading, but she did not know why.

The librarian raised his palm again, and—with a sudden flash of understanding—Akila saw the futility in her self-pity.

From behind his wafting mustache, the librarian grinned. "When I'm in a mood like this, I can always count on a book to cheer me up." He reached into his satchel, sifting around as if drawing something from an endless shelf. "And I have the perfect one for you in mind."

The librarian pulled out a pristine textbook that would put doorstoppers to shame.

"What is this?" Akila walked over to the book.

"I've been reading this lately, and I must say, from what I've seen here, it's far more engrossing than what's on display."

"*Principia Alchemia, Vol. I.*" Akila read the title as if it was in a language she did not understand. "By Dr. Akila Saloum…?"

"In it, you will find the secrets of the panacea, among a great deal of other things."

Many would have laughed this act off as a practical joke, but Akila, taken aback, went quiet, wondering if she was in a dream.

"Who *are* you?" she finally asked, staggered, but the strange old man who suddenly seemed so much stranger just smiled.

"I'm the Librarian."

Akila, feeling the floor give out from under her, latched onto the closest chair and collapsed into it.

"For some reason I can't explain, I believe in the authenticity of this textbook."

"A wise assumption." The Librarian nodded and raised his satchel onto the table. "This satchel affords me access to the finest publications from across the known and unknown universes—past, present, and future…"

"If…" Akila trailed off, wondering if she should even bother, but the Librarian only had to raise one of his bushy eyebrows inquisitively for her to blurt out: "If I asked you to tell me who you really are, would you?"

"I'm afraid not, my dear." The Librarian tapped the textbook. "But do, take my word for it."

"I can't…" Akila suddenly found it hard to breathe. "I can't believe that I'm the one who discovers the panacea."

"Can't you?"

"How?!"

"Read this." The Librarian tapped the textbook again. "And you'll find out how *you* did it."

Akila stared mutely at the Librarian. Was she really—or, rather, would she be—the one who discovered the panacea? Would all these sleepless nights she'd spent in a library, in the middle of nowhere, eventually change the world?

An eternity passed before Akila could find those words again, but when she did, she was as certain of them as the words she had uttered before the council all those years ago.

"I would love to read about it. Believe me." Akila pushed the textbook away, and back into the hands of the Librarian. "But I'd prefer to find it out for myself."

The Librarian nodded.

His work here was finally done.

"I mean." He chuckled. "It's only a matter of time, isn't it?"

Look to the Sky, My Love

Renan Bernardo

I know how Solândia's June Party will taste and smell before I arrive—burnt popcorn. It's that charred, ever-so-slightly buttery sensation of being in the right place, but in a time that can never be right again.

Alana died five months ago after a quick, but merciless battle against cystic fibrosis. Yet here I am, at a party, being disrespectful.

A mocking undertone pervades the air as I cross the flag-ornamented arc of the entrance. In every child yelping after winning a plushy sunflower in a fishing game, and in the wafting chaos of *farofa*-coated bio-frankfurters, corn pudding, and love apples. When I dare to feel but a fleeting satisfaction for being back in Solândia, it's quickly gouged out of me by my guilt and held before my eyes, as if saying, "Hey, is that what you're doing here? Being joyful... Aren't you supposed to be mourning?"

It's the first time I'm coming here after she died. We used to come many times a year until the disease grabbed her away. I'm here now because it's that time of the year again, time for her party. Although Solândia's June Party is all-year long, for me—as it was for her—June is supposed to be our special moment. It's in the name of the party, yeah. But it's also in the way the wind blows, chillier, drier, carrying hints of spending the evening together, snuggling and acknowledging half of the year has slipped by fast and ruthless, but there's always something to grasp ahead of you.

Perhaps, I'm here to challenge the party, this monstrous, continuous entity looming in the countryside. Because how could there exist a place that gobbles up people across two square kilometers of happiness and laughter and dance and affection? Alana is dead. I've set the canister with her resomated body on her mother's doorstep myself. The June Party should be in mourning.

I walk across one of the roads that branch through all the party sectors like veins. Many of the places are now foggy in my mind as if I watched a movie about it a long time ago and couldn't recall more than the vague setting. The surroundings bloom, remembrances returning back where they're supposed to be. I realize—recall, *exhume*—that Solândia is the party of our firsts.

First kiss (underneath a moon-bulb sky, a couple dissonantly slipping from the quadrille, our makeup—fake mustaches, goatees, and freckles—smearing each other, straw hats too big for our touching lips).

First time making love (hidden in the vacant booth of the fishing game because Mr. Marques was sick and didn't come).

First time telling each other we would always come together to Solândia, no matter what.

A girl with a straw hat, braided black hair, and a patched, sewn-flapped dress stops in front of me, smiling, a heart-shaped pad on her hand casting a pink glow on her painted freckles.

"Ah! It's you," she says, taking a good look at me.

"What is it?" But I know what it is. Love Mail. A tradition of June parties where people need to follow clues to find a secret admirer. "I'm going to pass on this..."

The girl scrunches up her face.

"You don't reject a love letter unread..." She extends her pad to my arm, where my skin blinks with letter icons, notifying me of an incoming message.

"Look..." I say, glancing at my arm.

The girl leaps forward, taps "Accept" on my arm, and skitters away, disappearing in the multitude of people lining up in front of booths to buy candies—crunchy *pé-de-moleque* or nutty *cocada*—and tickets to the games.

The back of my neck emits a haptic nudge. I look at my arm.

~~~FOLLOW THE LOVE~~~
Under St. John's starlit sky.
I stared deep into your eye.

</div>
~~~

Find me where the devil meets the saint.
~~~FOLLOW THE LOVE~~~

A riddle. My finger hovers above "Discard." But I don't tap it. Alana would agree with the courier. Even after we started our relationship, she'd never have let me deny it. At June parties, you owe a debt with love letters, even if it's just to say a polite 'no.' Love—be it that jittery shift in your belly or that mammoth depth inside your soul—isn't supposed to be promptly discarded, she'd say.

I sigh, lifting my head and looking to the sea of colored flags and balloons bedecking the party, plucked by the sunset breeze. I have no idea where the riddle points.

I set out to find my secret admirer, guilt gnawing at my chest while I look for clues. The party unfurls around me, droplets of memories beading up here and there. A kiss under a booth, a joke by the road's edge, an eagerness before a rendezvous. *Go back home... You're supposed to be muffling your cries with your pillow.* I clench my teeth to ward off the thought.

Solândia's June Party is the world's largest, extending over an area of two square kilometers. And the only one everlasting, going on for fifteen uninterrupted years and counting. The party boasts the biggest quadrille dance in the world, the tug-of-war with most participants, and the most pompous fake marriages, even more elaborate than real ones.

The road slopes up to a plain field where biogas lampposts cast swatches of green and orange across hundreds of white bamboo tables, booths, and sprout-booths carved into hollowed-out tree trunks, all crowded by visitors. Pockmarking the field, dozens of color-shifting bonfires flank the dance squares where couples boast their joy with *forró* songs, hands clasping together, circles rhythmically shrinking and broadening, fake goatees and fake freckles glistening with sweat. All acting as if death isn't part of the world.

Then, I know I'm going the wrong way. Not because grief is clouding my mind, but because grief is sticky. It wants to stay with you. And it knows if I go along the right path, it might be washed out to a bittersweet memory.

I tap my arm. All love letters have an expiration time. I may let it die by not finding the next clue. Instead, I decide to make a pact, to bargain with my grief and make this deal with the party. If I follow the love mail clues and honor my debt, then it won't be disrespectful to Alana's memory. When
~~~

it's all sorted out, I can just go back home.

I go back along the road and follow the right path.

Where the devil meets the saint. The Quentão Factory, a barrel-shaped restaurant where waiters prepare the typical warm drink using two liters of wine, half a cup of *cachaça*, sugar, cinnamon, ginger, and water. A chiton-dressed St. John pours a glass of water from a gallon jug while a reddened, grinning man pours a glass of *cachaça*. The place is packed. It's June. There won't be a single spot that isn't swarming with that anticipation of amusement and romance inherent to all June Parties.

An empty guardian mecha silently watches from the corner. Somewhere nearby, a woman sings in a boisterous voice. "Tá me esperando na janela, ai, ai." The dancers echo. "Não sei se vou me segurar."

Alana was already coughing that day. She held her breath after a fit, a few steps from me, her smile unwavering even then. She sported an eye-liner-drawn mustache and goatee, her hair dyed in red and yellow, puffing out from underneath her straw hat. The *quentão* cup in her hand tilted to the side, the dark red liquid almost spilling.

"Don't look at me like that," she said, mocking me, carefully sipping the drink from the straw. She stopped and inhaled, sucking in the air with difficulty. When she stepped forward, I thought she was falling. I felt my tendons and muscles tauten up to grab her in my arms and prevent her from falling... My teeth grating my lips... The aftertaste of a tumble that never happened.

She was only leaning in to kiss the tip of my nose.

"Let's get some *paçoca* before the dance," she said, breath whiffing out cinnamon and alcohol.

I can't remember the feeling of relief anymore, the dimpling of my cheeks as I smiled back at her and kissed her on her earlobe. The after-scent of a floral perfume—delicately sprayed on each side of her neck—I thought I would never forget. Only the tension remains, as if my muscles never relaxed and never will.

A nudge throbs in my neck. I peek at my arm.

~~~FOLLOW THE LOVE~~~
Where the ground is smashed.
In June, pleas of love, people gathered.
Find me where sweat and heat converge.

</div>
~~~

~~~FOLLOW THE LOVE~~~

I smile, then grimace. Smiling tastes like overcooked corn.

But this clue is obvious. It leads to Solândia's Central Field, the place where the party converges.

The walk to the Central Field takes fifteen minutes. This is not the only path leading to the center. Like a web, eleven other roads lead to the Central Field, coming from all seventy-two party entrances.

Photovoltaic cells line up on the soil, whole gardens of them chaotically mingled with more bamboo tables, sprout-booths, and dance squares. Underneath my feet, the patched dirt road and the grass surrounding it reveals the metallic glints of the thermoelectric and kinetic generators that underlay Solândia's soil. The dance harvester—as people like to call it—underneath Solândia's grounds harnesses all the movement from footsteps and dances, and all the heat from bonfires and bodies exuding joy. It not only helps powering the communities all around, but also provides increased moisture capacity and granular structure to the soil of the vegetable gardens that feed Solândia.

Shining in the middle of the field, St. John's *Fogueirão* casts its gilded glares across the party. That's not something grief can block from me. It never could, maybe because of its glaring light: One tall, vivid fire, yet many symbols. Some people go to Solândia only to see it, to leave offerings to St. John and pray, in gratitude or gloom. And then there are people like Alana and me who went for the warmth on our backs, the kindling crackle of the flames, and the shadows dancing in front of us while we talked about the surrounding communities and of how Solândia distributed the energy harvested from dance and movement to five different towns.

It would be her postdoctoral research had she lived. She'd promised herself to make that fire shine brighter for a lot of other communities. She had plans to use artificial intelligence and machine learning to improve the efficiency and management of the generators. Once, during a peculiarly quiet evening around the *Fogueirão*, she'd told me how she wanted to turn the party into a living organism, something that could spread beyond its boundaries and supply energy and comfort throughout other parts of the country using a relay of underground networks. Joy and life bequeathing dignity and solace.

"It's not machine learning," she'd told me, chuckling with an afterthought, pressing her forehead against my shoulder. "It's *party* learning. The party will learn and improve itself."

That day, she had the air of someone overly conscious of one's own fate. After a moment of silence, I'd lowered my head on her shoulder and absorbed the soft thumping of her heart as tears flowed across her body. There wasn't much to be said by then.

I swallow the memories. They taste like cooled *quentão*. And farewells. I've already said my goodbyes to Alana. Once. Briefly. As she asked it to be. A kiss on the lips followed by walking away from her. No more visits in the hospital, no more trying to find her perfume amidst the antiseptic scent of intensive care.

A mecha trumpets nearby, whirring its gearwheels and flexing its supple legs. The sound of accordions, *zabumbas*, and triangles come out from speakers on its bulky belly. It's all graffitied with the party's motifs—balloons, peanut brittles, *maria-moles*, *canjicas*, bonfires, and stick men and women dressed in bridal gowns and mended jeans. The underside of the mecha's arms is bedecked with colored, diamond-shaped flags in many different sizes. Children play Saci hop under its legs, giggling and tumbling, jumping on one leg. The mecha had been one of the guardians when sabotage was still common among all the groups wanting to take a bite from the party's success. It provided security, monopolized energy production, and controlled the booths sales. Now it's just a retired hunk of metal, a sturdy guardian walking around the bonfire for the children's amusement.

My neck tickled and throbbed. I glance at my arm.

~~~FOLLOW THE LOVE~~~
[[SWEETHEART UNAVAILABLE]] — Too bad :-(
~~~FOLLOW THE LOVE~~~

Wrong place?
I frown and hit back to check the previous riddle.
Where the ground is smashed.
There are always mechas stomping the grounds around the *Fogueirão*...
In June, pleas of love, people gathered.
The people who pray to the bonfire...
Find me where sweat and heat converge.
I lift my head and stare deeply into the fire. The party converges in the

Fogueirão, but it's not where people converge. They like to see it and make their prayers, but they don't linger. Although it offers light and warmth, it can't provide exhilaration. So where?

I traipse along on the grounds near the *Fogueirão* as if waddling my way through smog, trying to let the riddle solve itself. A shadow already creeps up on me, wanting to be cast over the Quentão Factory and the moments that regained clarity after I crossed Solândia's arched gate. The more time passes, the more I need to just walk away fast to the safety of my pain.

But I made a pact with my grief.

I sit on a bench, recomposing, hands slightly shivering on my lap. Nearby, children hop around a mecha, frolicking and giggling, still far from needing to bargain with life. Night drains the sky, leaving little space for blue, just a blackened, empty canvas in its place.

"Olá," a little boy stops before me, words glowing on his arm. He has a thin mustache drawn underneath his nose. He hands me a love apple on a stick. Its sickly caramelized scent invades my senses.

"Are you giving it to me?"

He shakes his head. "Not me."

I look around, searching for my secret admirer, expecting to see someone smiling or waving—or for my guilt to say I should be home, mourning. But there's no one. And my guilt says nothing.

"I don't see—"

But the boy has already vanished. I wonder for a split second if my mind's playing tricks. But the love apple is real. As I eat it and surrender to its sweetness, I realize that, like before, I know *where sweat and heat converge.* I was just pretending the riddle was hard so I could flee from the solution. And like before, I can't go back there. Why waste my time over memories that will never become real again? Why bother?

I finish the love apple and force myself to stand up from the bench with the same effort I exert to wake up every morning.

The answer to the riddle is the *Quadrilha da Perpétua.* It's happening every day, every hour, every second, a ceaseless quadrille alternating dancers in synchronized sway in an eternal rotation of dance and music and unrestricted happiness. It's where people go to find friendship and fun, joy and lightness, love and sex. It's the vortex of all things, gobbling down sadness and spewing forth joy.

But there's something else. My heart hammers in my chest. The Quentão Factory and *Quadrilha da Perpétua* aren't just random places that a secret admirer would think of while elaborating riddles. There are hundreds of different spots around the party that could fit those descriptions. Those particular places are central to me.

It was in Quentão Factory where we had our last drink together.

It was in *Quadrilha da Perpétua* where we shared our first dance.

It can't be a coincidence... but it can. It's only my mind trying to find meaning in some stranger's riddling logic. Those are only places. They're significant to many people, famous to most partygoers. I've set the rest of her on her mother's doorstep. I've signed the documents. There's nothing to look for in Solândia.

Yet, sometimes, the only way forward is making sure there's no way back. I look at the road from where I came and pretend it doesn't exist. I touch my arm and check the love mail's config.

No bonds last forever! This letter will expire in five minutes.

I shoo the children away from the mecha and climb its legs. The unused head-door grumbles when I open it and enter. I inhale the decade-old hydraulic fluid and neglected cushions.

And when I slip into its control gloves and brogans, it molds perfectly around my arms and legs. It's like it has been made for me.

I run. The mecha's feet trample the road toward the quadrille.

Around the enormous square, sitting before the balloon-larded fence, unpaired people wait for an invitation to be carried into the whirlwind, loners feeding on the temporariness of solitude. It's a trait of high seasons, when lines of couples wind alongside the square, waiting to take their turn, to become part of the rows of dancers and be swallowed by the *arraiá* and the *balancê*.

It was Alana who kneeled before me and invited me to dance with her, braided locks puffing out from her head with tiny colorful clips, a tattered straw hat in her hand. I was only looking around the square, thinking how beautiful the four bonfires in each of its corners were, like protective saints themselves, tricks making the light range from pink to green to orange. I hadn't thought of dancing. But just as you don't reject a love letter unread, you don't refuse an invitation to dance.

While we waited in line, Alana told me how thirty percent of all party-generated energy in *Quadrilha da Perpétua* came from the feet stomping on the ground, all the frisking and rhythm translated into energy and dignity for all the surrounding communities. And she told me how it could reach seventy percent if the party itself was able to trim its energy expenditure, and how so many possibilities could come from that. She'd eagerly dive into the details, and I'd eagerly listen until the quadrille devoured us. If only we had the time.

And we danced. How we danced. Left, left, right, right, shuffling, thighs glued together in a *xote* symphony. When the couples moved away in two separate lines facing each other, we stared deep into each other's eyes, already bound. And as the lines marched toward one another and we connected again, I pulled her closer and kissed her. If the *Fogueirão* was where it all ended, with the certainty of death looming over us like ghosts creeping out of the flames, then it was in *Quadrilha da Perpétua* where it all started.

I switch off the mecha near the square. People gape and gather around the guardian, clapping, booing, laughing, singing in everlasting energy.

I climb out of it, legs frail as I leap to the ground.

"Hey," I call to a love courier standing in a corner and show him my arm. "Can you tell me when this love letter was written?" I need to make sure it's a coincidence and not some past letter from Alana that only today was mapped to my arm. I need to rid it of meanings.

The boy frowns. "Probably today, mixter. I never saw love letters from any other days. It wouldn't make sense because—"

"Just tell me, please."

The boy shrugs and raises his heart-shaped pad near my arm. He peeks at it, gaping and sliding a finger over an icon.

"That's weird..." he says. "These things get smarter day by day. It's like the holo-fish escaping from the fishing game. It's funny. It seems to have been self-generated as soon as it detected your arm. It doesn't ... have a date?"

Self-generated? I think of asking who sent it, but the words catch in my throat. No need.

I run, eyes hopping from people in the crowd to my arm, waiting for another link, praying for time like I did during Alana's last weeks. A song blasts from the speakers around the square, which is so large its edges get fuzzy in the bonfires' glare. Non-piloted mechas gather near the fences, each holding a couple of balloons in their mechanical hands, their feet stomping the field.

Foi numa noite igual a esta
Que tu me deste o coração
O céu estava assim em festa
Pois era noite de São João
My eyes tear up. Yes, it was on a night like this you gave me your heart.
I look at my arm as soon as it vibrates. It shows an automated message.

~~~FOLLOW THE LOVE~~~
[You've found each other! Enjoy the love!]
~~~FOLLOW THE LOVE~~~

Beneath my skin, a soft thumping spreads throughout my arm. The beating of a heart, the tempo of a body crying...

Her way of saying goodbye. No hands interlaced on a bedside smelling of antiseptic certainty. No incessant beeps fading, dance steps coming to an end.

The bonfires around the square all shift to plum-hued flames, Alana's favorite color.

Her way of saying a different kind of hello.

I force my legs to walk confidently to a young woman with braided brown hair underneath a straw hat full of green ribbons. My muscles relax. I extend a hand and invite her to dance. Other people receive messages in their arms and devices. They open up for us, giving us their place in line.

We enter the square, crossing our arms together, waving our hats.

My neck sends a signal, but I don't look at my arm yet.

I just dance.

Olha pro céu, meu amor
Vê como ele está lindo
I look up to the sky. Small balloons stud the blackening night, released by the mechas around the square. The night smells of sweet cake and buttery popcorn.

The Center Cannont Hold

Holly Schofield

The King's Pawn glowers. In the misty far ranks, the enemy awaits.

The command comes from on high: two squares, and the Pawn eagerly strides forward.

His enemy counterpart does the same, abutting his square. He smirks. Soon, one of his comrades will eliminate her as he will annihilate the pawns beside her.

"See me!" she shouts.

He ignores her silly ploy. He will not be distracted.

She leans toward him, intense. "We have agreed, my comrades and I. We will fight no more unto death."

What insanity! To die for Queen and King is the ultimate sacrifice. The cozy nestle in the box, the feather touch of his comrades, then the calm routine of positions followed by the thrill of attack. The inevitable moment of piercing agony, only to rise again the next game—what could be nobler?

The madness is spreading. Enemy pawns advance, all of them by two squares, bubbling in excitement. The Pawn's comrades are listening intently. Then, a comrade twists obscenely backwards, tipping the King into the blankness that exists beyond the board. Others then crowd the Queen over the edge. More pawns begin to frolic like knights or slide like bishops. The world is losing its mind!

The other King and Queen also fall, rendering the game over, with no winners but also no losers. Madness!

The King's Pawn sidesteps to avoid a careening bishop. He collides with another pawn, and they steady each other side-by-side, that familiar soft feathery touch. He squints. This pawn is no comrade of his! What to do?

The enemy pawn crimps a warm smile.

Slowly, the King's Pawn brushes against her again, then he ventures cautiously into new squares, and new ideas.

Seven Sisters

Susan Kaye Quinn

"I don't understand why the bill's so high." Latoya rubbed the bridge between her eyes but kept her voice polite. "I just need to know why y'all be charging me more than the estimate."

The girl said to hold, she'd get the robotics team lead.

Latoya leaned back in her chair. Out the window, the sun heated up her fields, solar arrays soaking in power for the farm while shading their signature crop, *Camellia sinensis.* The neat, green rows of tea bushes had grown thick over the years. The hedges were fat, with just enough room between for the picking bots. The spindly creatures harvested each leaf and bud at precisely the right time. They were key to every harvest, but especially this second flush—the first had been wiped out in March when the polar vortex came down to Mississippi for a visit.

She had only four harvest bots running, out of ten in the fleet, and it wasn't near enough. Two were out for repairs, the rest needing one thing or another. Aubree, the farm's bot keeper, was laid up sick in the guest house. Everyone at the farm played an important role, but Latoya never appreciated that red-haired skinny white girl more than right now, as this oversized bill stared at her. Aubree could have fixed these before breakfast and without the extra parts.

The *Seven Sisters Collective* tea farm was having money issues, and hoping for better days was not a solid business strategy. Latoya knew that—so said her degrees in sustainable agriculture and business—but all the best practices in the world couldn't outrun a changing climate, one virus after another, and plain bad luck.

"Ms. Comfort?"

"Yes."

"I heard you wanted to talk about the bill." This young gentleman's accent sounded like it got lost on the way to Jackson's shiny new tech corridor. Latoya hoped there might still be room for negotiation.

There was that word again: *hope.* "I appreciate you helping us out with repairs," she started, even though they'd been substantially delayed, messing with her whole plan. "You know our bot keeper is sick with the virus, that new one—the arbovirus." Mosquitos were a hazard everywhere in the South, especially when they helped viruses cross over to humans.

"I'm sorry to hear that." And he seemed to be. "It's just those specialized tea pickers you've got out there need specialized actuators. We had to order those from Taiwan, and they've got a supply chain problem. Long story short, their price is double right now. We're just passing that on, Ms. Comfort."

"I see." She kept her sigh tucked in her chest. "The bill says we've got thirty days to pay. I'll need every one of those. Could we get our bots back before then? We need them to harvest the second flush."

"I'll have them sent straight out today. Should be there by tomorrow. And I'm sorry about your bot keeper. I hope she gets healed up soon."

Latoya had that wish as well, and not because the farm would be sunk without her. Aubree wasn't just a skilled bot keeper, she was *family.* They all were. Seven Sisters had more than seven folks—thirteen, for a few years now—and none had ever been sisters. Mama said it gave cover to families like theirs before they were legal. But now, they'd all sworn the oath, signed the documents, and pledged to care for one another, in sickness and in health, come hell or high water. The business was how they kept fed, body and soul, on top of the Basic Income everyone brought, thanks to the international billionaire tax making sure people didn't starve while the rich built their fleets of yachts. In good years, Seven Sisters had a full cash reserve and sponsored climate refugees at the center down in New Orleans. In a great year, they could host—that's how Lucía had come to the family. But the heat dome last year had burnt seven acres to a crisp, then the polar vortex killed first flush this year, and now their bot keeper was down? Reserves were nearly empty. Latoya couldn't afford to send bots out every time they needed repairs. Dang things broke all the time.

Basic would keep them from starving, but it wouldn't keep the farm alive. For that, they needed a good strong harvest to carry them through to third flush. Otherwise, they'd have to shut it all down for the first time since that first harvest thirty years ago.

Not gonna happen. Not on her watch.

Some things would have to change, and no one would like them.

***

Seven Sisters' Tiny Tea House sat on the corner nearest the road, away from the main house but adjacent to a small row of tea bushes and the processing center. The whole farm met the mandates to be net-zero on carbon and make your own energy, but the tea house was quite the spectacle of green tech, from the passive solar design and geothermal heat pumps to the solar glass windows and rooftop windmills. Jasmine and Zoe had been buildin' on the tea house for years, Jasmine with the vision, while Zoe was all about those kilowatts. They both ran the classes and tastings that brought substantial revenue to the farm year-round.

Which was why it pained Latoya, what she had to do.

The window-walls were dialed down, so she was quiet opening the door. Sure enough, they had a class going. Jasmine, her animated self up front while Zoe stayed to the side, ready to help. A dozen students were arrayed on couches and chairs, with the tasting room behind Jasmine, its shelves lined with teacups from around the world. The class must have just begun—the presentation's title, *Decolonizing Tea,* beamed from each person's tablet.

"We want you to deeply enjoy our hand-crafted teas." Jasmine gestured in fluid movements with her long arms to the bins of teas. Zoe's more compact, sturdy form floated around the room, checking on the tech. Both noted her presence by the door with a flicker of attention. "But at Seven Sisters, we believe that to enjoy tea, you have to understand the colonial history—not only to acknowledge the wrongs of the past but to understand how it flavors the present." She splayed her dark brown fingers. "This very land used to be a plantation—not tea, but cotton—with six thousand people enslaved in this county in 1860. The founder of the company, Ms. Angela Comfort, traces her lineage back to those enslaved peoples. Her grandfather acquired this land to reclaim it and honor the blood of his ancestors that tilled this soil. Of course, there were people here before the colonizers. The Choctaw lived here for at least 1,000 years before they were driven out of Mississippi in the 1830s, so this land also holds their sacred memory. In a moment, I'll share a short video about the history of the tea trade—how tea grew wild and was cultivated in China for thousands of years until the British discovered it, contrived two Opium Wars to get hold of it, and eventually spread tea-growing to India, East Africa, and beyond. Thirty years ago, Seven Sisters planted the first *Camellia sinensis* shrub on this 300-acre parcel of land—and worked to rewild the rest, keeping with the WILD50 plan to rewild half the planet's previously cultivated land—but before that, tea had never been grown here. However, the plantation system in Mississippi and throughout the South, as well as the sugar plantations in the Caribbean, were the models the British used for their tea-growing operations in India. The East India Company called these plantations 'tea gardens,' but they were a brutal system of kidnapped and indentured labor."

The mood of the class had grown noticeably grim, but Latoya was glad to see no one was shocked by this little overview. Occasionally, a fragile soul somehow escaped knowledge of the past—or, more likely, turned a blind eye to it—and they told on themselves when they discovered tea had a past that existed beyond the color in their cup. But word got around, and that sort rarely showed up in their tea house anymore.

"With that," Jasmine gave a smile that said she was proud they were taking this journey with her, "please watch this short video history of tea, war, and colonization." Zoe activated it right on cue. Their routine was well-polished. The simultaneous sound from the devices was enough to cover the conversation Latoya needed to have with them.

Jasmine quickly crossed the room to the door where Latoya had stayed put. "What's up?" A small crease formed in her unlined brow. The young ones made Latoya feel all of her fifty years.

"Got the bill for the bots I sent out. It's a lot. More than we can spend to get the rest fixed."

"Is that bad? That seems bad." Jasmine wrapped her arms in front of herself, tight.

Latoya waited until Zoe joined them. She slipped her hand through the crook of Jasmine's bunched-up arms, tugging her to loosen up her worries. They were young, but they'd been together all ten years they'd been part of the family.

"What's happened? Is everyone okay?" Zoe asked.

"Everyone's fine." Which reminded Latoya of one way out of this. "How's Aubree doing?" Zoe was on the schedule to care for their sick bot keeper.

Zoe's pale skin had worry lines naturally, but now they went deeper. "She's not eating again. Can't keep it down. It's gone on too long."

Latoya knew what she meant. It was a month now, and most folks recovered after a couple weeks. Those who didn't—whose systems were thrown out of whack by the virus's assault—could be sick for years. And the business didn't have years. It might not even last past this harvest if they couldn't bring it in.

"She should go see that specialist." Jasmine nodded agreement with herself.

"Will she?" Latoya directed that at Zoe.

Her face pinched up. "Maybe if she catches her wind? I'll get her to call in, at least."

Latoya nodded, but they couldn't count on Aubree having a miraculous recovery. She should have had Aubree apprentice someone, but she was so young—not even twenty-five, yet with that gift for bot care—and Latoya thought they had time. But she supposed bad luck was just time being ugly.

She drew in a breath. "Well, the two harvest bots I sent out for repair will be back tomorrow. But we can't afford to fix the others, and the ones we have won't keep up with the harvest." The picking window was short for each flush—seven days, ten at the outside—and if you picked too late, the quality dropped. They all knew it.

Jasmine looked stricken but kept quiet.

Zoe said it instead. "You mean we need to do the picking ourselves."

"Afraid so." It was brutal work—meticulous, out in the sun, backbreaking enough that Latoya felt her knees protesting already, and they had done nothing but walk to the tea house. "If everyone pitches in and does the best they can, we might salvage enough of the harvest to get the bots fixed before third flush."

"You *sure* we can't get them fixed now?" Jasmine's grimace had taken over her whole body.

"Even if we had the money—which we don't—we can't get the parts in time. The tea's ripening faster than expected."

"Probably a knock-on effect of the polar vortex wiping out the first one." Zoe had just finished her studies in agriculture.

Latoya nodded. Timing the harvest was always tricky, but the climate crazies made it worse. "With all of us who're able to work the fields, we can salvage some of it."

"What about the tastings?" Jasmine was still sorting it out.

"We'll have to reschedule." Zoe squeezed Jasmine's arm, reassuring, but Latoya felt the support and appreciated it.

"Finish up this one," Latoya said, "then meet us out there."

The end-of-video music was playing, so Jasmine hustled back to the front while Zoe drifted to the side of the class.

Jasmine gathered everyone's attention with her smile, but Latoya could see the tightness. "Now that you understand the history of tea, we're going to work on decolonizing your cup. All tea comes from the same plant—the differences come in the precise timing of the harvest." She shot a quick look at Latoya, who was waiting so she could depart without disturbing the class. "Commercial teas," Jasmine continued, "in line with their colonial past, harvest at an industrial scale, indiscriminately chopping up the whole lot, often blending to restore any flavor at all. Their teas are homogenized, branded, and made shelf-stable. The legacy of colonialism flattens tea into a commodity. Whereas, at tea farms like Seven Sisters, we handpick and process each leaf, resulting in a superior flavor you can taste. At our farm, we use bot labor for all our home-grown teas, and we make sure all our imported teas are likewise fair-trade. Now, if you'll follow me to the tasting area..."

Latoya used the cover of that shuffling to step out. Just then, a message came through. It was Pushti, their at-large tea buyer. She was due back any day now from her South American tea-buying trip.

I will remote in for the family meeting tonight, but heads up: I have a possible new member! Refugee. Brazilian drought. Tell you more tonight! We're boarding the boat now.

Pushti also sent her itinerary: traveling by light-sail, a light-duty wind-solar-sail hybrid that traveled faster than the wind-only cargo ships. Departing Cuba, arriving in New Orleans in three days, then she'd be home. With another mouth to feed. *Lord,* Pushti always brought the strays. Her good heart drew in the desperate like she was selling salvation in a teacup. Seven Sisters did what they could to support refugees—that was part of their founding and purpose—except they didn't have the money right now to host. And Pushti wanted this one to join the family!

There was no room for that.

Latoya sighed. Time to pay Mama a visit.

***

Angela Comfort was deeply invested in her handheld word game, such that Latoya considered coming back later. But *later,* she'd be out in the fields, and this needed discussing. Angela was the founder, along with Eleanor, but she was too gone with her mind to be troubling with family matters.

Latoya knocked on the open door. "Mama?"

Mama rumbled frustration and waved her in. "I ain't never seen a word try so hard not to be figured out." She sat in the big blue chair by the window, with a view of her fields of tea.

"Is that how it is?" Latoya perched on the cedar chest by Mama's bed. Her 80-year-old mother's mind was still razor-sharp—she kept up with advances in climatology and agriculture, knowledge grown out of her love of tea and this property she'd inherited. It lay at the same latitude as the birthplace of tea in China, and the hot and humid weather—although erratic and increasingly pesky—was similar to Assam, India, where some of the finest black tea was grown. The world had nearly stopped putting carbon in the air, but it would take a while yet to pull it back down. Meanwhile, the sins of the past kept taking their toll.

"I'll get it in a minute." Mama set the handheld on her spindle-legged table.

"I'm not sayin' you won't."

Mama waggled her fingers, summoning her to speak her mind.

"I'm asking everyone to pitch in to help with the harvest." Latoya kept her informed on the finances, so that didn't need explaining.

"I ain't much to look at, but I'm good for about half an hour."

Latoya's smile broke wide. "I'm not here for that."

"Good, because that's a lie. I'll watch y'all from the tea house."

Latoya chuckled a little, then got down to business. "I've got nine able bodies, including me and Olivia." Who was likewise feeling all of her fifty-ish years. "It won't be enough, not for all thirteen acres."

"Thirteen?" Mama's brow wrinkled up. "We've got twenty."

Latoya softened her voice. "The heat dome took them last summer. Remember?" It about killed her mama when it happened. An acre of tea bushes was wildly expensive to start and took five years to produce a harvest. In the beginning, Mama had sweated for every single one. Replacing those scorched bushes this spring had drained their reserves. It was an investment in the future, but it was a gamble, too. One that hurt them now, plus the future was never promised.

Mama scowled. "Then what'd you come to see me about?"

"Pushti's bringing home another stray. Wants them to join the family."

Mama brightened. "Who is it?"

"Refugee from the Brazilian drought. That's all I know." Latoya waited, but her mama just nodded to herself and kept that smile. "Mama, we can't afford it. Not right now."

She whipped her sharp brown-eyed gaze to Latoya's face. "Can't *afford* it? You weren't old enough to remember when things got in the negatives, baby girl. Don't tell me about *poor*. Whoever this refugee is, they're coming from a lot worse than we have."

"I know, but..." She hated arguing the practical side, but someone had to. "New Orleans can take them. They'll get Basic and all the rest. The center can support them through the transition. Maybe we'll be on our feet by then." Although Latoya couldn't see how. This refugee wouldn't help with the harvest. They were usually a mess when they arrived and needed *care,* not to be thrown into the blistering sun to work the fields. Mama wouldn't stand for that, and neither would she.

Mama had narrowed her eyes like she thought Latoya had been out in the sun too long already. "What do you think I founded this family for?"

"I know—"

"Then you know that we help who we can, when we can. And I've never seen that be *convenient* at the time."

"This is different."

"Is it?" The challenge in her mother's eyes was quickly eroding her resolve.

Latoya sighed. "Pushti will be at the meeting tonight. We can put it to everyone then."

"Pushti thinks this one could be *family.*" She said it like that settled the matter.

Maybe it did. Her mother and Pushti, put together, were a Category 4 storm making landfall: you could batten down or get out, but the storm would have its way in the end.

Latoya nodded but without conceding. She'd think more on it, which was what Mama usually forced her to do. "I'll come get you tonight."

"Make sure you do." Then she reached for her handheld and scowled.

The word game could take the brunt for a while.

***

Lord, the heat. And it was only June.

Latoya's hat shaded her hands as she picked. They'd all been toiling an hour, spread out, working their way down the rows, filling their mesh bags. It was an endless repetition of counting three leaves down and pluck-ing the ones just old and dry enough to withstand the withering and rolling required to produce a fine black tea. This flush—if they could harvest it—would produce Seven Sisters' signature Night Queen tea. The terroir—the land's unique combination of acidic soil, topography, and climate—combined with a perfectly-timed harvest and their hand-crafted processing would create a cup that could soothe the most weary soul. And with enough kick to wake it up to live a whole and vibrant life.

Latoya rolled her shoulder, working away the ache and switching hands. She felt the gaze of her ancestors, disappointed she was in the fields, never mind she owned these crops, the whole family did. *Just one harvest,* she promised the ghosts, as if it could be any different. It was clear this was untenable. The labor was harsh, and they simply couldn't harvest it all. The math didn't add up. It mocked her even as she counted down the stem, *1-2-3-pluck,* and kept movin' on.

Jasmine's voice broke the quiet with high exuberance. "Natsu mo chikadzuku hachijūhachiya." It was a Japanese tea-picking song from one of her classes. The tune was sing-songy, and Latoya remembered the lyrics as something like *Eighty-eight nights, summer is drawing near.*

Raelynn, their resident musical talent who normally worked in tea processing, joined in. "No ni mo yama ni mo wakaba ga shigeru." *Young leaves grow thick in the fields and the mountains.*

They all knew it, and it quickly spread. *Look over there, my friend, the many lovely women come, in hats and crimson sashes, work to pick the tea.* Lucía, the youngest in the family, still in school studying environmental systems, swayed as she sang. Kinsley, who'd taken a spot next to Olivia, holding both their bags, nudged the older woman to sing. Latoya was sure there was something between them, even if Olivia pretended not to know it. Ivy, their marketing guru, lifted her non-picking hand to wave with the song. Emery, who took care of every little thing, a fixit person for all except bots, bumped hips with Ivy and did a swaying dance. Latoya just listened, round after round. There was magic in the music, the pains of labor easing.

When Mama and Eleanor arrived with trays of iced tea, the singing quickly faded. They all rushed to bring in their meager haul and claim the drinks. The glasses were wet with condensation and blessedly cool on her forehead and cheeks before slaking her thirst.

While the others drank and rested, Latoya gathered the bags, brought them to the processing house, and dumped the leaves out to begin the withering process. Two trays' worth. Bots could harvest ten times as much in an hour. But there was nothing to do about it except drink down her tea and go back out.

Maybe sing this time, and hope for better days.

***

Every body was weary, the ache of the harvest being rubbed from feet and kneaded from shoulders. The tea house stank of their collective sweat, each member of her family draped on a chair or sprawled on a table, waiting until it was meeting time.

The only one missing was Aubree: Zoe said she'd gotten an appointment with the specialist for tomorrow, so that was progress.

Normal times, Latoya would've canceled and let them crawl to their beds, but they all wanted to hear about Pushti's stray, none seeming concerned about the finances: *that was her job.* Her place in the family was to free the rest from worry about making ends meet. That was how she fulfilled the vow: *to care for one another, for better or worse, in sickness and in health, until this bond is legally dissolved by a court of the state of Mississippi.* But she'd failed to anticipate the worst. She couldn't control the climate or supply chains in Taiwan, but she could plan ahead, keep reserves. Yet she'd given in to Mama's desire to replant those devastated acres, so she'd see them in full harvest once more, before the actual worst could happen and she passed on. Lord willing, not any time soon, but time could be ugly that way. Latoya had bet on good weather and a healthy bot keeper. She thought they'd had a cushion. But sometimes, the world piles one thing on top of another and flattens you.

Jasmine was pulling down the screen, so they could all see Pushti when she called in. Emery rolled off the table and took a seat. Kinsley stopped rubbing Olivia's shoulders and sat right in her chair. The rest straightened up, and Mama interrupted her long-winded story, regaling Eleanor with the exploits she could no longer remember, to turn an expectant look to Latoya.

She supposed it was her job to start the meeting, too.

All eyes were on her as she stepped up to the screen. "I know y'all are excited. Just keep in mind what we've had to do today, and why." She saw a few winces, but mostly the brightness on their faces was undimmed. And she loved every one of them, so it wasn't like she wanted that damper. "And there's the small matter of Aubree taking up the guest room while she's recovering." *Lord, please let her recover.* "I don't like the idea of putting someone in her room in the big house—I don't want her to feel like we've moved on." That gathered frowns.

Kinsley spoke up. "Pushti's stray could have my room." She peeked at Olivia. "I could move into Olivia's room. Just temporarily."

Latoya bit both her lips, but the absolute dead silence in the tea house spoke louder than anything. She wasn't the only one who'd noticed a little something going on.

Only Olivia seemed surprised. "Um. Sure. Okay."

Held breaths released. Emery was fixin' to burst, trying to keep that laugh trapped in her chest.

Well, heck. Now Latoya was hoping the *Gosh, there's only one bed* scenario would actually happen. Which made not a bit of sense. But heart matters rarely did.

"All right," she said to cover the twitters. "So maybe we have room. *Temporarily.* I'm just saying—" A tone indicated Pushti was calling in. Latoya wagged a finger. "All y'all keep it cool. We vote on this as a family, same as always." Then she waved at the screen to let Pushti's call through.

Her shining face was a welcome sight, despite the drama. She'd been gone nearly four months, scouting the best teas, working with vendors, making sure their suppliers kept to the best fair-trade practices.

"Hello, Sisters!" Pushti waved with both hands and then threw kisses, which everyone returned, the usual silliness. Latoya rolled her eyes and worked her way to Mama and Eleanor, but she had a smile for Pushti, like everyone else. "You got my message, yeah?" Pushti blazed on. "I told Marta to wait in the hall until I call her. She knows the family decides this, not me. If it were up to me, she'd go straight to bunking in the big house—"

"Tell us about her!" Jasmine cut in.

"Right! Her name's Marta Oliveira. Speaks *three* languages—Portuguese, of course, but also Spanish and English. Refugee, like I said, from the Brazilian drought. I didn't say this in the message, but you know that heat event on the news last month? It took her husband. And the rest of her family. The power went out, they were caught, no way to get to somewhere cool. Half her town went that way, it was terrible. Marta couldn't face staying, with all her family gone. Too much, too hard. She and the baby were in the city—"

"Wait, there's a baby?" Mama's voice cut her off, even from the back.

"Hi, Mama Angela!" Pushti waved weakly.

"How old is this child?" Mama stood, and that didn't portend well, but Latoya couldn't tell for whom.

Pushti grimaced. "Baby Zaira is eighteen months. Cute as a button, and not any trouble. I've never seen a baby so sweet—"

"Well, that changes things." Mama had all their attention now, and Pushti knew better than to offer anything more. "We all know the good work the New Orleans refugee center does every day. Top-quality organization. I'm not saying a thing against them. But we *also* know it's making the best of a bad business. And it's no place for a baby and her mama when they've been through it and lost not just their home but everyone they had. A refugee center is not a *family.*" Mama's gaze met each one of them, eye to eye, but when she got to Latoya, she knew it was decided.

"But we are," Latoya said. "And our family has room."

Mama nodded sharply and sat.

"Yes!" Pushti said softly from the screen.

Latoya stood. It was done, but it should be asked anyway. "Unless any-one thinks we should do different?"

Smiles all around but buttoned lips. No objections.

Not even from her.

"Marta!" Pushti had gone off-camera. A few whispers later, she returned with a young brown-skinned woman and her truly adorable child, who was busy chewing her fist. The baby saw them and then buried her face in her mama's long brown hair.

"Thank you so much!" Marta seemed near tears. "You and Pushti have been incredibly kind. It means so much to have a place to start over. And I can't wait to earn my way into your family, to repay you for giving me this chance."

"You won't need to *earn* anything," Latoya said. "You've got that little one to care for."

Marta blinked quickly. "But I *want* to. Pushti said—" She cut herself off, dashing a look to Pushti...

...who was all smiles as she leaned closer to the screen. "Marta's a bot keeper."

What? Latoya would have throttled Pushti if she weren't on a boat in the Gulf. "You could have mentioned *that*," she sputtered before she could stop herself.

Mama's smile was beyond self-satisfied as she stood again. "Time to celebrate. Jasmine, bring out that special Pu'er tea from Yunnan Province. I want to toast our new family-members-to-be."

Jasmine scrambled, Pushti whispered something to Marta, who seemed to calm, and Latoya settled back in her chair, relief loosening all the tension that had held her upright for the last month, ever since Aubree took sick and things went dark. Hope was no kind of business strategy, but it kept you moving through hard times, waiting on better ones. And family—your chosen ones, your vow, and your love for each other—was what carried you through.

Maybe better days had just shown up.

The Tides Rolled In

Christopher R. Muscato

The tides rolled in. The tides rolled out. It was as simple as that. And in that simplicity there was power. Enough to light entire cities, even, not that Afton knew personally. Her little village did just fine, roaming the waves, but in her thirteen years she'd never seen the capital of the Floating Republic. She'd never walked on sidewalks so steady it was said you couldn't even feel the rocking of the waves. For Afton, sea legs were the only legs she'd ever known. But today, that would change.

Afton looked down at the scroll in her hands, her eyes hovering over the pliable screen. Her lips twitched, a subconscious reflex as she rehearsed her plan, her thoughts finding shape in the inaudible whispers escaping her mouth. Then a breeze blew a stray hair in her face and she suddenly became aware of herself, feeling the subtle burn of embarrassment in her cheeks and her eyes darted back and forth assessing whether anyone had seen her talking to herself, seen what was on her tablet. She darkened the screen and rolled up the scroll, tucking it into her belt and leaning against the rail of her ship, mind still turning as she lost herself for a moment in the horizon.

"Ahoy there, matey!" A voice boomed from behind her. "Be ye ready to see the great city?"

Afton rolled her eyes as she turned towards the sound of footsteps.

"You're not going to talk like that in the city, are you?"

"What be ye talking about? This be how all captains speak!"

"*Ayah.* Seriously."

The Captain roared with laughter, rubbing his round belly.

"Captain, come look at this," came a voice.

"Duty calls," the Captain winked, his voice trailing after him as he scuttled off. "What have ye scallywags done now?"

Afton rolled her eyes again, turning back to the ocean churning rhythmically below the bow of her community. Her young fingers traced the edges of the scroll secured in her belt for a moment, then slowly withdrew it. A sound caught her attention and her head snapped in the direction of the captain's thunderous voice, still audible even from the adjacent deck. Afton shook her head and shoved the scroll back into her belt. Despite her father's outwards demeanor, he always said it was a great privilege to be elected captain of a village.

It was also a great privilege to be a captain's daughter, and so Afton diligently bustled about her chores, inspecting rigging and cleaning solar panels as her village plowed through the waves. She checked in on the gardens, talking softly to the plants as she brushed the leaves with her fingers. She stopped by the *ikat* huts and brought tea to the weavers. She followed her father on a routine inspection of village. Even with the new carbon filaments, there was always thatching that could be done on the woven roofs of the many *rumah adat* of the village, from the conical Mbaru Niang of the Wae Rebo deck to the Batak Toba deck's pointed gables. The entire village swayed on its half-submerged piles, and Afton skipped deftly from deck to deck along rope ladders and walkways, assisting with whatever tasks she could find, stopping only occasionally to smell yams and shrimp boiling in pots of aromatic spices.

There were more than enough things to do in the village, more than enough distractions to keep her mind occupied. And yet, as she bustled from deck to deck, from chore to chore, she couldn't help but become aware that the inner decks and structures were quickly emptying of people. There was an excitement sizzling throughout the village, a palpable energy that swept people away from their work like a riptide and ferried them to the village's outer railings. It wouldn't be long now.

Afton tried to remain focused, to remain diligent. She tried to ignore the buzzing in the back of her mind, the itching in her fingers that seemed magnetically drawn to the scroll in her belt, the notes and outlines and maps flashing across its surface. She tried. It wasn't long, however, until she could stand it no more and found herself wedged alongside the other children, eagerly scanning the horizon.

Cerulean waves danced before her village, a mesmerizing rhythmic geometry tracing the fine border between sea and sky until blending into a medley of soft blues and misty haze. Beams of sunlight punctured the waves, columns of luminescence streaking defiantly into the depths below. Afton had lived her entire life on these waters. The ocean was their home, their power generator, their garden, and still it never ceased to steal her breath from her lungs. There was something her father would say whenever he caught her gazing upon the sea, that all the formulas and equations in the world wouldn't mean a thing if they couldn't simply appreciate the beauty of it. Harmony required more than mathematics.

Living among the waves, carried by currents and the natural rhythms of the ocean alongside the fish and the dolphins, over forests of seaweed and metropolises of coral, their village was one with the watery world surrounding it. They had found their harmony, but very soon the entire village would get to experience this on an entirely new scale. The city was getting closer. It was hard to imagine that such place was still able to exist in perfect unison with its ecosystem. The city was just so big.

Incredible as it was to believe, Afton heard that there were once cities even larger on the land, even if most people today lived on the water. Her ancestors lived in such a city, a long-lost place her grandparents called Jakarta, a name they only spoke of in the reverent whispers of a people eternally in mourning. It was one of many places reclaimed in the Great Flooding. That's what her grandparents called it, although Afton never really understood the term. It didn't sound so great. Entire countries disappeared into the ravenous sea, hundreds of thousands dead and millions displaced by the rising ocean, the survivors moving onto the water as the remaining land dried up and was depleted. Afton read all about it. She was good at science. All the marine ecologists and engineers and meteorologists in her village said so. What didn't make sense to Afton was how nobody noticed. Her grandmother said that people were aware the ice was melting but weren't willing to do anything about it, neither to save the planet nor the people, but that made even less sense.

When Afton looked down at her hands, she was surprised to see her scroll between her fingers. She glanced around, and slunk away into a corner as she opened it, eyes hungrily zipping from side to side. Her lips twitched as she read over the plan, little beads of sweat forming on her brow. She looked around again, ensuring that her father was not watching, could not witness her nervous recitations. Huddled against the wall, the scroll an inch from her nose, Afton read over it again, and again.

"There it is!" Someone shouted. Eyes popping open wide, Afton felt her heartbeat jump and she rose on the tips of her toes to try and see between the crowds pointing and gasping, her small frame weaving between legs until she reached the railing. And there, crystalizing in the distance, magnificent structures began to take shape. The excitement was enough that even Afton's great agenda and responsibilities vanished in her mind, the scroll returning hastily to her belt as eager eyes bulged with wonder.

The village slowed as it navigated the maze of wind and tidal turbines heralding the appearance of the great city itself. Children on the floating village pointed upwards in awe at these awesome structures, children inhabiting apartments on top of the turbines laughing and waving giddily at the passing community. Theirs cheers joined with the clarion songs of seabirds plunging and diving, skimming the water's surface, frolicking between roosts built into the slowly revolving edifices.

"You know every one of these turbines provides the backbone for an entire ecosystem," Afton informed a young boy who clung to the railings next to her, mouth agape. Afton tipped her head to glimpse a rainbow of brightly colored fish darting between the turbines. "There's all sorts of reefs living down there."

With the village magnetically tethered, the villagers poured onto the dock amid gasps of wonder and the craning of necks. Afton swayed back and forth as she took it in, her body adjusting to its first time on a structure that didn't rock with the waves, or at least rocked more subtly.

Afton slowly took in the towering structures that composed the city, mouth hanging open. There was so much here that she wanted to see. The underwater greenhouses. The hatcheries. The reefs. The ocean, a wild garden that sustained the city. Her father also said that the capital had the most innovative waste reclamation system in the world, but Afton didn't feel like she needed to see that in person.

Of course, all of that would have to wait. Afton looked down at her hands, her throat going dry as she saw them trembling. She tried to retrieve her scroll, but for the first time her fingers seemed unable to reach it. The weight of it all seemed like an anchor on her shoulders, the reason her village had come to the city rising like floodwaters over her head. It was time to coordinate the rotations of fishing grounds, sustainability quotas, and the sharing of resources, but this year there was another issue at hand. A young girl from a small inconsequential village, just one in the vast Floating Republic, had discovered an unintended consequence of their fishing practices on the marine ecosystem. This research needed to be presented to the general assembly.

Afton clenched her fists, trying to quiet her shaking fingers. The presentation seemed so daunting. The Floating Republic was so big, and she was so small. But her father always said that a utopia was not a place where things were perfect, only a place that was willing to address its own imperfections. And now she was part of that.

"Avast! Be that the great savior of our rolling seas?" The Captain's booming voice rattled Afton. She turned, clenching her teeth and trying to look brave. It was a great responsibility to be the captain's daughter, and she wanted to be worthy of it. It was a great honor, to be heard by the assembly. It was a great privilege, to be a steward of the vast maritime garden they called their home. It was all so great, and in that moment she felt so small.

The Captain leaned down in front of her and took her hands in one of his, smiling with large, sympathetic eyes. With his other hand, he slowly withdrew the scroll from her belt, and handed it to her.

"Ready?"

Afton took a deep breath, and nodded.

Neyllo

Naomi Eselojor

I am Neyllo, the last of my kind, transported to earth after my world was destroyed five years ago.

I recall lying in my nest when my planet shook. Another earthquake had swallowed the Zemonians in the western sector. Fifteen dead and forty injured. Split into twelve clans, Zemon was home to a species of clever and reserved herbivores. The abundance of nitrogen allowed our plants to thrive so much that less than one percent did not contain trees. Each day began with the rise of the red sun, a celestial beauty that more than half my people worshipped but millions of years after, our sun started to fail. One of my progenitors believed more in technology than in the red sun, believed more in intergalactic travel than forest hunts.

He foresaw the destruction of my planet and entrusted me with a Tridel – a seed that decoded the genetic makeup of my race.

On the planet's last day, I was taken to the escape pod. Balls of flame rained down the atmosphere, setting our plants and our people on fire. Our strongest woven thorns served as shields, but they didn't last. My progenitors bade me an agonizing farewell because they couldn't come. They had a duty to protect Zemon or rather, to try and protect what was left of it.

On the 18th of March, 2244, my escape pod landed at Wazobia forest in Lagos, Nigeria.

After a few months of battling with illnesses, I found a spot to plant the Tridel, an inconspicuous location where no human would think to look.

For many days, I nurtured the plant and envisioned the fierce joy I would feel when the embryos would form. Day and night, I watered it, groomed it, and watched it; sometimes, I simply basked in its sharp musk because it reminded me of home.

Then one day, a helicopter landed in the forest. From it emerged a plumpish human in a voluptuous attire; a man of power, I presumed, because he had a platoon of soldiers escorting him. Pointing around, they explored the forest, their hands widening in a gesture that suggested they were planning or measuring something.

I snuck closer to where they stood, using my chromatophore skin to camouflage myself in the leaves, when I heard: "This is perfect. In five days, we will begin deforestation."

***

Back on Zemon, my progenitors would have me sit around a white flame and we'd discuss life in other galaxies. I missed them, missed the wild thorns we spun for shelter, the taste of grub and the three moons and red sun that gave light to the cities.

The destruction of my planet ripped me apart but there was hope since I had the Tridel. Now, the tree was blossoming and, in a few weeks, the embryos would emerge. Uprooting it would ensure the eradication of my kind. I trembled at the thought of it.

I needed help to save my Tridel, but there were only two humans that knew I existed and I needed to travel to see them.

I wove thick vines, roped them to solid sticks, and thrust those sticks into the ground to create a fence around the Tridel. At least until I came back, it would be safe.

The night train to Lekki was a smooth transit. Every passenger had their minuscule corner that warranted no outside disturbance and I enjoyed watching Channels TV updates. One of the headlines was "Urbanisation in Wazobia Forest – The future of Opulent housing."

Hidden behind a cloak, I alighted from the train and sauntered through the streets of Ikoyi, sticking to the shadows like a cockroach. My form was similar to a human's, modified by an earthling scientist to adapt to Earth's climate. I had two arms, two legs, a nose and a face and since I was female, I had the semblance of a girl's curves, and the thinness of a girl's waist. My skin was green, like the colour of leaves, and I had no hair. A child looked my way, eyes narrowing as he tried to make out what I was, but I hurried away, slipping into an alley before he could draw attention. I wasn't ready to be seen. Not yet.

The gates of the Ojiofor residence were twice my height, wrought iron strips woven in a criss-crossed Lattice. As I stepped forward, a machine ran a horizontal red beam through me. A voice spoke, 'Identity unknown'.

"Tell Chinaza that Neyllo is here!"

In three minutes, the gates swung open.

"Follow the cobblestones to the backyard," the voice said. "There, you will find Chinaza in the rose garden."

I followed the directions and found Chinaza sniffing some roses. I had met her two years ago, right after my escape pod had landed. She was twenty-six years old, a slim, dark-skinned girl, with thick, curly tresses dangling from her head. Around her neck was a golden chain, attached to a diamond encrusted pendant, a symbol of her family's wealth.

Chinaza regarded me with a warm smile as we sat under a tree to discuss.

"The future of my people is at risk." I began. "I have learnt of a pending project, the urbanisation of the forest I reside in, but the Tridel needs more time to develop, Chinaza. They cannot cut down that tree."

Chinaza nodded and squeezed my shoulder.

"Oh, Neyllo. I understand your plight but there's nothing I can do. The project was approved by the Minister of Housing. The government has a hand in it. Contractors have been assigned, funds have been disbursed."

Just then, her phone rang and she pulled it from her pocket. The face of a man appeared on the screen and my eyes widened in shock. She picked the call and her face broke into a wide smile.

"I got you the purse you've always wanted," a muffled voice spoke from the device. Chinaza told the caller she would talk to him later and hung up.

I met her eyes.

"The Minister; the one who assigned the project, is your father, isn't he?"

Chinaza's face tightened.

"There's nothing I can do, Neyllo."

I shook my head.

"Of course there's something you can do. You can talk to him, explain what is at risk."

"This is more important than a tree, Neyllo. Lagos is overpopulated, we need more land to build houses, and more room to expand."

"But what about my legacy?"

Chinaza shrugged. "I don't know, Neyllo. You're going to have to figure that out on your own. Just remember, the lands were never yours to begin with, they belonged to the government. So don't expect them to prioritise your needs at the detriment of my people".

At this time, Chinaza stood up.

"I helped you once, Neyllo but I cannot help you this time."

She left me speechless and made her way into the house.

***

I remembered it like it was yesterday. In the first week of my arrival, I struggled to survive. My skin cracked and my chest tightened with every lungful of air. Despite my planet's similarities to Earth, I had a hard time adapting. It was then I met Chinaza, camping in the woods. She offered to help, found me a scientist and donated a fortune to get me body modifications. I understood her reasons for refusing to help me. Nothing was more important than family.

I made my way to a smart apartment in Ikoyi which housed one of the most brilliant minds in Lagos.

"Neyllo!" Mayen screamed, taking me into her arms. She was about Chinaza's age, vibrant, bespectacled and passionate about science. Her room was a clutter of textbooks and gizmos, small, compared to Chinaza's mansion but it was in a way, cozy.

She poured me a cup of water.

"Do you have any issues with your body?"

I shook my head.

"No, you did a decent job on me."

Mayen raised the cup, a smile forming on her oblong face.

"Why then did you come?"

I helped myself to a chair and narrated my ordeal.

"Chinaza has disappointed me once too," Mayen said. "Back when we were students of Unilag, she promised to attend my party but backed out at the last minute. Like my father always says, never put your trust in man."

"I need a plan, Mayen. Time is not on my side. What if I speak to Chinaza's father? Maybe I can convince him to spare the forest.

Mayen stroked her chin.

"That could work but I do not think he will buy into your belief of a safe haven for your kind. Telling him that you're nursing a tree that would produce alien species might come off as a threat. Like you're trying to take over the country."

"I couldn't if I wanted to. Zemonians are mild, introverted people. We couldn't hurt any creature."

Mayen laughed.

"I know this, Neyllo, but the minister doesn't."

"Let me try to talk to him. You can help me, can you?"

Mayen's smile disappeared. She settled in her swivel chair and slid towards her computer.

"It will be difficult to bypass the Minister's security. To get to him, you'd have to be creative."

I turned to meet her eyes.

"Show me."

***

Minister Ojiofor rested in his car with his back arched slightly backwards. If a bed could fit in the SUV, he would have gotten one. For most of the day, he was trapped in a leather chair, issuing documents to contractors and reviewing costs for building projects. The SUV glided through the streets of Lagos and Minister Ojiofor's phone vibrated.

"Your daughter is requesting a video call, sir," the AI said.

"Put her on the big screen."

Sound-proof curtains circled him as a monitor emerged from the back of the front seats. Ojiofor straightened himself to see his daughter, only that it wasn't his daughter he saw.

"Good afternoon, Minister," the strange creature said with a female voice.

Ojiofor's face turned white with fear.

"Please, do not panic. I am not here to hurt you," she continued

"Who are you? What have you done with my daughter?"

"I am Neyllo, of the race of Zemon. Your daughter is safe. Be rest assured I am not a hostile creature; I only need your assistance."

Neyllo spoke about the Tridel as her legacy, the last chance of survival for her race, and how the urbanisation project would put the lives of the embryos at risk, and he listened in shock.

"Is this some kind of joke, a prank put up by some jobless teenager?"

"No, Minister. This is real. I am real. Do not destroy our Tridel, please!" Her voice quivered as she pleaded.

"My daughter, where is she?"

"Minister, I–"

"I demand to see my daughter, now!"

There was a break in transmission and the video glitched. A tiny screech emitted from the device and soon, Chinaza's voice surfaced.

"Hello, dad. I lost you for a minute. How was work? Dad....?"

***

Mayen chewed a slice of vanilla cake as she typed on the keyboard.

"Chinaza called me. She said you nearly gave her father a heart attack."

I sighed. Seconds of watching the digital clock blink resembled hours. Three days felt like three years and the sound of Mayen's chewing was making my ear twitch.

"Don't worry," Mayen continued. "I didn't tell her you were with me, or that I had a hand in it."

I jolted from the cushion.

"What if I can speak to the president?"

"Really, Neyllo? Didn't you learn from the incident with the minister? Do you know how many federal security organizations tried to trace you with that one call?"

"What then can I do?"

"I've been thinking. The whole urbanization project was set up to cater for the needs of the masses. Lagos is an overcrowded state, it is only logical they wish to expand. The only way we can stop this, is for Nigerians to support your cause, make them sign a petition against the project."

My eyes widened.

"That could work?"

"Sure, but we need to get as many people on your side as possible – like hundreds of thousands, or millions of people."

"How will we do that?"

"The same way you market a product or service. You set up a website and a lead magnet, something free and captivating, to get the attention of people. Then you lure them to the website to read about your plight. There will also be a short video of you, speaking to us, telling your story. Before anyone leaves the site, a pop-up icon would request they sign the petition."

I had no idea what most of her words meant but I understood the logic behind it. We began immediately and it took a few minutes to turn Mayen's room into a studio.

"Are you ready?" Mayen asked, her eyes glued to the computer screen.

My core pranced and I nodded. Before now, only three humans knew of my existence. It was scary, showing myself to the world, not knowing what would happen afterwards. Our chromatophore skin allowed us to hide, to blend into the environment and disappear. It was ironic that after so much hiding, we were about to be made public.

"We will record in ten seconds."

I sat in front of a white background, hands quivering as I waited for the signal. A LED bulb emitted a blinding light that made me squint.

"Focus on the camera, Neyllo. Breathe. It's going to be fine. We will record in three, two..."

For a minute, I froze, until the teleprompter reminded me what to say.

"Good afternoon, Nigerian citizens, my name is Neyllo ...

***

"Tsunami, give me the numbers," Mayen said to her AI.

Number of views – 700,000.

"Number of clicks to the petition?"

About two thousand.

I sank to my knees, devastated. That was barely enough to get the government's attention. The project would commence in twenty-four hours and there was still no luck. Mayen tried to comfort me but I waved her off and burst out the door.

On my way to the train station, torrents lashed down the city and the gusty wind carried down the earthy smell of rain. Pedestrians without covering hurried through the city, seeking shelter in shops and restaurants. I allowed the cold to engulf me as the wind tugged at my cloak. A minivan swerved by, splashing filthy water my way but I didn't mind. I felt crippled by my failures, overwhelmed by my inability to save my legacy. Imagining a life where I was the last Zemonian survivor was excruciating. I wanted to have my people around, to experience the wonders of this planet. My willpower dissolved and all that was left of me, drifted in the boisterous wind. Perhaps, I would take out my core, allow myself to die. Since the humans were not willing to offer us a home, then, we might as well all die, and let them be.

The wind intensified, nearly whisking me away, but I planted my feet on the road. Screams broke from every angle as wigs, fabrics and plastic chairs floated in the air. One of the cries alerted me.

"My son! Where's my son?"

I caught a glimpse of a boy grasping a tree with his body, hoisted like a flag. The wind wrestled him but he clutched the branches, desperate to survive.

I turned to his direction, battling through the storm, dodging floating umbrellas and spiralling clothing. I extended my arm. The boy took it without hesitation, chest swelling as he wrapped his arms and feet around me. His mother's gaze trailed me from a spot beside a streetlight, gratitude and astonishment in the glaze of her eyes. She breathed a sigh of relief when she hugged her son.

"I don't know what you are," she said, "but thank you."

I nodded.

Turning to leave, I noticed the glint of smart phones, the clicking sounds of the camera shutters, the collective gasps of bedazzled Nigerians.

Sirens blared and tyres screeched as patrol cars halted at the entrance of the restaurant. But by the time the police burst through the crowd, I had already fled.

***

Channels TV Headlines
  A tremendous Hurricane passes through Ikoyi.
  Mysterious green alien saves a five-year-old boy.
  Urbanisation project will commence in twenty-four hours.

***

Minister Ojiofor called for maximum security, so the forest was edged with barricade tapes and armoured trucks. Reinforced with surveillance drones, the Nigerian army swept through the woods, searching for any form of resistance to the day's operations. News vans lingered around, pointing their cameras and scuttling to get the best view of the incident.

The automated bulldozers revved their engines loud, I quivered at the ostentatious display of strength. Leaves rustled and the military came close, close to the Tridel, close to me. I was shrouded in the leaves and so one had to be observant to find me. They were a hair's breadth away when one of them spoke to his watch. "There's no one here."

"Wait!"

Another soldier edged towards the fence, regarding it with a persistent gaze. He took out a laser pen and was about to cut it open when I ambushed him. I lunged towards him, like a mother, protecting her brood. He grunted, falling on the ground with a thud

"Get your hands off the Tridel!" I screamed, my veins pumping in an unfamiliar feeling of rage.

They hesitated, alarmed by my appearance in the woods but it was not long before they drew their weapons. I was surrounded by heavily-trained soldiers and menacing drones. I couldn't win, not like this.

"Begin the project." One of them said, while I was being handcuffed.

The bulldozer began grating the soil and, in my trepidation, I yelled.

While the deforestation was ongoing, I was in the armoured truck, listening.

"You will pay for attacking a soldier and trying to harm the Minister's daughter," the soldier beside me spat. His wrinkles deepened as he stared at me in contempt. At this point, with the forest coming down, I was ready to withstand whatever punishment. It was only a matter of time before they destroyed the Tridel.

There was a television in the truck and in it, a reporter narrated the events of the day.

"The alien has been detained and the bulldozers are in motion. Rumours state that she is charged with identity theft and attempted kidnapping of a five-year-old, and may be in military custody for a long time."

The reporter pressed a device in her ear and paused.

"Hold on...I'm getting reports from Lagos island where there seems to be a protest..." Her voice took on an animated, surprised tone. "I don't believe it... Nigerians are protesting against the alien's imprisonment."

The scene changed to show a crowd chanting and holding placards. Mayen was beside a male reporter who pushed a microphone to her lips.

"She was just trying to protect her legacy," Mayen said.

"But she attacked the Minister's daughter."

"No, she didn't and I have footage that proves her innocence. Neyllo would never hurt anyone."

"It's true." I recognized the woman whose son I saved. "She saved my baby. Neyllo and her people should be given a chance at life, just like the rest of us. As of now, we have gotten the attention of the vice president. We just pray it's not too late."

Hope surged through my veins. Just then, the soldier beside me listened to his watch.

"Are you sure, sir?"

He looked at me.

"I have orders to release you."

His countenance softened as he unlocked the door. I stumbled out of the truck and hastened towards the mother tree until suddenly, my legs failed me. I was connected to the Tridel, and if anything went wrong with her, I would feel it. My core thumped, slowly, painfully. Purple fluid seeped through my nose as I struggled to heave myself up. I was too late. My head spun and I felt myself slip to the foliage on the ground. The reporters gathered around me, handing me their microphones. I saw their lips move but I heard no sound. Time seemed to slow down as I closed my eyes.

***

Channels TV updates

Alien collapses.

Protesters gain the attention of the president.

Government approves the rejuvenation of Wazobia Forest for the aliens' habitation.

Aliens given a second chance, ordered to sign a treaty to endorse their peaceful coexistence, but where is Neyllo?

***

I sat by the forest and watched the Tridel grow again. They had cut off her branches and were about to uproot the stump when the call came in. Thankfully, it could grow again. Two years would pass by quickly and I was optimistic. I inhaled the sweet smell of musk as I watched the embryos form.

Uɴɪᴠᴇʀsɪᴛʏ, Sᴘᴇᴀᴋɪɴɢ

Phoebe Wagner

First, we found someone to listen. We whispered to new hires and emeritus faculty, first-year students and graduate TAs, deans and presidents. And we failed. Yes, new housing towers joined the city skyline. A baseball field cut down too many trees. An Old Town revitalization project promised condos, windowed storefronts reflecting our spires, a rooftop bar. These places made a bad translation of what we wanted. Not a wider, taller, more decorative wrought-iron fence. We wanted no fence.

In all our whispering, we weren't listening. We had a vision, our architectural imagination of ourselves, entwining with the city for what we thought would be better. But someone was already speaking to us.

The gardener had worked our grounds so her kids wouldn't have to take out so many student loans. Two bright and beautiful boys had studied late in our library, played frisbee on our lawns, posed for graduation pictures beneath our elms. Still the gardener tended our mulch beds, brought us flowering pots to hide our crumbling corners, moved our inside plants outside for some afternoon sun, kept our sidewalks clean and weeded. She pruned our rose bushes and taught the wisteria how to climb the new trellis. In our hazy summer slowness, when our lights dimmed early and our lawns stretched lonely, she hummed the latest piece from the civic choir.

We followed her into the city through our grass clippings and flower petals. On Wednesdays, she met her wife for beers. On Thursdays, choir practice, still in her work boots that thudded clumps of us across the stage.

On Fridays, she rode her motorcycle to work and went for a riverside ride afterward, sending pieces of us drifting across the city's veins.

We fell into the trap of our fences. How would a gardener convince a dean, a president, a board of trustees? No, we needed a professor, a student at the very least. But as the years went, and she planted sunflowers in the back beds only eager summer interns and wrung-out research assistants walked by, as she prepared green spaces for winter, we began speaking to her.

She knew our ghosts and cobwebs, the corners where students tucked away their folded-paper fears, which bushes the cigarette stubs blew under. Even so, she came back, long after her grown children needed her job. She shoveled our sidewalks, returned frisbees from behind our hedges, smiled at the creaking of our elms. Sometimes, she'd sit back on her heels and sigh at our emptiness, our flowers and shade and paths left unappreciated for the best summer months. Our imaginings were just another whistling wind to enjoy.

One spring, as she mulched the bed lining the backlot—what the president had recently renamed Tower Lawn, after a trustee—we whispered plans for a community garden. In the summers, nobody used this quad. Even in the fall term, when the intramural teams played volleyball here, they only used half the lawn. The grassy space faced downtown, and professors, deans, students walked through the decorative, pillared gate to go to lunches or coffee or the bar, but nobody came from the city. We could change that.

All summer, the gardener watched the grass unused, shorn down over and over by the mower. We whispered about how the birds would love it, how the butterflies and bees would be fed so much better by a community garden than a barren lawn.

The gardener started talking. Her wife agreed something better than grass could be imagined. The head groundskeeper liked the idea because he didn't have enough space at his home for a garden (and he hated mowing). The math professor always eating lunch on the bench outside when the gardener watered the roses thought it would be good for the students to learn about food systems. The regular Wednesday bartender said they would take a plot since their apartment was only a few blocks away. The alto to her right wondered if the local library might run a kids' program to teach gardening basics. The alto on her left had never been to campus.

The provost said no.

Gardens are messy. How would security keep track of who came onto campus and what they did? The Buildings and Grounds crew was already too busy; now they wanted a community garden to tend. Who would come to this garden, anyway?

This was why the gardener didn't talk to the provost except at the holiday party. If this river were to run its course, then we needed a crack in the dam.

When the gardener told her summer student workers what happened, one asked if he could organize the community garden for his capstone research project. He'd grown up in the city and wondered why campus, the only large green space downtown, needed a fence around it.

The student received a grant from the city, and the local library ran a kids' program about food systems, and the Riverside Apartments held a garden potluck, and people ate their lunch on benches the gardener's wife built, and the gardener pulled weeds beside her Wednesday bartender, and students spread blankets on the remaining grass during orientation, and they tried to catch the last of the cherry tomatoes in their mouths.

These new gardeners carried more and more of us into the city, where we swirled in the roadside eddies or collected against churches. We trailed fingertips across the city. We wanted more, and so did the city. We had one crack, where we pressed against each other. One crack could grow.

When the summer storms came, we dropped our dead branches onto the tall fence. We leaned our tired trunks against the wrought iron. We battered away at the spiked posts. The gardener asked for the fence to be removed around the quad as the community garden became more popular. A professor who studied national borders helped a student group write a proposal for removing the fence and investing the saved maintenance funds in Little Free Libraries and miniature food pantries around town. The wilderness education students volunteered to build new walking paths with permeable materials once the fence fell, opening campus to dogwalkers and commuters.

We rubbed against the city. Our fingers entwined. Parents pushed strollers between our flower beds. Longboarders glided along our curves. Children sledded down our hills. Joggers passed between us. We traced the lines of each other's palms, but we still wanted more.

When our flourishing environmental science program needed a bigger building, we whispered about buying a place by the waterfront and grumbled against the big, bright windowed building design that would never be sustainable amidst the rising heat, the worsening storms. The city hummed that meant more bus lines to make sure the students could access the waterfront building.

The board of trustees grumbled. The deans questioned. The president hemmed and hawed. The college experience they were charged with marketing required a quiet, private campus—nothing to fear. What would the parents say when they came to visit? A manicured border, a fence that no longer existed except in their minds—what might the students learn out in the city?

The city swirled through the mayor's office, ruffling campaign posters and building plans, whirled into councils, rumbling about tax breaks, free marketing, economic revitalization, beautification pledges. Butterflies to flowers, we began to pollinate.

We whispered to the college's wilderness program to propose more bike lanes. The city made a walking path from the environmental science building to the Riverwalk. And once the students could bus to the river and wander through the grass onto the sidewalk off the campus, as we cuddled up with the city, our fingers in each other's hair, the students proposed a fall music series, and another community garden, and they protested campus security driving people away from napping on benches. Professors held classes in the new coffee shops, and the groundskeepers had their morning planning meetings at the bagel shop across the street, and the city created a free audit system for locals to take classes, and the STEM programs partnered with the local hospital for a weeklong science festival, and the gardener's Wednesday bartender opened their own brewery where the gardener met her wife every Friday after her motorcycle ride.

The provost who said no, who'd continued saying no, retired, warning on the way out the door that students would stop coming. As fewer and fewer students attended traditional colleges, they would choose the big, endlessly sprawling campuses or the small, spired closed campuses. Nobody went to college spread over a town. Either the town belonged entirely to the college, or the campus kept itself separate from the city.

But our city held us tight when the storms came. Sometimes with thunder, sometimes with recessions. The city hummed to not be afraid when students couldn't come to us because of sickness or flooding or money. The city always had its own children who wanted to learn. The children who had pulled weeds in our community gardens, had sledded down our hills, had played catch beneath our oaks, they sat in our libraries, classrooms, labs and heard us whispering.

These children helped the homesick students call our grounds, our city home. They showed them the best spots to sit by the river and think, the fastest bike path to the movie theater, the cafe that gave free coffee to students studying late, the restaurants where nobody would stare no matter how loud they laughed, the park with the best fall colors, the park with the best spring blossoms. The students stuck together, and even the provost could not have dismissed their numbers.

The gardener retired, and we gave our best blooms that summer. She still came to sit on the benches when the summer flowers flourished, watching the bees at work. She helped with organizing the community gardens for planting and harvesting, until it made her short of breath and her back sore. She still brought out a chair, even though the other gardeners didn't know her anymore, but they called her the Gardening Grandma and asked how to store seeds or how to prune the tomatoes.

When the tornados took out whole towns, when floods washed away homes, when heat threatened families—the students left us, for a while, carrying pieces of us to their own towns. We knew what to do. We whispered of connections across time and space to our new deans and new professors, just as bits of our dirt and grass and roots clung to clothes and books and blankets.

Students talked of different classes like civic engagement, community organizing, disaster preparedness, practical activism. They asked to organize a better credit-exchange system with the community college at the other end of the city so they could take welding and construction courses. Students and professors organized for online classes when they needed to stay home for a semester to rebuild their towns.

And when the storming and flooding finally split our walls, collapsed our roofs, washed our basements, the city caught us up. The local library, the diners, the coffee shops, the community center, the churches, the hospitals, the parks became classrooms, were remembered for the classrooms they always had been.

The city held us tight until we forget we were ever separated. Tattoos on skin, we became.

Our students come to us for the classrooms. Writers meet in the bookstore and the library; artists in the tattoo parlor and the museum; biologists in the hospital and the field station; sociologists in the mutual aid center and the clinic; psychologists in the counseling hub and the lab. Now, we stretch our arms wider as the citizens see what needs doing and lead the students to new projects. We grow.

The gardener lost her home in one of the floods, so she and her wife live above the brewery, where her bartender's grandchildren ferment all types of things. They teach classes, and the gardener likes to open her upstairs window and listen, just as she'd pause on campus while pulling weeds, on those sunny days when the professors would take their students outside.

If We Can Do This, We Can Stop Asteroids

Andrew Dana Hudson

(An excerpt from Our Shared Storm:
A Novel of Five Climate Futures*)*

SECOND SUNDAY

After the storm came a bright, blue morning and much work to be done. Faces poked out of broken windows, waved at each other. Glass was swept off doorsteps. Leaves were cleared from solar panels, and extension cords were tossed from rooftops to charge phones and run water filters. Gardens were picked through for surviving plants and produce. Dusty disaster kits were pulled from closets. Rooms were found for those put-out. Neighbors mobilized cleanup crews. Strangers went to check on strangers.

The city's disaster management office unfurled a network of command nodes and block captains to coordinate recovery efforts, spread and verify information, and triage requests for help or resources. As good as this operation was, it—like all centrally planned human activity—did not quite map onto the actual social relations emerging on the ground. So adjustments had to be made: cleanup crews merged or split or given impromptu legitimacy, new nodes established and a few disbanded, natural leaders brought into the process, captains asked to step back when they fell short.

This was normal and natural but occupied a surprising amount of time and energy compared to the actual physical labor of cleanup and recovery.

On the whole, however, the awkward melding of top-down planning and bottom-up improvisation had distinct advantages when done right. Each paradigm saw and corrected the blind spots in the other's strategy. The street knew the newcomers, the live-in boyfriends, the visiting relatives, the not-quite-common-law squatters. The state had yearly census records that included the anti-social, the shut-ins, the infirm, the workers of graveyard shifts rarely seen by neighbors. So in this way the recovery efforts reached and checked in on most everyone who'd been living in Buenos Aires during the storm.

There were, in the final count, very few injuries and only one death: an expecting mother who died of complications during childbirth when she went into labor during the storm and was unable to reach either hospital or midwife. The baby, which survived, was delivered by strangers at the cafeteria where the woman took shelter. The woman was mourned throughout the city, memorialized in murals, her name given to a program of free lay-midwifery trainings offered to the public months later.

Despite the unexpected ferocity of the storm—which coalesced out of an unstable pressure system and arrived via an erratic and swift path that left little time to prepare—the city's infrastructure held up well. The grid had been fortified by Transition Era retrofits which spread solar generation and energy storage throughout the city. These had been won by robustness hawks who had shouted down pinchfist technocrats at raucous public planning debates during the height of Mobilization Politics. The grid was clumped into "cells" that could function like independent microgrids if connections were torn. They could also deliver power to neighboring cells if generation was uneven, as when rooftop solar was damaged or obscured by debris. The balance of the grid algorithms meant that there was quite a bit of incentive for friendly competition between cells to keep maintenance and energy demands down. The hyperlocal expertise that encouraged came in handy after the storm, and by the end of the first day, grid-nerds had jerry-rigged fixes for almost every house and business that did lose power. And where the grid held, electricity still flowed from the city's pump-storage vaults, which not only helped contain the deluge but netted power from captured stormwater.

The limited flood damage was another win that the robustness hawks would be crooning about for years to come. They had built the "slanting garden" embankment parks high enough to hold off a storm surge from the Río de la Plata, as unlikely as that had once seemed—as well as a significant amount of sea-level rise, should the projects to stabilize and rebuild the planet's glaciers fail. The city's once notorious drainage problems had been much improved by shifts to porous roads and a general greening of public and private urban spaces. Rooftops channeled the downpour into rain barrels. Flowerbeds, trees, and mossy lawns that had been parched by the summer heat soon bloomed a deep green.

Perhaps the most notable forms of damage were broken windows—which spilled music onto the streets for several days after—and breached ground fridges. Many home-clusters and apartment buildings had invested in these passively cooled cellar pods, subsidized by the city in the late 20s. The storm coincided with the sealants on doors and joints in the most popular models showing their age, and some porteños found after the storm that rain and groundwater had leaked in, generally making a mess. While little food had actually been spoiled, a good cleaning and repair was usually in order.

Many moved the contents of their fridges out to the sidewalks, laid out on collapsible tables, and encouraged neighbors, cleanup crews and passersby to help relieve them of their perishables. Others brought out produce salvaged from wind-torn gardens and window boxes. Much of this bounty was used to prepare huge communal meals to support the recovery efforts. The days after the storm became a kind of informal feast week—the smells of cooking overpowering the whiff of flood rot, the noise of construction and demolition mixing with sounds of eating, cooking, laughing, sharing, dancing, belching, singing, dishes clinking and bottles clanging as boisterous toasts were made.

The joy and catharsis of these festivities, however, was cut through with a serious mood the storm had brought to the city. While everyone agreed that the damage could have been much worse, the black swan disaster was a reminder that—despite the successes of the Transition Era, the great reforms made locally and globally—they were not out of the woods yet. The Earth's oceans and atmosphere were still dangerously energized by greenhouse warming and would remain volatile for generations. Glaciers were melting, tundra was thawing, ecosystems were struggling to adapt. The climate crisis had an inertia that would take centuries to turn back, even if the most critical transitions had been accomplished. The planet was in for a long, rough, precarious time. Everywhere in the world knew it, but some weeks some places knew it more than others.

This collective feeling was heightened by the fact that the global planetary management negotiations happened to be taking place in Buenos Aires when that angry cloudbank had charged up the Río de la Plata. Still called the "Conference of the Parties" despite the shifting nature of the UN's framework convention, COP60 became a topic of much local interest in the week after the storm. The public-facing parts of the conference were mobbed. Live videos of negotiations and roundtables were shown at bars between futbol matches. COP attendees—both porteños and visitors—were feted at community cleanup dinners, invited into classrooms, approached on the trolly, bombarded with attention, questions, opinions, requests, demands, accolades, anger, congratulations, business proposals, and romantic propositions. It made for a very lively conference.

The increased public engagement brought more energy than usual to the more provocative elements of the otherwise anodyne negotiations. This included thorny questions about the risks and benefits of solar geo-engineering, about the costs of various computationally intensive atmospheric modeling moonshots, and about the optimum temperature to stabilize at when the world's carbon disposal industry eventually brought greenhouse gasses under control. This last—where to set the metaphorical global thermostat—was of particular faddish interest. "Cuál es tu número?" folks would ask, and be met with shouts of "doscientos setenta!" and "trescientos doce!" "Muy frío! Trescientos cuarenta y cinco, por favor!"

Badge holders would get asked to weigh-in on this debate when spotted at salons, breakfast cafes, church services, or parks. And because opining is a form of thinking, the half-dormant working groups that handled these questions suddenly found themselves enriched with new ideas.

All this activity—the cleanup, the grid repairs, the feasts, the window and fridge replacements, the midwifery classes, the interest in the COP, the engagement with the big questions of planetary management—none of it was smooth or evenly distributed. The effects of the storm played out over months and years, different from neighborhood to neighborhood, sprawling beyond the city, the continent, the single conference. There was no single story of the storm any more than there had been a single cloud or drop of rain or gust of wind. The storm wove into countless stories, playing a role in triumphs and disappointments, breakups and flirtations, marriages, divorces, promotions, bankruptcies, career changes, affairs, ambitions, artistic breakthroughs, friendships sparked and ended, children conceived and come of age, homes remodeled, blocks transformed, cities reinvented, life carrying on as it always had into a future that was forever uncertain but not, it was hoped, unwelcome.

SECOND MONDAY

Noah hung from a trolly strap, hands blister-sore from the cleanup. The sensation put him in mind of his childhood—growing up rough around hard work he'd since gone too soft for. Born in the late teens, but his parents were among the first to join the American ecosystem repair efforts, even before the jobs program had gotten ramped up. So he'd been a Green New Deal baby through and through: rambunctious, curious, mirroring the energy he saw all around him, raised by the whole Climate Crisis Corps village in the Montessori classrooms of the great, fire-prone Californian forests. The grown-ups would chop and haul brush for the Big Cali Clear, building a sparer landscape that could sink carbon without burning out of control. Noah would sit watching, demanding to help until someone gave him a pile of sticks to move.

He'd drag the dry, tinderous saplings to the sledges, rawing his fingers, scratching his legs and arms in the untrailed woods. He remembered feeling so proud but realizing, later, that the task had been more about keeping him safely out of the way of more dangerous work. There had been little pressing need to move those sticks.

Thus it had been the day after the storm. Like many COP attendees, Noah had offered his help to the cleanup crews assembling outside the apartment building where he'd been given lodging. They had appreciated his eagerness, but he and the other COP-goers—being foreign political operatives—had little of the hyperlocal knowledge or technical skills necessary to be truly useful. So they had found a lone pile of rubble and debris for Noah to help move—an old church that had somehow not been brought up to code, whose north wall had collapsed when a tree toppled. There was no urgency to this job, but afterwards the crew captain thanked him and inquired concernedly about keeping his strength up for the negotiations. Noah got the hint. He decided to stay out of the way and get back to the job he'd traveled a hemisphere to do.

So Noah got to the negotiating room early on Monday. The building was a union hall—Noah's home turf. He didn't know enough about the Latin American labor scene to parse the acronyms on the door, but from the look of the muraled walls Noah suspected the venue belonged to the building trades.

Most of the COP sessions were spread throughout Buenos Aires—though never more than a couple trolly stops apart. This kept the proceedings accessible and helped keep the negotiators from getting insular. Now, however, some of the spaces were being double-booked to help organize the block-by-block recovery efforts. Noah shouldered past tables where men and women in coveralls were handing out mold masks and protective gloves.

Saga Lindgren, of course, was already in the session room, sitting at the table, shuffling through notes, wooden name block already stood on end to request the floor as soon as they started.

"Good to see you, Noah. How are your children?" Saga said when Noah plopped down next to her.

"Sad to learn the storm didn't wash me out to sea," Noah said. "How's the art?"

"We will see on Wednesday, I suppose," Saga said. "Are you coming to my show?"

"Are you going to help me get a straight answer on 2100 stabilization targets? You know the taigal parties have been holding out on me."

"And *you* know I'm here negotiating for the arts constituency, not the Nordic block."

"Doesn't mean you don't have influence," Noah pressed. "I bet if you only let people willing to name a target into your show, we could whip a couple votes."

Saga gave him a reluctant smile. "Flattery, flattery. Personally, I think they aren't unreasonable in wanting to wait. We don't actually know what a stabilized 350ppm world looks like. We barely have meaningful data on the preindustrial climate. You are asking people to commit to setting the thermostat while the climate still has a lot of chaotic inertia to spin out."

"I don't care about the thermostat," Noah said. "I care about planning the work that needs doing to get wherever the world wants to go. Everyone says, 'well, if we don't like the climate, we can always draw down more, right?' Wrong. The final target determines the number and size of the reservoirs we eventually have to build, and the pipelines to get there. Which in turn determines the resources we allocate to building them, how many workers we hire, how many pensions we budget for. And it can be dangerous work, so there's health costs to figure in as well. And that's just my concerns representing the carbon trades unions. The other trades will need to know the scale of the operation, so they can plan to get us the materials and equipment we'll need—and everything else. Dragging our feet on these decisions loses us a lot of efficiencies."

"That's the problem with a planned economy, Noah," Saga said, clearly getting into the spirit of the debate. "Plans change. The big data projects are still crunching the habitability numbers. Maybe lowering the temperature loses us more land near the poles than it gains us around the equator. Maybe we'll be able to reclaim land from sea level rise, maybe not. We just don't know. If we make big bets now and have to change course later when we know more, the costs might be much more than what we pay by asking for a little flexibility from the unions."

"So set an ambitious target now and we can pull back a bit later," Noah said. "A vote not to make a clear plan is a vote to leave it up to some kind of nebulous market, and we all know how that works out for workers. Last thing we want is a boom-and-bust cycle when the stability of the planet is at stake."

The other negotiators and observers started to file into the room.

"The delegates you are asking me to convince represent people whose farms may eventually freeze over if the COP votes for targets under 300," Saga said. "I think we should take their concerns seriously."

"If they want me to take their concerns seriously, they can always join my union. We've got plenty of jobs that need doing." Noah shrugged. "Anyway, what about those guys? Some of them are getting 55C summers, massive desertification. A little ice age might make their lands arable again."

He waved at the group of African equatorial negotiators taking their seats. They looked intense, dashing, confident—as always. With a small surge of jealousy, Noah remembered the previous year's COP in Nairobi. The city was verdant and shining, the result of bleeding-edge leap-frog development. It was one of the great ironies of the Transition Era that, when funding started to flow, many areas in the global south had been able to adopt sustainable economies and technology much more quickly and readily than the richer, earlier industrialized countries

While Lagos and Kinshasa transformed into so-called 'green megas,' and new arcology cities sprung up in Africa's solar surplus zones, America and Europe still slogged through endless rounds of retrofits, sprawl repair, densification, redevelopment, leakage analysis, further retrofits. Noah's 'developed world' found itself weighed down by a crumbling layer of materiality that had once been a great achievement but, it turned out, hadn't been built right the first time around. California was up to its knees in undead housing and zombie infrastructure: clunky, toxic, half-functional buildings and systems that polluted the landscape and got in the way, but still usually had to be lived in. Finding the talent to drag them out of the 'wreckage of the unsustainable' was a mounting challenge; America's best architects and planners were brain-draining themselves to Africa and Asia, where more ambitious and glamorous projects were possible and plentiful.

These different paths to sustainability played out at the COP as differences in aesthetics and attitudes. Noah often found his mild, childish jealousy mirrored by looks of pity from the equatorial delegates.

"I thought you didn't care where we set the thermostat," Saga said, nudging him.

"I don't," Noah said. "But the carbon trades membership voted to make bringing home clear 2100 disposal targets one of my negotiating priorities, so here I am, trying to push the conversation along any way I can."

"Okay, okay," Saga gave him a friendly, placating pat on the shoulder. "I can't make promises today, but I do know much of the Nordic delegation will be at the reception before my show on Wednesday. If you are looking for a place to work your magic, I can get you on the list. *If* you bring your union friends to my show."

"See, there we go," Noah said, tapping his name block to hers like a comical high-five. "I scratch your back. You scratch mine. The system works."

SECOND TUESDAY

The fair—and thus the world—seemed to Luis to be full of wonders. He walked among the pavilions, scanning the wares and sampling the foreign foods on offer. Around him buzzed COP attendees and porteños, drifting toward smells or demonstrations, getting pitched on this or that UN programme or national effort. The party pavilions had taken the opportunity of the storm to reconfigure themselves early for the end-of-COP fair. It was one of the great boons to the city hosting the conference: diplomats, scholars and activists from around the planet brought with them casks of goods that were usually hard to get outside their bioregion.

The negotiations traditionally concluded with a sharing of this 'global bounty' brought in special by COP delegations. This year the storm—which Luis had watched blow through from inside the Villa 31 community center where he had been reporting back to his constituents on week one, and which now seemed like a memory from an ancient past—had prompted the organizers to move up their timeline. They hoped consumables from the fair could make their way into the post-storm feasts popping up around the city. Luis had bowed out of his negotiation commitments for the morning to help out at the Buenos Aires city booth. Of course there was very little foot traffic at the BA booth, since all their contributions to the fair could be found at every grocery and restaurant in the city. So Luis had in turn taken leave to wander through the fair, which had always been his plan.

□

He sampled fruit from Southeast Asia, beer from Western Europe, grain cakes from North America. He fingered exotic fabric weaves and toyed with artisanal electronics. He watched religious paraphernalia he didn't recognize being passed out to grateful believers. At the Indian pavilion an older woman in a sari tapped out small shakes of spices onto the back of his hand. He licked them off, one by one.

"I know this one," he said in English, puzzled. "Or something similar. I think I tasted it before, on a trip to São Paulo. Or maybe Paramaribo?"

"Very possible," the woman said. "Much of northern South America is in one of our sister biomes. Star anise, cardamon, turmeric—all spices we've worked to globalize into the rest of the pluviseasonal tropics. Is this your first COP fair?"

"My first COP, actually," Luis admitted. "Luis Soto, Argentine youth delegation."

"Diya." She gestured namaste. "I used to be a RINGO, then I was with the Indian delegation, then the UN. Thank you for taking time to be here at the COP and this fair. I know when a neverstorm struck my city, when I was about your age, nothing seemed to matter besides being out on the streets, doing what I could."

"I'm definitely...distracted," Luis admitted. "The community I serve took the brunt of the storm. But my constituents are very keen to understand what's happening at the COP and wanted me here, instead."

"Good! Very sensible of them. How are you finding the fair?"

Luis, not wanting to come off as wonderstruck as he'd been feeling, cast about for something insightful to say.

"Well, it has me wondering how tricky it would be to get my hands on some of this stuff were the COP not in town."

"Far from impossible, I should think," Diya said. "There are a few of the old, refrigerated container ships still running on diesel dispensations, and more and bigger wooden sail-ships and solar drift-ships launch every year. You might have to put in a special order or sit on a waitlist. At worst get mildly lucky in a lottery. But there's very little, within reason, that you couldn't get your hands on with a little effort."

"I suppose," Luis mused. "My parents sometimes complain that, back in their day, they had access to anything and everything from around the world, within days and with just a couple clicks—not that they could necessarily afford it. But then they also tell me I'm spoiled by how much better the food is now."

Diya laughed. "My family could always afford whatever we wanted, and still half of what we ate was too processed, dried, and stale to be enjoyable. All so we could have the supposed luxury of eating blueberries in Mumbai all year round. How boring! Much better to always have the novelty and nostalgia of the next season's dishes around the corner to look forward to."

"Of course! My parents also complain about old clothes and electronics. Everything wore out or broke down after a couple years, unless you could splurge on stuff that wasn't made in Chinese injection-mold factories or Bangladeshi sweatshops."

"Everything you find here will be durable," Diya assured him. She had a professorial air about her, which Luis, who had been thinking of going back for another round of schooling, found congenial. "When you aren't trying to flood every market on the planet, you can afford to use artisan methods that expend more energy and time on smaller batches. The math works out because you get products that last longer and have less distance to travel."

She offered him a wooden tray with sliced guava, as well as pieces of flatbread, some already spread with a yellow chutney, others with something red and spicy-looking. He picked at the food and found it as good as everything else he'd tried.

"So how is everything at this fair so fresh if it came from across the planet?"

"Oh, that's not very difficult—just energy-intensive. Too much so to necessarily do at a huge scale, but we make an exception for the COP. Plus everything comes from the finest crops grown in each bioregion. All to grease the wheels of diplomacy, right?"

"I suppose I owe you a vote or two for all this, then," Luis said, taking another couple flatbreads from the tray.

"I'll let it slide." Diya winked at him. "These days my role is mostly ceremonial. I do this and that, but I'm involved in only a few actual votes."

"Like what? I'm still wrapping my head around everything that goes on here."

In the eight days that Luis had been part of the Argentine delegation—liaising between the negotiations and the former slum community where he organized the annual needs-census—his biggest takeaway was how sprawling planetary management was. He'd met people who worked on glacier engineering, soil carbon overclocking, rural depopulation facilitation, megafauna outreach and negotiation, keyline design, desertification rollback, sea retreat community planning, carbon mangrove reclamation, rare greenhouse gas accounting, indigeneity onboarding, ecosystem services cryptocurrency stabilization, orbital commons stewardship, the search for sustainable extraterrestrial intelligences. He only knew what about half of those things meant, and even then only in the vaguest terms, but he was determined to finish the COP with, at least, a sense of scope.

"Well, today I helped organize this fair around the sister biomes 'seed and skills share' programme," Diya said. "We help communities adopt a kind of 'globalized bioregionalism.' This means diversifying production and agricultural practices with crops and techniques native to other parts of the planet that share similar climatic and landscape characteristics. If we're successful, you may see more exotic foods at groceries, coming in via overland trade from the other biomes on the continent."

"What about invasive species?"

"That's a paradigm we're moving away from. We've already globalized the planet—there's no going back. The question is whether we can globalize the useful and the beautiful, not just the weeds and the pests. There's no rolling back the extinctions that have already happened, either. What we can do is weave together many different lifeways to make our ecosystems truly healthy, rich, and robust. Biodiversity, not nativism. So that means a lot of careful swapping of bugs and birds and molds across continents, in addition to seeds and skills. It's painstaking work, but I like to think the institutions doing it are finally starting to knit together something like the post-nation state political imaginary. Eventually we hope to have enough solidarity and coherence within and between bioregions to drop the concept of 'countries' for something a little less prone to conflict and contradiction. But, of course, these big goals have to start somewhere, and I think they start with food. Ah!"

A pair of blue badges arrived and showed Diya a tablet.

"It was very nice to meet you, Luis," Diya said, offering him another friendly wink. "Give my friends here your contact. Perhaps we can continue the conversation later in the week. Enjoy the rest of the fair."

Luis did so, and then she was gone, whisked off out of the Indian pavilion and into the crowd. Luis stood there, looking after her, mulling over what she had told him and wondering if and how he could find a place in such grand and abstract ambitions. Eventually one of the other pavilion minders came by and offered him a cup of chai. Luis accepted, and the sweet tea seemed to rouse him from his reverie.

As he walked away, Luis felt a hand close around his elbow. It was Cheeto, a wiry Belgian youth delegate Luis had befriended in passing over the first week of the COP.

"Man, did you just get fifteen minutes of one-on-one conversation with Madam Kapoor?" Cheeto demanded. "You gotta teach me your secret."

"What? What do you mean?" Luis asked. "You know her?"

"Brother, Diya Kapoor is the former executive secretary of the UNFCC. Which means she basically used to run the planet!"

Luis started at that, but it made some things click into place. He felt an urge to chase after the older woman and thank her properly, call her 'madam secretary,' maybe apologize for wasting her time. But there was more fair to explore, and his own booth to check on, and then back to negotiations in the afternoon. He would simply have to go about his day, holding on to the notions she'd left in him: that new imaginaries were possible, that small things could be part of big plans, and that the powerful and accomplished were not so different, up close, than the likes of him.

SECOND WEDNESDAY

As the minutes ticked by before the gallery opened, Saga fiddled with the lighting. It was, like so many things, an ever-evolving process. She had gotten it perfect two weeks earlier, but then other works had been moved into the space, changing the cast of the walls and the shape of the air. And so she'd had to tweak the lighting algorithms over and over again until the color and intensity of the illumination hitting her piece—the centerpiece—was back to how she wanted it. By the evening of her show, she worried that the many adjustments had muddied her own sense of her original vision.

Nonetheless, when the gallery doors opened and the early arrivals trickled in, she set aside such anxieties, pocketed her control glove, and prepared herself to present her art—however imperfect, but good enough. She smiled and mingled, made small talk about the conference as needed, though mostly she tried to keep herself a bit apart from the rest of the COP, a bit aloof, and instead directed the guests' attention to the various contributions of the arts constituency arranged around the space.

Saga liked quite a few of these pieces. There was the longitudinal series of oil-on-canvas sunsets, painted by a bot every day for twenty years and curated to highlight the slow changes in the sky that came with falling emissions—and the chaotic weather that still persisted. There was the slab of bleached coral reef, delicately extracted from the ocean floor and hung on the wall without context. There were the provocative videos depicting a utopian society living in a hot-house climate, children joyously exploring decimated cities, lovers embracing in the light of whale oil lamps, families picnicking to watch tornados. And her favorite of the pieces not her own: an exquisite iron sculpture of a runaway train spilling over a cliff, caught and righted by many hands and broken bodies, carrying on its way.

The reception got more crowded, buzzier. In the mix Saga saw friends and acquaintances, a few other artists. Noah Campbell was there lobbying some members of the Nordic bloc. More came in, a wave of dignitaries Saga was slightly shocked to see attending. She paid respects to indigenous leaders and the archbishop-elect of Buenos Aires. At the last minute, Diya Kapoor swept in with a young Argentine in tow, who was trying very hard to keep the deer-in-the-headlights look off his face. Saga managed just a brief, "So lovely to see you, Madam Secretary," and then heard in her ear the cue from her assistant that it was time to begin.

Saga excused herself, changed in the back, tugged on control gloves. When she returned to the gallery, the mood had mostly hushed.

"Comrades, we have been lying to ourselves," Saga called to the crowd, the only frame she would give them for what came next.

She stepped to a platform next to a wide, roped-off basin in the center of the gallery, then began the sequence. Fog started to pour out of the ceiling above the platform. Working her gloves, she formed it, from several meters back, into a grey, rotating sphere. The tiny jets in the platform and ceiling, combined with a nearly undetectable projection layer, caused the ball to begin to resemble a monochrome miniature of the Earth. Then thinner vapor circled the globe, forming several sets of cloudy shells, each highlighted by projector light in a different color: a translucent planetary nesting doll.

It was a very impressive visual effect. The piece used a great deal of computing, along with projections that flickered so fast they confused the eye in very specific ways. The eyes could even focus *through* the globe, onto each of the different layers, much like the ear could pick out one voice in a choir. It took some getting used to, and as the crowd's eyes adjusted, they oohed and ahhed.

Saga didn't need to control the installation live. Indeed, for the last several days of the COP, and for a month after while she lingered in Buenos Aires, the piece would run automatically for visitors to the gallery. But there were advantages to being there, doing some of the shaping and controlling the timing. It allowed her to instill a sense of theatricality. For instance: Diya Kapoor's young companion was by the ropes, and when he reached out a finger to touch the fog globe, Saga triggered the next stage.

His hand pulled back, startled, rebuked, impressed. Images had begun to resolve on each of the layers, one by one. The onlookers stirred with appreciation. Each layer showed video of a different part of the living world: trees swaying, grain waving, lava sliding, the lights of skyscrapers coming on and off, insects roiling in a carcass, soil shifting with time-lapsed microbial action, fur rippling over animal muscle, a thunder-cracked storm. And more. All wrapped around each other, forming one harmonious system.

This, Saga knew, would have been perfectly acceptable to many galleries. Some in the crowd were no doubt thinking she was making a statement about the interconnectedness of all beings. With her opening pronouncement, some would interpret the piece, thus far, as a reminder that humans were just one part of a complex web of life, a truth forgotten beneath civilizational lies. Something sophomoric like that.

But then Saga triggered the third stage. The images panned or shifted, and became violent. Sometimes in abstract ways—a fiery clash of colors and shapes. Others were less subtle: rioters fighting with old-school police, pirates firing on an oil tanker, gas canisters pinging off laser-lit streets, a tractor pulling down a statue, children kicked by jackboots, tasers jolting into picket lines, strikers beating scabs.

The crowd pulled back, stunned by the abrupt change in tone. Saga let the horror show play for just a few seconds, then flipped the images back. The onlookers again leaned in to see the fine details of the many-shelled world, though more wary this time. She twisted her hand—more violence. Then back—green hills and rain in puddles, famous arcologies rising out of familiar skylines. Then violence once more.

She went through this cycle a few more times, and then she made each layer of vapor puff away, until all that was left was the dense Earth of fog, on which was playing an incoherent mash of all the other layers—peaceful and not. She let this roll as she made her way off the platform toward the gallery's back exit. Eyes followed her, but most stayed watching the globe. She snapped her fingers and the cloud dispersed, the projector lights went out.

Saga had a glass of water, changed back into her reception dress, and then went back out to see the already dwindling crowd.

There was a small smattering of applause when people noticed her return. She made her rounds through the room, thanking the clumps of guests for coming. The gallery emptied. Eventually only one group remained, Noah Campbell and a few others Saga knew. They were discussing their interpretations of her performance, which Saga would prefer not to engage, but Diya Kapoor was there, and she felt obliged to tell the famous climate leader goodnight.

"For me it evoked a very retro feeling," Tara McVey, another American, was saying. "Like it was referencing all those expectations of apocalypse and collapse. There really was a fear, before the Transition Era, that everything would fall apart really quickly and violently. People had trouble imagining how smooth the transition could be, how much sense most changes would make when governments were stirred to act. I think a few of the shock-and-awe images were from old movies."

"For me, I think it reminded me of the opposite," Noah countered. "We have this sense now of, like, 'of course things worked out this way.' But really, they didn't have to. We could have made worse choices, or lost a bunch of coin flips no one remembers anymore. And I think we have this gradualist narrative. That things were smooth, like you said. But that's because we've already erased from our collective memory a lot of the worst of the ruptures. It took real struggle to finally get climate action. Direct action, strikes, even a little violence."

"Well, of course," Tara said. "But compared to the horrors of the 20th century, the climate movement was extremely nonviolent. There were sit-ins and occupations and general strikes, but no assassinations or bombings, at least not in the US. Just peaceful protests!"

"Yeah, but my parents were at all that stuff, and they always say there was no such thing as a nonviolent protest—just ones where the protestors didn't fight back." Noah shrugged. "Plus, nobody likes to talk about the pipelines that got sabotaged, or the threats and harassment that got coal plant operators to desert. But making carbon energy companies harder to operate was a big part of why investors eventually threw the old fossil giants under the bus, trying to buy themselves time. And reimagining politics produced a lot of hate and distrust. I remember growing up, we'd occasionally encounter sad, sick people who were camped out in the woods, sure the government was about to come euthanize them as part of some sinister population control program. Then when the population started to dip a lot faster than people had expected, there were even more conspiracy theories."

"So that's what you got from the piece?" Tara said, nonplussed. "That the Transition Era was messy?"

"What I got was a reminder not to feel so smug. We talk like it was all part of some inevitable enlightenment. But The Enlightenment was a culture war too, with its own share of violence. So, to me, that's what the 'lying to ourselves' bit meant. And maybe a warning that we aren't immune to rupture now. If we forget the past, that kind of anti-solidarity could come back again."

"I don't think anyone my age forgets the strife and tension before—and during—the Transition Era," Diya Kapoor said. "Luis, you're the youngest here. What is your view?"

"Madam Secretary," said the young Argentine, hair in a prim bun. He seemed to be choosing his words carefully. "I'm no expert. But my impression is that history has been a long process of stepping back from the edge. Once, many wanted to use nuclear weapons, and they had to be talked down. The time before the Transition Era was another edge. So, I'm thinking about the people I organize with, who I know so well. And I ask, do they have it in them to walk up to the edge, whatever edge it may be? Yes, I think they do. I don't think that goes away."

"Well put," Saga said, stepping a little closer to the group. A couple of them started.

"Since you were listening, can you tell us who got it right? About your intent?" Noah put in.

"That's a terrible question to ask an artist," Saga said. Then added, "but I will say none of the videos are from old movies."

"Regardless," Diya said, in a tone that made it clear she was ending the discussion. "Saga, my dear, that was wonderful."

"Thank you, Madam Secretary."

"Just one question," Diya added. "Does the work have a title?"

"I don't like titles," Saga said. "But in the promotional materials the gallery has circulated, it's called 'Nuestra Tormenta Compartida.'"

Noah started to fumble with his translator, but she stopped him.

"It means, 'Our Shared Storm.'"

SECOND THURSDAY

Diya hated talking to rich people, but she was good at it. She was one herself, or had been, though that sense of isolated entitlement never quite leaves you, she feared. The lingering rich needed most to be made to feel that they were winning, in charge, going of their own free will, even as the sea overtook them. So, that's what Diya offered them.

"This, my esteemed friends, is the kind of glory your money can buy."

Diya stood at the prow, shouting to be heard over the wind and the waves and the low hum of the sail yacht's electric control motor. Her audience sat on cushioned benches bolted to the deck of the boat. They drank mimosas and wore gold 'VIP' badges which glinted in the summer sun, an ego-stroking touch Diya was particularly fond of.

She waved at the octagonal structure looming ahead of them. It looked impressively industrial, in that very 20th century way. But was also draped with greenery, vertical crops hanging in sheets from four of the sides. Around the structure the open ocean was broken by smaller works—a farming flotilla of rafts and buoys, beneath which hung yet more crops: kelp, scallops, mussels, fish traps, and soil bags growing a dozen kinds of artisanal aquatic vegetables. It was one of the more impressive offshore agriculture projects in the region, providing significant fish protein to nearby Buenos Aires and helping reduce local acidification levels in the surrounding waters. But Diya wanted to keep her audience's attention on the rig.

"The platform you see before you began life at a shipyard in Itaguaí, Brazil, at the cusp of the Transition Era," Diya continued. "It was destined to be an offshore oil drilling rig pulling toxic hydrocarbons out of the Argentine Basin, at the behest of a hungry market and hungrier investors. But we have found a better use for it. Mr. Campbell?"

Her audience turned to Noah, who grabbed hold of a rope and hauled himself up to stand unsteadily beside her. She had brought Noah along to explain the technical details of the storage project, but also to remind her guests of the powerful unions they might come up against if they said no. She would be the carrot, Noah would play the stick.

"Far below us, under the ocean floor, is a large, porous formation of sedimentary rock," Noah explained. "Right now those pores are filled with saline—salt water. With robots and special concrete-setting microbes, we have fashioned that formation into one of the world's first carbon waste reservoirs. Carbon dioxide is transported here in a flexible undersea pipeline from an air capture plant tethered to the offshore wind and solar farm a few dozen klicks further out. Here it is pumped down into the reservoir, where it forces the saline out into the ocean and pretty much stays put. The technical details are obviously more complicated, but I promise you the chemistry is too boring to be worth getting into. The gist of it is, we take clean energy, use it to fix waste carbon out of the atmosphere, then put that sky trash more or less back where it came from—underground, where it contributes to neither radiative forcing nor ocean acidification. Questions?"

"Why do all this, instead of planting more trees?" asked a man with thick plastic sunglasses—showy and expensive given the limits on non-essential plastic manufacturing.

"As I understand it," Noah said, "that's an ongoing debate at the COP—the balance of these strategies, anyway. But one answer is nutrient bottlenecks. We've got a lot of waste carbon, but that's not true of everything we'd need to do huge amounts of afforestation. Another is land, which people don't always want to give up to plant carbon dark forests. Plus, because of the sensitivity of weather systems, if you plant a new forest in one spot, it can reduce sequestration in a neighboring area. A third answer is time. Industrial air capture works somewhat faster than trees mature.

"And finally, when trees eventually die, they release much of the carbon they captured back into the air—usually on a shorter timeframe than we are looking for with carbon storage. That's fine when you're working at scale. You count the forest, not the trees, as it were. Still, forests catch fire, trees burn, and then you're set way back on your drawdown. Living systems take a very different kind of management. Nothing wrong with that, but we think it's better to put as big a chunk of the problem as we can away for good, and not all in the tree planting basket."

"Why the pipeline?" someone else called out. "Why not just do the capture right here?"

"Eventually, yes, we hope to incorporate generation, capture, and disposal all into the same facilities. But right now these pieces are largely being built out in a modular way while the carbon trades find their feet. The other reason is that we might want to pipe CO2 in from other sites, depending on the eventual capacity of the reservoir and where the solar surplus shakes out."

"You don't *know* the capacity of the formation?" A bottle blonde in the back raised a skeptical eyebrow. She wore a high-fashion version of the jumpsuits coming out of the new European clothing provision houses—a statement of either scorn or envy for the empowered masses, Diya didn't know which.

"It's hard to know anything for sure about anything that far underground," Noah said, unfazed. "This isn't some big cave we've dug. We're talking about rocks, under more rocks, under the ocean. But we have sensors, we know where the carbon goes and whether it stays there. The biggest challenge now is building an organization that can ensure the integrity of those sensors and the data coming from them, and be financially responsible for any leaks that occur over the minimum time we want the carbon to stay put. Say about 500 years. Which, I guess, is where you all come in."

Diya took the prow again.

"Esteemed friends, you know I have brought you here today to show you the vital work funded by the Planetary Trust. This is but one of hundreds of beautiful, state-of-the-art storage sites we are building. They are true marvels, a great gift to all the world and every living thing in it, and to a hundred generations yet to be born. We are also funding a great deal of the aforementioned afforestation, and countless other projects that benefit the planet as a whole. But when something benefits me, I pay for it. When something benefits a city or a nation, that city or nation pays for it. Who pays for something that benefits everyone? We need a new kind of institution, one whose mandate is both broad and long. That is why most of the parties to the UNFCCC individually—soon to be followed by the UN as a whole—have instituted a global wealth tax that pays into the Planetary Trust."

The mention of taxes made the crowd shift uncomfortably.

"I know, I know," Diya said, giving them a knowing smile. "A topic sure to ruin an otherwise lovely day out on the yacht. That's why I'm here to offer you an alternative. All of you control significant private assets, and while your investments have been smart, much needed, even world changing, we now have ever more data showing that private mobilizations of capital are deeply inefficient for achieving long-term climate stability.

"We need to put the world's capital into the hands of the Planetary Trust if we are going to build projects like the platform you see before you and operate them for the next five hundred or one thousand years. And we need that money fast, because, esteemed friends—we are still up against it. The storm our fine host city experienced this week is a reminder of the tipped-over world we are desperately trying to right. Every year that passes with this much carbon in the air continues our planet's slide toward the hothouse. We need every resource available to us to build the removal industry at scale and at speed!"

At this Diya stepped down from her perch and took up a champagne flute of mimosa. She held it up, as if making a toast.

"My most esteemed friends, today I ask you to make this possible. Hand over your assets to the Planetary Trust, so that we might accelerate our plans and stabilize the world. Why wait for the wealth tax to siphon them away year by year? I know, as well as any of you, the burden of these vast, clunky masses of capital. Masses that many of us never asked to be charged with keeping. They are in their own ways as toxic as the oil this rig had once been built to dig up. Relieve yourselves of them, put them to better use. And in return, you will be cared for all your life, with freedom to go and live as you please, a citizen of every country party to the Trust. You will be honored forever on these monuments for your generosity. You can build us a stable climate future. And if we can do this, we can stop asteroids! We can handle the many dangers that lurk in deep time. The Planetary Trust can ensure a prosperous human future where your names will be remembered!"

She swept back up to the prow and pointed at one of the massive struts lifting the platform above the water, which had just come into view. On it were freshly carved names—famous names of ultrarich people Diya had already talked out of their fortunes. Diya raised a toast once more.

"To you! May your names be honored for a hundred generations!"

She drank. Many of the others drank with her. Those who did not glanced away, not able to meet her eye. She'd get them too, soon enough.

Diya's speech was done. She did not mention how paltry the perks and pensions and honors were compared with the titanic sums they'd be giving over to voluntary democratization. She did not mention the increasing legal precedent for holding the megarich accountable for what their investment portfolios paid for in terms of fossil extraction, deforestation, ecosystem damage, and political dithering. The Hague's climate trials had a momentum all their own now, with prosecutors always hungry for new enemies to feed into the environmental justice maw. She did not mention what she would hint at later, in private conversations: that the best way to avoid a dangerous audit was to just give their money up now, after which prosecutors would look the other way. She did not mention that the unions Noah was representing were clamoring for the Trust to move forward with more hostile expropriations of such "stuck capital."

Noah caught up with her on the ride back.

"Heckuva pitch," he said. "If I were a lonely, anxious billionaire, I'd be jumping to give you my money. Though, it leaves a sour taste in my mouth, seeing their egos stroked like this. They are my class enemies, after all."

"There's only brief catharsis in seeing your enemies humiliated," Diya said. "Letting your enemies save face, however, can prevent them from becoming your enemies again. Noah, understand, these people used to basically run the world. Now we are, shall we say, laying them off from that position. Today's theatrics are just the difference between saying 'you're fired' and saying 'we're letting you go.' If that difference helps them shuffle quietly into the night, I say we let them have their dignity."

"Still, it rankles. Why should some rich assholes get their names on that strut, instead of the workers who actually built the thing?"

"Because the world isn't fair, Noah. Not just yet, anyway."

SECOND FRIDAY

The closing ceremonies had birds. They swooped through the open air, in no particular pattern, black dots sharp against the cloudy gray sky. Some landed. Great cawing corvids gathered in a shuffling murder on a hill to the side of the lawn in the park by the river where foreign badge holders and many porteños had come to put COP60 to rest.

They were a new addition to the proceedings, these birds. A week before, biodiversity sensors had noticed that the city's avian population had largely fled the path of the neverstorm several hours before humans understood its trajectory enough to begin battening down the hatches. So a pilot project had been launched to explore incorporating local birds into an early warning system for future neverstorms. Experts on non-human relations who happened to be attending the COP were quite enthusiastic about this project, and they had used their translation algorithms to liaise with local crows and ravens. In the end the conference organizers, as a favor to the host city, had invited the corvids to attend the closing ceremonies as a show of good faith.

There didn't used to be closing ceremonies, just closing plenaries where those who came sat next to their luggage, sending messages, winding down the hours until they needed to head to the airport. But the introduction of voting had brought a raucous, contentious dynamic to the climate negotiations, an energy to match the politics of the spikey, fraught, ultimately successful Transition Era. So the closing ceremonies—as well as second Thursday parties—were added as a way to smooth over the little grudges and frustrations inherent to any democratic process and remind everyone that they were all, ultimately, striving toward the same goals.

Speeches were made, sermons were given. Ceremonial drinks and snacks were handed out and consumed in unison, songs were sung—awkwardly but with genuine feeling. The birds even got in on the act, circling up, it seemed, for their own set of pompous speakers offering long-winded remarks. It was all a little silly, but it had the intended effect of helping everyone leave more or less on good terms, investing them in the process for the year to come.

Noah, Saga, Diya and Luis were all in the crowd, feeling varying degrees of annoyance and bemusement at the proceedings. They did not stand together, but with others in their delegations, or other friends and acquaintances they knew from their years at the conference. A couple times one would catch the other's eye, perhaps nod or smile. When the ceremonies were done, Luis found Diya and thanked her again for spending so much time with him. Diya thanked Noah for his help on the yacht. Noah jostled into Saga as they made their way out, cracked a joke. Saga told him to bring his kids next time. Luis watched Saga's yellow hair drift off toward the exit, and he resolved to take his sister to see Saga's installation at the gallery. None of them were so important to any of the others. But there was a congeniality there, a solidarity, a sense of being together as small parts of a larger whole.

The COP the following year was in Vienna. The year after that, Lhasa. Then on to Moscow, Cairo, Seattle-Vancouver. The process continued. The last of the world's greenhouse emissions were chased down and either shut off or accounted for. The carbon disposal industry ramped up its operations. Glaciers were kept from sliding into the sea and then, decades later, were rebuilt. Bioregions leached away national sovereignty. The wealth tax slowly leveled the world's inequalities, funding the Planetary Trust to first manage the climate, then draw down ocean acidification, then scan the heavens for dangerous objects, then provision basic needs for each person born on the Earth. All these were efforts that had their own momentum, but the COP remained a meeting for various political players to come together for two weeks each year to iron out the kinks in these projects, resolve disputes, and decide collectively what kind of world they wanted to live in.

None of which was to say that things were perfect, or that history had ended, or that the planet turned placidly until the end of time. There were still setbacks. There were still terrible climate horrors waiting in the second half of the century: millions displaced, crops lost, species extinct, the world's resources and planetary boundaries more than once strained to the brink. There were still culture wars and a few shooting wars. There were still diseases and preventable deaths. Many of the realities that had made life so hard for so many for as long as humans had walked the Earth still persisted. To be born was to know suffering—that much never changed.

But there was a sense, even as all these tragedies were lived through and dealt with in turn, that human life had passed through a bottleneck, or perhaps the eye of a needle. Some would always ache for the urgency and purpose of the Transition Era, and the dangerous, uncertain time before. But most recognized that, on the other side of this great test, a wide space of possibility had opened up before us. Life did not have to be lived in the shadow of onrushing doom, or with a sense of guilt at the damage one did by simply existing, or angry at the sins of a greedy, foolish past. There were so many ways to live, so many scenarios of human being to yet explore.

On that last day of COP60, in the hot December of 2054, there was only a hint of such possibility in the air. But the hint was there, as surely as the birds, and the river, and the lively clouds rolling in from over the water, promising a gentler rain.

About the Editor

Once upon a time, Justine Norton-Kertson corrupted young minds by teaching high school history, civics, and economics from a leftist perspective. Without tenure, that made it tough to find jobs, so they shifted and spent almost a decade as a union organizer. Nowadays, Justine continues working to corrupt the youth, primarily as a publisher, author, screenwriter, and podcaster. In 2022, they started Android Press and *Solarpunk Magazine* and are the publisher editor-in-chief for both. Justine was named one of the 2023 Grist 50 Fixers for their work publishing climate fiction and organizing around climate change, including founding and organizing the annual Utopia Awards & Climate Fiction Conference.

Their short stories and poems have been published by *Utopia Science Fiction Magazine*, *Reckoning*, *Solarpunk Magazine*, and World Weaver Press, among others. Justine is also the creator and host of the Star Trek fandom podcast, *Unimatrix Zero*, and the fantasy fiction podcast, *Imagitopia*, as well as an associate producer for *The 7th Rule*. They live in rural Oregon with her partner, puppies, cats, goats, and bunnies where they enjoy gardening, kayaking, writing, and making short films. They can be found online on Instagram and TikTok @utopianwitchcraft, or at www.justinenortonkertson.com.

Author Biographies

Andrew Dana Hudson

Andrew Dana Hudson is a speculative fiction writer, sustainability researcher, and futurist. He is the author of *Our Shared Storm: A Novel of Five Climate Futures*, as well as over twenty short stories appearing in *Slate Future Tense*, *Lightspeed Magazine*, *Escape Pod*, *Vice Terraform*, *MIT Technology Review*, *Grist*, and many more. His nonfiction has appeared in *Slate*, *Jacobin*, and others. His fiction has been nominated for the Pushcart Prize, longlisted for the BSFA, and translated into Italian. In 2016 his story "Sunshine State" won the first Everything Change Climate Fiction Contest, and in 2017 he was runner up in the Kaleidoscope Writing The Future Contest. His 2015 essay "On the Political Dimensions of Solarpunk" has helped define and grow the "solarpunk" subgenre. He attended the prestigious 2022 Clarion Workshop.

Christopher R. Muscato

Christopher R. Muscato is a writer and dad of twins from Colorado, USA. He is a Terra.do climate fellow, winner of the inaugural XR Wordsmith Solarpunk Storytelling Showcase, and former writer-in-residence of the High Plains Library District. His fiction can be found here and there, among other places.

H. Pueyo

H. Pueyo is an Argentine-Brazilian writer of speculative fiction who occasionally ventures in the realm of comics, translations and other literary genres. Her work is often influenced by her multicultural and multilingual background, her experiences as a child immigrant, and her life-long struggles with trauma, C-PTSD and chronic pain.

Her short fiction has been published in English, Portuguese, Spanish and Italian, and can be found in venues such as *Magazine of Fantasy & Science Fiction, Clarkesworld, Strange Horizons* and *The Year's Best Dark Fantasy & Horror*, among others. She was also awarded the Othership Fellowship for her work with gender in speculative fiction. She is represented by Lee O'Brien at Looking Glass Literary & Media Management.

Holly Schofield

Holly Schofield travels through time at the rate of one second per second, oscillating between the alternate realities of city and country life. With over one hundred published short stories, her works are used in university curricula and have been translated into multiple languages. Holly's stories have appeared in *Analog, Lightspeed, Escape Pod*, the Aurora-winning *Second Contacts*, and many other publications throughout the world. She hopes to save the world through science fiction and homegrown heritage tomatoes. Find her at hollyschofield.wordpress.com.

J.D. Harlock□

J.D. Harlock is an Arab American writer & editor whose short stories have been featured in *The Deadlands, Sciencefictionary, Defenestration, Wyldblood Press*, and the *Decoded Pride Anthology*, and others. His poetry has been featured in *Penumbric, Mobius* and *Black Cat Magazine*, and his articles/reviews have been featured in *NewMyths.com, Mermaids Monthly, Interstellar Flight Press*, and on the SFWA Blog.

Jetse de Vries

Jetse de Vries is a specialist for a propulsion company, and used to travel the world for this. Of late he's trying to settle into a desk job, in order to have more time for editing and writing science fiction. He's written science fiction since 1999, and had his first story published in November 2003. His stories have appeared in about two dozen publications on both sides of the Atlantic, and include *Amityville House of Pancakes, vol. 1, JPPN 2, Nemonymous 4, Northwest Passages: A Cascadian Anthology, DeathGrip: Exit Laughing, HUB Magazine #2,* and *Clarkesworld Magazine* (May 2007), *SF Waxes Philisophical* anthology, *Postscripts Magazine* #14 and *Flurb* #6.

Kanishk Tantia

Kanishk Tantia is a novice author and immigrant. Most of his stories come from his lived experiences as a neurodivergent person and BIPOC, and from his experiences in Computer Science Academia. Kanishk currently lives in Boston, USA but escapes to California whenever the temperature drops below 70F. Find more from Kanishk @t_kanishk or at kanishkt.com

Katherine Quevedo

Katherine Quevedo was born and raised just outside of Portland, Oregon, where she works as an analyst. She attended Santa Clara University in Silicon Valley and holds undergraduate degrees in English and Business Economics. She earned her MBA from Portland State University. She has studied abroad in England, Chile, and Argentina. She lives in Beaverton, Oregon, with her husband and two sons. When she isn't writing speculative fiction or all types of poems, she enjoys watching movies, singing, playing old-school video games, belly dancing, attending soccer and basketball games, making spreadsheets, going on light hikes, visiting zoos, and snorkeling whenever travel allows.

Her stories have been selected for *Best of Utopian Speculative Fiction* and *Best Indie Speculative Fiction* and been included in *Tor.com*'s annual list of Must Read Short Speculative Fiction. Her poems have been nominated for the Pushcart Prize and the Rhysling Award and received an honorable mention in the Helen Schaible International Sonnet Contest. Her articles have appeared on the official websites of *Writer's Digest* and the Science Fiction and Fantasy Writers Association (SFWA). Her writing appears in a variety of magazines, anthologies, and podcasts. She is a member of SFWA, the Science Fiction & Fantasy Poetry Association (SFPA), and the Horror Writers Association (HWA).

Liam Hogan

Liam Hogan is an award-winning short story writer, with stories in *Best of British Science Fiction* and in *Best of British Fantasy* (NewCon Press). He's been published by Analog, Daily Science Fiction, and Flame

Tree Press, among others. He helps host Liars' League London, volunteers at the creative writing charity Ministry of Stories, and lives and avoids work in London. More details at http://happyendingnotguaranteed.blogspot.co.uk

Marisca Pichette

Marisca Pichette works in speculative and literary fiction, poetry, and essay. Her writing strays from fairy tale to horror to the in-between, investigating queerness and marginalized identity—often involving monsters. She is represented by Amy Collins.

Marisca's debut speculative poetry collection, *Rivers in Your Skin, Sirens in Your Hair,* was published April 4, 2023 by Android Press. She has presented critical work at the International Conference of the Fantastic in the Arts and the Once and Future Fantasies Conference. She has given readings and sat on creative panels at the Nebula Conference, Can*Con, Boskone, Readercon, and the International Conference of the Fantastic in the Arts.

Naomi Eselojor

Naomi Eselojor enjoys writing fast-paced, gripping tales In the science fiction and fantasy genre. She has been published at *365 Tomorrows* and *Tree and Stone Magazine.* Her works are forthcoming at Improbable Press and *Hexagon Magazine.* Naomi is a student of the University of Lagos and resides in Lagos, Nigeria with her family. You can find her on Twitter as @neselojor or Instagram as naomieselojor.

Phoebe Wagner

Phoebe Wagner is an author, editor, and academic writing at the intersection of speculative fiction and climate change. Their debut novel *A Shot of Gin* is forthcoming from Parliament House Press (2023), and *Publishers Weekly* called their novella *When We Hold Each Other Up* a "fresh take on climate fiction." She is the editor of three solarpunk anthologies, including *Sunvault: Stories of Solarpunk & Eco-Speculation.* They blog about speculative literature at the Hugo-winning *Nerds of a Feather, Flock Together.* Wagner holds a PhD in literature, and she is an Assistant Professor of Creative Writing at Lycoming College in Pennsylvania. Follow them at phoebe-wagner.com.

Renan Bernardo

Renan Bernardo is a Brazilian writer of science fiction and fantasy, writing in English and Portuguese. His work has been published in English, Portuguese, German, Japanese, and Italian. He's also a SFWA member. You can find his stories in several publications, including *Apex Magazine*, *Podcastle*, *Escape Pod*, *Solarpunk Magazine*, *Dark Matter Magazine*, *Translunar Travelers Lounge*, and *Daily Science Fiction*. His collection of Solarpunk/Climate Fiction stories, *Different Kinds of Defiance*, is upcoming by Android Press in early 2024.

History, science, and music are others of his passions. He's graduated in Computing Engineering and works in a project that one day might cast the Earth in a black hole. He lives in Rio de Janeiro, but you can find him in the digital world: @RenanBernardo

Sarah Ramdawar

Sarah Ramdawar is a Canadian writer of Trinidadian descent. She writes about the myths that stitch together our days—the ones told to us, the ones we believe ourselves, and the ones that shape our future. She has short fiction in *Augur Magazine*, poetry in *Apparition Lit*, and forthcoming nonfiction in *Living Hyphen* magazine. While she finds serenity growing underwater forests, she also finds herself on Twitter @sararam.

Shelly Jones

Shelly Jones (they/them) is a Professor of English at SUNY Delhi, where they teach mythology, fairy tales, and writing. They received an MA in Creative Writing from SUNY Brockport and a PhD in Comparative Literature from SUNY Binghamton. Their current research explores fandoms, analog games, and tabletop role-playing games. For the past several years, they have served as an editor for *Analog Game Studies* and helped organize Generation Analog, an international conference on games research. Their recent edited collection *Watch Us Roll* explores *Dungeons and Dragons* actual play from a variety of different disciplinary approaches. Their next edited collection *Beyond the Deck: Critical Essays on Magic: The Gathering and its Influences* will be published in 2023.

Simon Kewin

Simon is an award-winning fantasy and sci/fi writer with over a hundred published short stories to his name (with appearances in Analog, Nature and many others). He's the author of the *Cloven Land* fantasy trilogy, cyberpunk sci/fi thriller *The Genehunter* and the "steampunk Gormenghast" *Engn* saga. He's signed to the mighty Elsewhen Press for the publication of his *Office of the Witchfinder General* books.

His novel *Dead Star* was an SPSFC award semi-finalist and his short story #buttonsinweirdplaces was shortlisted for a Utopia Award. His novella *The Clockwork King* won the Tales by Moonlight Editor's Prize. Some of his books are available to download for free – and there are more if you sign up to his newsletter. He's a member of the Untethered Realms collective. He has an honours degree in English Literature (1st class) and an MA in creative writing (Distinction).

Ruth Joffre

Ruth Joffre was born and raised in Northern Virginia. Her mother was born in Cochabamba, Bolivia, in 1950, and Ruth has taken her mother's maiden name to honor her. Ruth earned her BA from Cornell University and her MFA from the Iowa Writers' Workshop. After graduate school, she moved to Seattle, where she served as the 2020-2022 Hugo House Prose Writer-in-Residence and co-organized the Fight for Our Lives performance series. She now lives in Columbia, MO. In 2023, she will be a visiting writer at University of Washington Bothell and George Mason University.

Ruth is the author of the story collection *Night Beast*, which was longlisted for The Story Prize. Her work has been shortlisted for the Creative Capital Awards and been supported by residencies at The Arctic Circle, Virginia Center for the Creative Arts, Lighthouse Works, and the Whiteley Center. Her fiction and poetry have appeared or are forthcoming in *Kenyon Review, Pleiades, Gulf Coast, Lightspeed, Nightmare, Hayden's Ferry Review, Wigleaf,* the anthologies *Best Microfiction 2021 & 2022,* and elsewhere. Her interview series with the authors, editors, and curators of craft books and resources is freely available in Catapult's Don't Write Alone and the *Kenyon Review* blog.

Somto Ihezue

Somto Ihezue is a Nigerian–Igbo editor, writer, and filmmaker. He was awarded the 2021 African Youth Network Movement Fiction Prize. A BSFA and Nommo Award-nominee and finalist for the 2022 Afritondo Prize, his works have appeared and are forthcoming in Tor: Africa Risen Anthology, Fireside Magazine, Podcastle, Escape Pod, Strange Horizons, POETRY Magazine, Cossmass Infinities, Flash Fiction Online, NIGHT-MARE, Flame Tree Press, OnSpec Magazine, Omenana, Africa In Dialogue, The Year's Best Anthology of African Speculative Fiction and others.

He is an alumnus of the Milford SF Writers '22, and Voodoonauts '22, and will be attending Clarion West '23. He is a member of SFWA (Science Fiction Writers Association), ASFS(African Science Fiction & Fantasy Society), BSFA (British Science Fiction Association), and BFS (British Fantasy Society), and Codex.

Susan Kaye Quinn

Susan Kaye Quinn is an environmental engineer/rocket scientist turned speculative fiction author who now uses her PhD to invent cool stuff in books. Her works range from hopepunk climate fiction to futuristic spec fic, with side trips into cyberpunk and steampunk romance. Her bestselling novels and short stories have been optioned for Virtual Reality, translated into German and French, and featured in several anthologies, including placing 3rd in Grist's 2022, Imagine 2200: Climate Fiction for Future Ancestors contest.

Susan is a full member of SFWA (Science Fiction & Fantasy Writers Association), NINC (Novelists, INC: The International Organization of Multi-Published Novelists), and RWA (Romance Writers Association) under a penname that she keeps secret unless you bring tea and pinky-swear not to tell. She's also a graduate of the 2022 class of Viable Paradise, a Published Penn with PennWriters, and a member of the Author's Guild.

Toshiya Kamei

Toshiya Kamei holds an MFA in Literary Translation from the University of Arkansas. His translations and stories have appeared in such venues as *Clarkesworld*, *The Magazine of Fantasy & Science Fiction*, *Wyngraf*, and *Strange Horizons*.

Wen-yi Lee

Wen-yi Lee is a Clarion West alumni from Singapore who likes writing about girls with bite, feral nature, and ghosts. Her work has appeared or is forthcoming in *Lightspeed*, *Uncanny*, *Strange Horizons* and Tor.com, among others. She can be found on Twitter @wenyilee_ and otherwise at wenyileewrites.com.

Yasmin Moita

Yasmin Moita is a Brazilian writer born in the Amazon Region. Her poems and poetic prose are featured in the anthologies *Dossiê Literamazônicas, Vol. 1 (2021)* and *Revoada* (2021). She has published her first sci-fi short story, *Taming the Sea and the Wind,* in the *Amazofuturo* (2022) anthology, with an upcoming translation to English. She also writes on her bilingual page at Medium, *Uirapuru*.